With the bow between my knees and an arrow laced on the string, I lean back and rest. A sharp pain shoots up my leg. I breathe deeply and evenly, willing the pins and needles to settle. My foot is hot, but even the throbbing can't keep my eyes from closing. What's the big deal if I close them for a moment? Nothing bad can happen in a moment…

**Praise for Susan Antony**

First Place winner of
the Missouri Romance Writers of America
"Gateway to the Best" contest

# Cherokee Summer

by

Susan Antony

## Acknowledgements

I am forever grateful to my friend Susan J. Bickford, talented writer, wealth of knowledge, and first responder to my many writing crises. Thank you for putting up with my endless string of questions, late night emergency readings of not-ready-for-prime-time pages, and countless requests for advice. Your help navigating my journey to publication has been invaluable.

To Alexander Chow-Stewart, thank you for choosing me as the winner of your Twitter contest. Without your encouragement I might never have attempted to write.

To Barbara Rogan and Merrel Davis, past writing instructors and gifted wordsmiths, thank you for being there in the beginning and nurturing a very "green-seed" writer. Your help and positive support helped me to blossom.

To Chuck Roberson, Jenny Elliot, Natalia Jefferson, and all the others who have read my work countless times, I want you to know your input has been one of my greatest assets.

My family is my blood and soul, breath and life. Dustan, Kirby, Antony, Stella, Donna, Dean, and Chloe, thank you for always having my back. Each of you gives me a reason to strive to be my best.

And finally to my editor, Kinan Werdski, thank you again and again for taking a chance on me. It's not often a girl's dream comes true, and I am forever indebted to you for helping me realize mine. Wow! I'm so lucky to be an author with The Wild Rose Press.

## Chapter 1
## Ace McAllister

I'm late. My self-imposed curfew ended an hour ago, but sometimes I have to get away just to breathe. My hand trembles as I sweep the key card through the lock mechanism. The green light blinks, and I let myself in. A warm lamp burns in the large living area, but the sharp angles of the ultra-modern furnishings keep the place from looking like a real home. Who am I kidding? A suite in a casino resort in Cherokee, North Carolina isn't a real home, but thanks to Dad's job, that's where we're living for the summer.

"Mom, I'm home," I call.

No answer.

*Oh, no.*

I toss my purse on the counter and run to the bedroom I share with my twelve-year-old brother, Zack, to be sure he's okay. He's in bed asleep with the light on, an encyclopedia draped across his chest. The book rises and falls with each of his shallow breaths. I sweep his long brown bangs to the side and kiss him on the forehead. He would never let me do that if he were awake. He's sensitive to touch, so he only lets me show him the love he deserves when he doesn't know he's getting it.

*Now to check on Mom.*

I only make it halfway to her bedroom before my

stomach cramps, and I have to stop. I really have no reason to worry. She's been fine since we got here, even happy. She's probably just sleeping.

A couple steps further and I'm knocking on the door. "Mom, are you awake?"

No answer, still.

I take a deep breath to keep my anxiety in check, then let myself in. The room is dark and quiet, lit only by the full moon bleeding through the solid glass wall.

I squint while my eyes adjust. My mother sits in the Jacuzzi in the far corner of the room, a mere silhouette, a lonely black ghost. She rolls in my direction and mumbles something. A glass slips from her hand and shatters on the tile floor. Before I have a chance to react, she sinks into the tub.

"Omigod!" I dash to her side, grope through the water, and fish her out. She coughs and sprays chlorinated saliva over my favorite shirt—the blue one with the beadwork horse on the pocket. A design I spent hours creating.

I shake her. "Wake up. You have to get out before you drown."

She fights me, but I hold strong while glass crunches beneath my sneakers. To my advantage, she isn't very big—a whole size smaller than my size seven frame—and I'm able to get her on her knees. While this isn't the first time I've had to take care of her, I've never seen her this drunk. My mother is like a stranger to me.

She groans when I drape her over the side of the tub. With one hand on her back, I brush away the glass shards with a neatly folded towel. Then I ease her forward, and she tumbles out with a wet thud.

"Don't move. You might cut yourself," I say.

She lies sprawled like a naked rag doll while I run to get a clean towel from the bathroom. I return in a flash and help her to a sitting position, then wrap it around her middle.

Mom scrubs her nose with the back of her arm and rasps, "Your father left me. He's with another woman."

*Here she goes again.* The alcohol has damaged her brain. There's no other explanation. I mean, they fight a lot, but Dad loves her. He loves us. "Stop with the nonsense. You're imagining things. He's working. You know that."

"You left me. Zack fell asleep early. Why does everyone always leave me?" Her breath is ragged and tears flood her already damp face.

I'm mad as hell, but her sobs, as usual, evoke pity in me. I don't want them to, but they do. I knew Dad was going out, and I left her. It's my fault she's in this condition. Now I have no choice but to undo the damage I've done, right my wrong. I've got to fix things before anyone finds out.

I hug her and kiss the top of her head. "Don't cry. It's okay now. I'm home. I won't leave again tonight."

"Swear you'll stay?" she whimpers.

"I always do," I say under my breath as I jump up to flip on the lights.

My mother's usually perfect blonde hair is matted to her head in stringy wet noodles. Trails of black mascara stain her cheeks, and there's a smudge of red lipstick on her chin. Beneath it all she's still beautiful. Even when my mother's a mess, she's a hot mess.

I find her satin, multi-colored birds of paradise bathrobe—her favorite—then I coax her to her feet. She reels a bit but cooperates and slips into the robe. I tie it snugly around her waist and tug at the skirt part until it hangs evenly the way she likes it. Mom totters to bed with me guiding her by the elbow. She flops onto the mattress, and I tuck her in under the covers.

Snatching a tissue from the silver holder on the bed table, I wipe her face clean as best I can. "There. You're all better," I lie colossally. A real whopper. "Do you need anything else?"

She grasps my wrist, digging her manicured nails into my flesh. "Ace, I don't know what I'd do without you. You're the best daughter in the whole world."

She deserves my wrath, but how can I be mad at her? She's nice to me when I'm playing nursemaid. It's the other times that suck.

I sit on the edge of the bed and pat her shoulder. "Get some rest, okay, Mom?"

She nods and closes her eyes. It's not long before she's snoring. I turn her on her side and prop a pillow behind her back, adjusting her position until her breathing quiets. After cleaning the broken glass off the floor, I turn out the light and leave her to sleep it off.

In the living room, a half-empty pint of vodka sits open on an end table near the couch. I take a sniff. The stench stings my nose. It reminds me of a floor cleaner. Which one? I can't remember. I screw on the lid, zip it in my backpack, and hide it in my bedroom closet under a bag of dirty clothes. Then I wrap the empty bottle of wine in today's newspaper and stuff it in the bottom of the trashcan. There's no point in letting Dad find out how much she drank. We've had enough family battles lately to classify the area as a combat zone.

My phone bleeps like a space laser, making me jump. Zack's been messing with my ringtone again. I dash to pluck it from my purse and silence it.

There's a text from Cameron. What does he want? It's only been an hour since we said goodbye in the hallway.

CAMERON 12:45 AM: *Meet me downstairs. Our moms did some serious partying. Mine's out cold. Is yours? We could sneak out and they'd never know.*

Oh, brother. I bet Dad thinks he's done everyone a huge favor inviting Cameron and his mother on our family vacation and paying for their room. Would he be so generous if he knew Susan drinks as much as Mom and Cameron's trying to lure me out of the house in the middle of the night.

I text him back.

ACE: *Can't. Mom's standing guard duty at the front door. LOL*

One more little lie couldn't hurt.

CAMERON: *Come on. Don't be a chicken.*

He gives me strange vibes, but I hardly know him so it's really not fair to judge. Mom wants me to be friendly to him so Susan will like her. Pathetic, I know, but her drinking has alienated her from most of her other friends. Her plea, "Be nice to him for me," swirls around in my brain. My stomach spasms as I peck out my next text.

ACE: *Maybe we can do something tomorrow.*

CAMERON: *Deal. Can't wait.* (I visualize all the exclamation points he lazily left off.)

ACE: *See you then.* (I leave off the sad face emoticon.)

Why do guys always have to push?

Between dealing with Mom, and now him, I'm in desperate need of a little distraction. I flip on the TV, press the mute button, and watch meaningless images flash across the screen. What the hell am I going to do when the sun comes up?

## Chapter 2
## John Spears

My eyes shoot open.

Stupid alarm.

The volume is set to just above audible, but at this hour, when the house is silent, it might as well be a foghorn. I poke at the off button and ease out from under the covers, careful not to disturb my brother, Victor, who's lying next to me, snoring his brains out. One day I'll have my own place and my own bed. For now, I'm stuck *status quo*.

My little cousin, Lenny, is sprawled out on the single bed in the corner. He's uncovered but the bed is dry *this* morning. Good thing, 'cause I'm not in the mood to change sheets. I pull the covers up to his neck, grab my clothes, and strut down the hall, ninety-eight percent sure there will be no fight for the bathroom. Living with as many people as I do, I can never be one hundred percent sure.

Rae, my twin sister, is conked out on the couch under a fuzzy blue blanket. Damn. Everyone in the house gets to sleep in but me. I don't really mind too much, though. My job is cool.

Once I'm locked behind the bathroom door, I run the water until it's lukewarm and hop into the shower. I'm going to get soaked rafting, but I don't want to start my day smelling rank. Tips are pretty good when my passengers like me.

I towel off and dress in my board shorts and work T-shirt. Then I braid my hair into two long plaits. Braiding long hair is a pain, but every time I think of chopping it off, my grandmother's words pound in my head. "Your hair is a part of you. It's an extension of your thoughts. Without it you'll be lost."

I've never had short hair, so I don't know if she's right, but I like the way I look and I want to please her, so keeping my hair long is a win-win situation.

When I'm done, I hang my towel on the hook on the door and hurry to the kitchen to grab a granola bar for the road.

*"Osda sunalei, ulisi atsutsa.*" "Good morning, grandson," my grandmother shouts from behind me.

I choke on pure air. Why does she always have to sneak up on me? Can't she say good morning face-to-face like a normal person?

I turn around. "Morning, Elisi." Ay-lee-see is the Tsalagi word for maternal grandmother.

She glares at my hand—the one with the granola bar. "What kind of breakfast is that? You'll starve to death." Shuffling past, she motions for me to follow. "Come on, I'll make you something proper to eat."

"Can't. I have to go to work."

"Then don't eat. There will be more for everyone else. But work can wait. I want to talk to you. Sit, please?"

By the tone of her voice I can tell I'm not getting out of this one. Elisi rules the house with an iron gavel. If I don't obey, she'll jab a finger at me like that lady judge on TV and hit me with, "Cherokee heritage dictates women rule not only the house but the children who live in it, too." Loosely translated, "While you live under my roof, you'll shut up and listen whether you like it or not." I heave out a breath and follow her across the cracked linoleum floor I've vowed to replace when I find the time.

While Elisi cooks oatmeal over the old gas stove, I sit in a wooden chair and drum my fingers on the table. Her silence is grating on my nerves. I'd rather she just get down to business so we can end the tension between us and move on with the day.

Finally, she stops stirring and stares at me. "Why do you work so hard at a meaningless job? After you graduate there'll be plenty of time for work."

My job is far from meaningless and pays well, but there's no point in letting her rile me up. "My scholarships aren't enough. I still need extra cash for when I'm away at the university."

Elisi puffs, popping out a p sound. "You torture yourself for nothing. You have a beautiful life on the reservation. Leave and you'll end up like your mother. Do you want that for yourself?"

My cheeks heat up to two hundred degrees, and I flex and release my fingers. I hate when Elisi predicts my future based on my mother's life. I hate it even more when anyone talks bad about Mom. I've been known to loosen a few molars of those who dared to disrespect her. Not my grandmother's, of course. Elisi can say what she wants about her own daughter. It's her right, but I don't have to listen to it.

My chair squeaks against the floor like chalk on a board as I push away from the table. A few steps later, I'm at her side, leaning on her shoulders. "You know I love you, old lady, but I have to go."

"Go, go." She waves her hand around as she speaks. "You're always in such a hurry. No time to appreciate life." She gestures toward the pot boiling on the stove. "Or good food. Go ahead and eat the white man's processed junk. Work in the white man's world until you drop dead. Don't listen to an old lady like me. I don't know anything."

I kiss her cheek, then say, "You know plenty," as I head for the door.

Elisi grumbles but doesn't try to stop me. Both of us know which way our conversation is heading. We've had this argument too many times before. She knows I burn inside when she talks about my mother, and I know she gets depressed when I talk about leaving the reservation. After we get done exhausting those topics, Elisi will break into a lecture about the darkest abyss in my life—my dead father. She always has plenty to say about him, and I can't dispute it like I do with my mom. All I remember about my father is the long braid that hung down the middle of his back—and my mother crying for days when he was killed in a car wreck.

I hesitate with my hand on the doorknob. Leaving without some sort of parting words will hurt her, and that's the last thing I want to do. I lean back and peek into the kitchen until she notices me.

"*Stiyu*," I say to her.

It sounds like I'm saying "see you," but it means, "be strong." My family says this because the Tsalagi language doesn't have a word for goodbye. It's too final.

Even though Elisi crosses her arms and shakes her head, I know now it's okay to leave. So I do.

Outside, the pale yellow sun peeks over the

horizon, kissing the eggplant-colored sky. The cool, clean, mountain air clears my mind. I jog across the overgrown grass, while dew wets my shoes and splatters my ankles.

When I reach my ride, I run my hand along the fender. Old Blue was built by Ford Motor Company back in 1956, but with new paint and a rebuilt engine, she carries me around town just fine.

I settle behind the wheel, grab my shades off the visor, and turn the key. The engine growls and the floorboard rumbles beneath my feet. When my lap belt's fastened, I slip the transmission into first gear. Gravel spits and crunches under the large wheels as I roll down the driveway and on to the road.

Though it's not far to the Nantahala River, I'm late so I step on the gas. Old Blue hugs the road, shifting hard to the right, then left, in an S-shaped pattern as I climb higher into the mountains. When the road straightens out, I roll down the window and settle into my seat. The fresh air bears a slight hint of wildflower and tickles my sinuses. I'll miss the mountains and my people when I leave for Duke University, but I'm ready to get on with my life.

A little while later, beyond the reservation, I reach the Adventure Center where I work. Just as I swing into the parking lot, a black BMW ignores the stop sign and darts in front of me. I slam on the brakes and simultaneously lay on the horn. The girl in the passenger seat stares at me, eyes wide, jaw hanging open as the distance between my front bumper and the Beemer shrinks. If my truck doesn't stop, she'll get killed. How could the driver of that vehicle be so careless with her life?

My tires screech to a halt inches before we collide.

The guy driving reaches across and flips me off.

What the hell? I avoid a major catastrophe that he almost caused and he has the nerve to give me the finger? Only a guy in a pink polo shirt would be a big enough idiot to do something like that.

Then, just as I think no one can be more obnoxious than this guy, the kid in the backseat presses his nose to the glass and torments me with a goofy grin.

The car whizzes past, exposing New Jersey tags. That explains it. Tourists around here are getting ballsier every year, but the ones from the Northeast are the worst. Good thing no one was behind me.

As soon as my racing pulse slows, I let off the brake and go park my truck. The only place left in the employee section is the end spot farthest from the building. Damn Elisi for making me late.

I climb from my truck and check out the sky. The heavens are clear blue without any clouds. The weather will be beautiful—a Southern scorcher, but rain free. If the morning delay and a near accident are the worst things that happen, the day might still turn out okay.

Without further hesitation, I hustle inside to take on my first assignment.

"Hey, Tim. Sorry I'm late," I blurt out, knowing my boss will be behind the desk where he usually is.

Tim looks at his watch. "You were due ten minutes ago. What gives?"

"I had battery trouble." I lie to him because it's better than telling him my grandmother controls my life.

"Well, hurry up. Your victims are waiting on the deck."

I double-step to the door to greet my customers and stop dead. Outside, the guy in the pink polo, the girl, and the kid with the goofy grin are sitting on the bench, undoubtedly waiting for me. I turn to Tim and point at the three. "Those are my passengers?"

"Yup." Tim nods.

"No way. You've got to give me someone else. That jerk cut me off and almost caused me to wreck this morning."

"You're the best guide I have, John, but if you want choices, git to work on time."

There's no use fighting with him. He never changes his mind, especially when he's making a valid point. I turn slowly and focus on my future as I walk out onto the deck. If I flip out and tell the guy off, he'll just have to wait for another white-water rafting guide. I'll lose my job. Besides, I can deal with it. In a couple of hours, the guy, the kid, and the girl will all be a blip of history in my life.

# Chapter 3
## Ace McAllister and John Spears

Cameron, Zack, and I are waiting on the bench outside when a guy wearing a shirt with a White Water Rafting logo walks onto the deck.

*Oh no*. It's the same guy Cameron cut off in the parking lot. My stomach knots. Just my luck that guy would be *our* guide for the day. Talk about uncomfortable.

He clears his throat. "Are you ready to head to the river?"

From the flat tone of his voice and the stoic look on his face, I suspect he hasn't forgotten us either.

Cameron uses my knee to push himself off the bench. He puffs out his chest. "You're our guide?"

"'Fraid so. Name's John Spears." He offers Cameron his hand.

Cameron ignores it and coughs out a one-syllable laugh. "Well, I sure hope you steer a raft better than you do a truck."

Ouch. He's been acting like a jerk all morning—bitching about having to take Zack along, and driving like a maniac. I know Mom wants me to like him as much as she likes Susan, but besides good looks, he doesn't have much going for him. Not only does Cameron have a bad temper, he's a jerk too.

John's hand drops to his side and his lips form a

hard line. Frankly, I wouldn't blame him if he walked away. "Look, dude," John says, "no hard feelings. Let's hit the river, huh?" He looks at me. "You ready?"

We came all this way. Zack would be disappointed if I bailed, so I smile and nod.

Cameron smirks. "Okay, man. Just don't kill us."

Zack leaps off the bench as if propelled by a rocket, and a familiar look of panic masks his face. "I don't want to die."

Autism. Not only does it give him hair-trigger anxiety, it makes him take everything literally. I need to calm him—and fast—before he has a meltdown. I rush to his side, careful not to touch him. He doesn't need any more stress. "It's okay, Zack. It was only an expression. Cameron didn't mean we'd really die."

John studies Zack, then looks at me and cocks an eyebrow.

He doesn't understand, but I don't have time to explain. Zack won't look at me, and his breathing grows increasingly labored while tears pool in his eyes. "You lied to me, Ace," he whines, "You said the trip was going to be fun, but it's not. He's going to kill us." He throws his arm out and points to John.

John's eyes widen and he holds up his hands. "Whoa, kid. I'd never do anything to hurt you."

Zack doesn't listen. He paces in front of the bench, muttering about dying.

Cameron crosses his arms and grunts. "I told you it wasn't a good idea to bring him."

I stiffen and glare at him. "Don't talk about him like he's not here."

Cameron frowns but doesn't say anything, which is good because I really don't want to go off on him in public. Instead, I maneuver in front of Zack to block his path. If I can make eye contact, maybe I can get through to him.

Zack arches his back and twists around me. He hits himself in the head with the heel of his hand, grunting, "Uh! Uh! Uh!" with each blow.

Cameron swears, then says, "Get him under control before he hurts someone."

John takes a step toward Zack. I motion for him to stop, but before I can tell him that Zack hates to be touched, John has both hands planted firmly on his shoulders. I cringe, waiting for Zack to unleash holy hell for all to hear.

"It's okay, buddy," John says in a firm yet soothing voice. "I've been steering rafts my whole life. You're going to love it. I promise."

Zack's eyes are wild and he tosses his head side to side, looking at John's large hands. He twists his shoulders, but John holds firm.

"You're safe with me," he says.

Thinking there's still time to intervene and stop the meltdown, I move closer.

Zack sniffs and grunts. He opens his mouth so wide I can see his tonsils. His body writhes, but then suddenly, as if something snaps in his brain, he throws his head back and goes still. His eyes follow the line of John's six-foot plus body from head to toe and back again. He rakes the tears from his cheeks and lifts one of John's black braids and examines the plaits between his delicate fingers. "Are you a real Native American?"

"Have been since the day I was born," John says.

Can this get any worse? "Zack, don't touch his hair and don't ask him—" I start, before John gestures for me to stop.

Zack's brows scrunch together. He seems to be processing John's revelation. A minute, maybe seconds later, his face relaxes. "My encyclopedia says Native Americans are great survivors."

I exhale in relief. Or is it awe? Zack hardly ever talks to people he doesn't know, much less allow them to touch him. This is new behavior, but I don't want to question it and risk firing him up again. Grandma always says it's okay to accept what you can't understand as long as no one's getting hurt.

John slowly peels back his fingers until Zack is free. "Ready to gear up, kid?"

"Hey, my name's not kid. It's Zack."

John presses his lips together in a hard line as the corners of his mouth threaten to twitch into a smile. "Well, then. Come on, Zack. Let's go."

Zack nods and the two of them take off down the ramp, my brother appearing gawkier than ever, mimicking the length of John's strides.

Cameron frowns. "Are you sure you want to do this? I mean, do you think Zack can handle it? What if he wigs out again?"

"Keep your voice down. He might hear you," I whisper. "He really wants to go whitewater rafting. He'll be fine."

Cameron shrugs. "He's your responsibility."

At the end of the walkway, we come upon a large wooden building. We go inside and get suited with life vests and helmets. John passes us each an oar and plucks a large inflatable raft from the wall. Then we head for the river.

Several feet from the sandy shore, the smooth

water feeds into a rush of current. Thick green trees line the rocky bank. The air is thin and fresh and tinted with something I haven't felt in a long time. Happiness.

John places the yellow raft on the ground near the water and sits on the seat in the back.

He goes over safety tips, and what to do if we fall in. Using the oar as a prop, he demonstrates rowing techniques. His muscles flex and twist, and the material of his shirt clings to his body, showing off a six-pack below.

When he's done he places the oar on the raft bottom and looks at the sky. The sun hits his face at just the right angle to create shadows beneath his cheekbones. He lifts his shades and rubs the bridge of his nose. His dark, piercing eyes catch mine, and I realize I've drifted off. His gaze sets my face on fire.

I turn away, feigning nonchalance by taking undue interest in the river.

I'm reeled back in when John says, "Hope you all have sunblock on."

Am I still blushing?

I touch my cheek. "Ah…I put some on before I left."

Zack sniffs his arm. "Me, too."

Cameron gives John a sideways glance. "I'll be fine."

John shakes his head. "You're pretty fair-skinned, and you don't have a base tan. We sell sunblock in the office."

"I'm fine." Cameron huffs. "How about you forget my skin and worry about doing your job?"

"Just trying to be helpful," John says.

"Whatever," Cameron mumbles.

John looks at Cameron, his eyes twinkling "If you're ready, I guess there's no point in delaying any longer. You're going to have a blast. I promise."

****

The dude takes the girl's hand and pulls her toward the river. She stiffens for a second before letting him lead her along. I'm left with the kid and the raft.

*What am I, a pack animal?*

The kid grabs one of the handles and lifts. At least he has manners.

"Thanks for the help." I say, loud enough for the dude's benefit.

The kid stumbles and sways under the load, only managing to slow me down. It would be easier to lift it over my head and haul it myself, but that might mess with his psyche, so I let him set the pace.

Stupid me. Here I thought these three were history, and I'm stuck with them for the next few hours. The kid has some sort of special need, but he's cool. It's the boyfriend who's going to cause me to crack. At least the girl is cute—not so bright for hooking up with a guy like him—but definitely cute. Maybe if I concentrate on the ruffled bikini top peeking out from under her life jacket and the shorts that barely cover the curve of her butt, I can refrain from killing the dude.

Finally, the kid and I make it to the river's edge, and I toss the raft into the water. I wade in up to my knees and tell my charges to follow.

"Hey, man," I say to the boyfriend. "I need you in the front on the right."

He hops in and pats the seat beside him. The girl sits and he moves so close to her their thighs touch. A dull ache hits me in the gut. If I didn't know better, I'd swear I'm grappling with a green-eyed monster. It doesn't make sense. The girl's nothing but a passenger to me, but I'm a guy. I can't help it if I want to save a pretty damsel in distress—even if she doesn't realize her sad situation.

*Focus on your job, John.* I shake my head to erase my thoughts before I freak out and go all fatal attraction on him. No bunnies will die today. Besides, she's preppy—not my type at all. I usually go for NDN women with dark hair and smoky eyes, but something about this girl trips up my thinking.

I clear my throat. "Excuse me."

She looks at me with her big blue eyes.

"You're going to have to slide over a bit or your oar won't reach the water." I assure myself I'm only telling her this for the purpose of rowing, not to put distance between her and the jerk.

Her cheeks color the softest shade of salmon I've ever seen, and she covers her mouth with three chipped baby-pink fingernails. "Oh, sorry, I didn't know. It's my first time."

How can I not forgive her? "No problem," I say, wondering if she's had any other first times recently, and if she has, hoping it wasn't with the jerk.

She dutifully slides to the edge of the raft, and my blood warms. The kid calls me. I look away, but the urge to turn back to her is too strong. "Hey, I didn't catch your name."

"It's Ace," she says in her husky girl-voice, "and this is Cameron." She hooks a thumb at the boyfriend.

His name I won't bother to learn, but hers—man-oh-man.

"Ace?" I repeat.

She nods.

"Sweet. That's a great name." I pretend not to notice the boyfriend in the background, snarling like a caged tiger I just poked with a stick. He's no dummy. He reaches across the seat and rubs her thigh in retaliation.

Her jaw drops. She lifts his paw and tosses it to the side. He's her man. He should know if she's into PDA's. *Way to diss a woman, guy*. My brain bursts into flames. *Stay calm, John. She is his girl, after all.* I count backward from ten in my head until the fire goes out. Then I mentally slap myself silly. This crazy attraction I have to her is all wrong. It's time to give up the fight. I don't like to lose, but I'm not sure I want to win this one anyway. This girl would probably bring me nothing but trouble, especially with the jerk in the picture. I turn away from her and help the kid onto the middle of the seat in front of mine, then climb in.

"Okay, paddles in the water," I say.

The kid sticks his out and rows the side of the raft. "I can't reach." He scoots closer to the edge.

"No wait, kid…I mean Zack. I put you in that spot on purpose. I need someone with an eagle eye to watch out for rocks. If you're too busy paddling, we might miss one."

The route I intend to take is only categorized as a class two rapid. Not much in the lines of obstacles or rough water, but I want to keep the kid near me just in case anything unexpected happens.

The kid wrinkles his nose and is silent for a moment. Uh-oh, I hope what I said won't set him off again.

He sucks in a breath, and his forehead wrinkles. "I

can do that. I'm a real good looker-outer."

He slides back to the middle of the raft, and the tension in my neck melts away.

Ace twists around to face us. Her eyes are wide and her expression is animated. "He'll do a great job. He's really observant, you know. He can walk into a room and notice if the tiniest item is missing or out of place."

Looks like she really loves that kid. "Is he your brother?"

"Yes, and a good one at that."

Zack beams.

It seems like family is important to Ace. *Hmmm...maybe we do have something in common.*

The boyfriend throws his hands in the air. "Are we going to take off or are we going to sit here yapping all day?"

He's really plucking my nerves. I jam my paddle into the river bottom and push off. "Okay, oars in the water."

Even with only three people paddling, we forge forward quickly and catch the current. The raft pops and bounces. Droplets of water spray across my bare skin, and I can't help but grin. The river is my peace, my escape, and the place where I take down all walls and become my true self.

The kid's grinning as hard as me. He pivots his head from side to side. Like he's drinking everything in. Ace is leaning back smiling, her hands gripping the seat. She's tripping on the experience, too. Even the boyfriend's scowl has disappeared. The spirit of the river doesn't discriminate when doling out its sacred calming forces.

Further downstream, we reach the divide. I steer

onto the novice pass. The sun is moving higher in the cloudless sky, sending some serious UVB rays our way. Sweat drips from my brow, and I wipe it off with the back of my hand. The jerk looks pink already. He should have listened to me about the sunblock. Oh, well. It's too late now.

Once we settle onto our route, I go into my spiel about the history of the river. How Nantahala is Tsalagi for "land of the noonday sun," and how it follows US Highway 19/74, which was once part of the Trail of Tears—the path my people travelled when the U.S. government forced us from our ancestral homeland.

"You got kicked out of your house?" Zack asks.

"Not me, my ancestors."

"Are you angry? Do you hate the white man?" he continues.

This kid is really something. I stifle a laugh as I shake my head. Yeah, when I think about the genocide inflicted on my people, I can't help but be mad. My ancestors live with me and are part of who I am today, but I don't want to project my anger on my passengers. "To hold a grudge would do me no good."

The kid nods crisply, seeming to get what I mean.

Once I have my law degree, I'll make sure Indigenous American rights are protected and our kids have a fair chance in this world. That's how I intend to even the score.

We finally sail into the white water. The raft gains speed and shudders and bobs. The kid whoops. Ace's hair twists around her helmet and tumbles in the breeze. A strand flies in her mouth and she swipes it away. No matter how hard I try, guy-thoughts get the best of me. The scenery fades, and I wait for her to turn so I can gaze into her large baby blues one more time. In my mind, my hand cradles her chin. With my thumb I gently tug at her lower lip until I see the tips of her teeth, then I press my mouth to hers. The thought of it makes my heart do a crazy dance and pump blood at warp speed though my body.

"So where are the rapids?" the jerk says, interrupting my mind-trip. "Are we going to paddle along all day like we're on a kiddy ride?"

Even the magic of the river can't placate this guy for long. There's no hope for him. Fortunately, I know the river well. Up ahead lies a place where I can give him the kind of action he craves.

We reach a slight bend in the river and the raft meets swift current and picks up speed. The wind blows the girl's hair every which way. She brushes it out of her face as she turns. Her eyes meet mine, but she quickly averts them to her brother still wedged between my knees.

****

"Are you having fun, Zack?" My brother squints as if he's searching for an answer. "Take your time and use your words."

"Rock!" he screams, jiggling in his seat. "Big rock." He's so excited he can barely form the words.

"Good job." John pats his shoulder.

My breath hitches and I spin around. Not far ahead, a large rock peeks above the river's surface. I thrust my oar into the water and power-paddle, trying to turn the front of the raft, but we continue full speed ahead.

"How do we stop this thing?" I shout.

"We can't." John says. "Hold on tight."

I let my oar fall to the bottom of the raft and clutch

the handle on the side with two hands. “My brother!”

John braces Zack between his knees. “I’ll take care of him.”

Cameron snorts like it’s all a big joke even though John doesn’t seem to be steering us away from the rock.

At this point, the only option I see is to jump off or trust John. I sure hope he knows what he’s doing.

The closer we get, the larger the rock grows. It’s gray and descends into the river like a boat ramp. We’re going to crash. A scream builds in my lungs. It bursts out as we bump into the hard surface. The rock is smooth as glass and covered in green slime, so rather than crash, we pick up speed and glide across.

“Hold on, Zack,” I holler.

Cameron cheers. "Woo hoo!”

Suddenly, Cameron’s side drops, and he flips into the water with a splat. The raft keeps going and plunges into the river. A giant wave splashes over us. I blink to clear the water from my eyes and swivel my head.

“Man overboard,” I shout as I turn to look for Zack.

Zack is between John’s knees, grinning like a loon. John’s eyes are wide as saucers and a smile tugs at the corners of his mouth. “There’s nothing I can do right now.”

Zack points at Cameron and laughs so hard he doubles over.

I smell a rat—a couple of them. These two have probably planned the whole thing. I glare at them, my eyes shifting from one to the other. “It’s not funny.”

“Wait for me!” Cameron screams, bobbing down the river a good ways behind us.

“You’ve got to do something,” I say. “We can’t

leave him behind. He has the car keys."

John turns around and cups his hand around his mouth. "Remember what I told you. Float on your back and put your feet out. That way, if you run into any rocks, you'll hit feet first. The river slows ahead. You can catch up there."

John picks up a small bucket and bails water out of the raft.

Afloat in his red life vest, Cameron falls further and further behind. "Do something," he screams. "It's friggin' cold."

"You." I point a stiff finger at John. "Quit bailing. You're making us go faster." I grab my oar and back-paddle like crazy. It's no use. I'm no match for the current. "Put down the bucket and help me."

"Paddle forward. When we hit smoother water, I'll dock the raft. Then I'll dive in and get him myself."

I change the motion of my paddle. John joins in and we move swiftly downstream.

"What the hell are you doing?" Cameron's voice fades into the noise of the rapids.

"Bye, bye, Cameron," Zack snickers.

I shoot him a look. "Cut it out. He could get hurt."

"He'll be fine," John says. "He fell off in the safest place possible."

"You should know." My voice oozes sarcasm.

"What do you see in that guy, anyway?" John asks. "He's a B...U...T...T...C...R...A...C...K," he whispers over Zack's head.

"Ha, ha. I heard you." Zack claps. "That spells butt crack. Ha, ha, ha."

I stop paddling and frown at John. My angry expression reflects back at me in his sunglasses. "How can you say that? You don't even know him."

"From what I've seen, I don't want to."

"That's not fair. He's going through a tough time. His parents just got divorced. Why am I even telling you—" I shake my head. Oh brother, now he has me defending Cameron, and I don't even like him.

"Don't try to sell him to me. He's a jerk and the sooner you figure that out, the better off you'll be."

Jerk or no jerk, there's no excuse for dumping him in the river. I press my lips together while I try to come up with the right words to tell him off. My mind draws a blank. It's hard to be mean to someone when they're trying to be nice to me—well, sort of.

"Enough talking," I say instead. "Pull over."

"Aye, aye, captain." He salutes me.

"I'm not kidding."

"Would you quit worrying? The calm water is a few meters ahead."

I puff out my lower lip and stew, crossing my arms on my chest and scowling, so John will get how angry I am.

The current slows practically to a halt and he steers us toward a sandy bank. Thankfully, true to his word, he hops out and beaches the raft. Cameron is a bobbing red blob of a lifejacket in the distance.

John stands tall on the bank, hand on forehead like a visor, scanning the river. He removes his sunglasses and bends toward me. "Here, hold these."

Our eyes lock for a second before his thick lashes sweep down over his dark irises and he lowers his gaze. My head feels fuzzy and flesh bumps shimmy down my arms. I hug myself, pretending I'm cold as beads of sweat form on my temples. I reach out to take his glasses and fumble. They fall into my lap.

"Oh, sorry," I say, recovering them to the safety of my loose fist.

John's mouth twists into a crooked smile, and he does a running dive into the water. He swims freestyle toward the middle of the river, his muscles bulging with each powerful stroke.

"Don't worry, Zackie, everything will be fine," I say.

"John is my friend," Zack says, bringing me back to the real world. The world where I'm looking at the wrong guy in the wrong way and not worrying about the one I should.

I sigh. "A person you met a few hours ago is not your friend."

"Yes, he is," Zack murmurs.

Arguing with him is pointless. Neither Zack nor I will ever see John again after today. As this fact sinks in, for reasons I don't understand, my throat thickens with a sandy ball of regret. I swallow hard. What is the matter with me? I'm crushing on a guy who just dumped another in the river in a testosterone-fueled rage. Damn, I'm a dope.

Cameron floats into the calm water, and John reaches out to grab him.

"Get the hell away from me," Cameron yells, interrupting my self-hate fest.

They exchange a few words that I can't hear, then Cameron leaps onto John's back and dunks him. There's major splashing before John surfaces, spitting water.

Cameron swims around him to the bank and marches onto the shore. He throws down his life vest, then strips off his polo shirt and tosses it onto the sand. His bare white chest showcases his arms, neck, and face, which are burned hot pink.

"He ditched me on purpose," he growls.

Zack giggles.

Cameron flashes Zack a death stare.

I stand. "I'm sure it was an accident. He warned you to hold on."

"Why are you defending him? He did this on purpose. He wanted to get rid of me so he could be alone with you. He's been drooling over you all day." His eyes narrow into slits. "I'll bet you were in on it."

"What are you talking about?"

He stares at me as he scratches the straggly patch of hair on his breastbone, leaving red ruts in his pasty white skin. "You've been looking at him funny, too."

A flush of heat moves from my neck to my cheeks. Were my private thoughts that obvious?

John wades onto the shore. Without making eye contact, I hand him his glasses and pluck Cameron's shirt off the ground, shake the sand out of it, and fold it.

Cameron pulls me into a side hug. "It's a good thing nothing bad happened to Ace, or I'd kick your butt."

I wiggle out of his arms and take a large step sideways. "Stop it."

Cameron frowns. "I'm filing a complaint with the management when we get back."

John shakes his head. "Come on, man. Chill. A little water never hurt anyone. Besides, you said you wanted some action."

"That's a load of bull. You'll be fired for what you've done, if I have anything to do with it."

John shrugs. "Okay, man, whatever you say."

"And another thing," Cameron adds. "Stay away from Ace."

He says this like he actually thinks he has a claim on me. I open my mouth to object.

"Whoa." John holds up his hands. "I'm not interested in your girlfriend."

My heart jolts, and I struggle to catch my breath. Cameron is no boyfriend of mine. Not that John deserves to know. The glimmer of attraction between us was obviously one-sided. It doesn't really matter, but still it hurts to hear out loud.

I pick up Cameron's life vest and hand it to him. He slips it onto his shirtless body. If we are ever going to get back—which I am more than ready to do right now—I have to get these guys to make peace. Or at least come to a truce.

"Listen," I say. "I came here to have fun and you two are ruining everything. If you don't stop fighting, Zack and I are going to walk back."

Zack jumps to his feet. "I don't want to walk. I want to ride the raft."

Now Zack is upset, too. This whole day is turning into a disaster and it's all my fault. I should have never suggested we come.

Cameron gets in Zack's face. "Shut up and sit down."

Zack rocks side-to-side and covers his ears. He hates being told to shut up.

I step between them. "Don't talk to him that way."

John closes in on Cameron. He has fire in his eyes. I push him back with both hands. "You've done enough already. Let me handle this."

John freezes, mouth hanging wide. Cameron smirks.

Zack takes off up the bank but stops after a few yards. He paces and flicks his finger in front of his eyes—a stim he uses to calm himself.

John scrubs his hands over his face. “Look, Cameron. I’m sorry you took a dive. I should have been more careful. I take full responsibility. Now, let’s get back in the raft.” He shoots a quick glance at Zack. “For the kid’s sake.”

“Fine,” Cameron says, “but don’t think your apology is going to stop me from complaining when I get back.”

John ignores him and pushes the raft into knee-deep water. “Come on, Zack.”

Zack stops stimming and runs for the raft.

Soon we’re in the current, paddling downstream in complete silence. Somehow, the river has lost its mystic effect, and the aroma of happiness has vanished. If it wasn’t for Zack, I wouldn’t be in the stupid raft at all.

## Chapter 4
John Spears and Ace McAllister

I tighten my grip on the steering wheel of Old Blue. Good thing steel doesn't bend. Damn it. Most of my rafting passengers like taking a nosedive into the river. They think it adds to the excitement. Some even request it. Not that bozo. He razzes me for taking him on a kiddie ride then morphs into a wimp when I show him some action. It's a good thing my boss likes me. Being sent home for two days for ticking off a customer is humiliating, but not as bad as being fired.

The worst part isn't my punishment; it was seeing Ace's expression sink when I told the jerk I had no interest in her. It's not my style to hurt girls. Especially vulnerable girls like her who can't see when the guys they are with are jerks.

Ah, whatever. It doesn't matter. I'll never see her again so there's no point in fretting. I've got a kitchen floor to fix, and I no longer have an excuse not to get started.

With no traffic, I'm home in a jiffy. Instead of a refuge, I find a sticky situation. My mother's rusted-out Toyota Corsica is parked on the grass. We haven't seen or heard from her in almost a year. What the hell is she doing here?

I get out of the truck and peek in her driver's window. Judging by the heap of laundry occupying the passenger side and the junk stuffed back seat, she might be moving back. Odd. Last I heard, she and Elisi were still on the outs.

With my heart pounding in fear mixed with excitement, I hurry to the front door. Even before I get my hand on the knob, I hear yelling. Damn it. Just once I want a normal visit with Mom—the kind where the family eats dinner together, tells stories, and laughs about old times. Why can't Elisi cut her some slack?

I step inside and head into the kitchen. Elisi stops mid-sentence.

Mom's back is to me..

"Hey, Mommy." I tend to revert back to a three-year-old when she's around. Lame, I know, but old habits are hard to break.

Her black hair swings on the middle of her back as she turns to face me. Dark circles fill the hollows under her eyes, and she's thin. Very thin. She hesitates a moment before walking toward me, arms wide.

I hug her and detect the slight hint of alcohol about her presence. Damn it.

My mother senses my discomfort and drops her arms to her side. "John." Her eyes widen. "You've matured so much I hardly recognize you. So, how have you been? I've missed you, baby."

"Missed him?" Elisi snaps. "Be honest for once in your life. You didn't come here to for a nice little visit. You came for money."

I slump against the wall. Does Elisi ever think before she speaks? Why not just punch me in the gut instead?

Mom stiffens. Her eyes dart to the door and back again. She looks as if bolting seems like a good idea.

"Don't believe her, John. She can't stop me from visiting you. I'm your mother, and I love you."

Elisi throws out her arm and points at me. "You've haven't been a mother to him in years. I have."

That's not completely true. I didn't come to live with Elisi until I was nearly four. I glare at Elisi. "She's my mother, and I want to see her."

Elisi flinches as if I've taken a swing at her. She grabs her purse off the counter, clutches it to her chest, and rushes from the room.

I don't try to stop her. I can straighten this out later. I hope.

Right now, Mom is here, and she needs me. "Do you want something to eat?"

She stares at the floor. "I'm not hungry."

"You're too thin. You need to eat."

"I'm fine. The only thing wrong with me is that I'm homeless at the moment. Martin kicked me out and it was his place so…"

"That sucks."

"He's a jerk? I'm better off without him."

We're in agreement on that. She met him a year or two after Dad died. He's drunk more than he's sober. While I know he doesn't pour booze down her throat, I blame him for Mom's drinking. She didn't touch alcohol until she met him.

She twists her fingers into a tangled mess. "Your grandmother won't let me stay. So I'll have to live in my car till I can come up with enough money to get a place."

Vapid silence looms between us, while images of a cliff with a large, jagged rock teetering on the edge high above fill my head. Elisi's screaming at me to run, but I stand there transfixed. Elisi screams at me a second time, but my hard head stops me from listening.

"Well, can you help?" Mom says, bringing me back to reality.

"If you promise not to drink, Elisi will let you stay. I'll talk to her."

"I'm not drinking, and she's still wants me to leave." She looks unflinchingly at me with her liar's eyes.

"How much do you need?" I ask, even though throwing money at the problem hasn't helped in the past.

"A couple thousand dollars should tie me over."

"A couple thou? It's taken me almost half a year to save that much money."

"Forget it," she continues. "I knew no one here cared about me. I shouldn't have come."

How can she say that? We all begged her to leave Martin and come home. The walls in the house shrink. I can't breathe or I'd scream, *I want a mother. Quit drinking.* I can't take the lies any more, but the stupid baby inside me, the one she once cradled in her arms, won't let me.

"Come on. I'll take you to the bank," is all I can manage.

****

When Zack, Cameron, and I return to the resort, Cameron hands the car keys to the bellhop and disappears inside, leaving Zack and me in the BMW. By the time we reach the lobby, he's already boarding the elevator. He looks straight at us but makes no attempt to hold the doors. They close and carry him away.

It's just as well. The way he treated Zack today is inexcusable. And I'm tired of hearing about his sunburn, and how I sided with our raft guide over him. Our guide made it quite clear we weren't in cahoots, that he wanted nothing to do with me, so Cameron has no reason to be mad—at least not at me. He better not tell my mother differently.

A loud group of map-clutching tourists flood past as they hurry for the shuttle. I chase after Zack as he weaves through them to reach the elevator. When I go to push the up button, Zack grabs my arm and hops up and down. I forgot. It's a rule. He always has to press the button. I let him, of course, a little jealous that I'm unable to get so excited over such a simple task, or anything else for that matter.

We reach the suite. My parents and Cameron's mother, Susan, are at the kitchen table drinking wine. It's funny how Dad doesn't mind if Mom drinks when he's around. Talk about a hypocrite. At least Susan's here. Mom saves her heavy-duty drinking for when she's alone. Hiding the severity of her problem is important to her.

"Hey, kids," Dad says. "Where's Cameron?"

"He went to his room." At least I think he did.

Zack's eyes flare. "We had great fun today. Cameron fell in the water and got real sunburned. Then he screamed at Ace 'cause she liked our river guide. I liked him, too. His name is John. Cameron wasn't mad at me for liking him, only Ace."

Susan jumps up from her chair and latches on to my arm. "Is Cameron hurt?"

"He's pretty sunburned, but he's fine. I think."

"I better check on him." Susan grabs her wine

glass, takes a big gulp, and clunks it back on the table. "I'll be back."

She brushes past me and hesitates, her eyes probing me as if she's looking for an unspoken answer. I take a sudden interest in the plain beige carpeting and she continues to the door. Zack and his inability to speak nothing but the whole truth has struck again. If he were closer I'd pinch him.

Once Susan leaves, I head for the bedroom.

"Stop!" Mom shouts. "I want to know what happened between you and Cameron."

Here we go again. Anytime Mom senses trouble, she automatically assumes I'm to blame.

I do a slow military turn and face her. "It was nothing. Zack's exaggerating."

"Nuh-uh," Zack grunts from the spot he's taken on the floor in front of the television. "Cameron's real mad."

I cut my eyes at him.

Dad comes up behind Mom, and, in a rare display of affection, rests his arm over her shoulder. Mom relaxes into his embrace.

"Don't let it ruin the night, Dawn," he says. "A little rivalry between boys over a pretty girl like Ace never hurt anyone."

I cover my burning cheeks. "Dad, stop. The river guide hardly knew I was alive."

Mom sighs. "Whether he did or he didn't, we invited Cameron and his mother as our guests. Try to be nice to him."

We did not invite him, she did. "Cameron's kind of rude, and he embarrassed me today."

Mom shakes her head. "Susan says he's having a

tough time since she and Ted divorced. You could try to be a little more sympathetic."

Sympathetic? Why not? That's my middle name.

On the bright side, Mom is much happier when Susan's around, and when she's happy she drinks less. Usually.

And it must be tough to have your parents divorce, then be shipped off to a boarding school the way Cameron was. If my parents divorced, they could do the same with me. A little distance from them might not be all bad, but what would happen to Zack if I wasn't there to take care of him? Zack needs me.

"You're right, Mom. I'll try to be understanding."

"Good." Mom says. "Now, I want you to help Zack get cleaned up. Daddy has to work, and I've invited Susan and Cameron to dinner."

Taking care of Zack is no problem, but Cameron? I think I feel a migraine coming on.

My phone rings. It's Grandma. She's probably calling to see how things are going with Mom. I can't talk to her now. She can always tell when I'm lying. If she finds out Mom's drinking, she'll insist Mom go back to rehab. My father threatened to leave last time. I can fix this without Grandma's help. I know I can.

"Ace, aren't you going to answer your phone?" Mom says.

I startle and stammer, "It's my friend, Marcy. I'll call her back after I get Zack ready for bed."

"Oh, okay. Well, scoot. Our guests will be here soon."

****

Through the large glass window in the front of the bank, I watch my mother puff on a cigarette. "Next customer, please?" the teller says.

I move forward, more sorry than ever I dunked the loser in the river and got sent home. I make a huge dent in my account, leaving some money to help Elisi with groceries and a little for myself.

Then I put on a poker face and march outside with an envelope full of cash. I don't want to hate my mother, but I'll hate myself more if I don't speak my mind.

She smiles. "You're a good boy. I'll pay you back."

She still owes me money from the last time she and Martin broke up, but I'm not worried about the money. I can make more. There's more important things to discuss. Where do I begin?

She sticks out her hand, gesturing for the money.

"Let me take you to rehab. Once you're sober, Elisi will welcome you home. We all will."

Mom's face twists into a scowl. "Here we go again. For the last time, I'm not drinking. I'm a little tired, that's all. Once I get my own place and can get some rest, I'll be as good as new."

"Mom, you're not fooling me. You smell like booze."

She stiffens. "So what if I have a drink now and then? It's legal."

Every muscle in my body tenses and pressure builds so tight in my head, I fear my skull will crack in two. I know it's the alcohol talking and not her. If I can convince her to get help, we can be a family again. I squeeze the envelope of money tighter.

She frowns at me. "If you don't want to lend me the money that's fine, but don't give me any more lip about my drinking. I don't have a problem."

I give up. I can't do anymore. It's time to give her a final ultimatum. The one I'd hoped I'd never have to use:

"All right. You win. The money's yours, but if you take it, I don't ever want to see you again. Do you understand?" I hold the envelope out, gambling with our future as mother and son. She has her problems, but she loves me. I know she does.

My mother kicks a rock on the pavement, sending it flying into the brick wall of the bank, narrowly missing the window. "You think you're smart, don't you? Well, no one, not even my son, can manipulate me." She raises her head, and her teary eyes lock on mine.

I hold her gaze, hoping she's finally ready to make the right choice.

"I'm sorry, John. I love you, but I can't do it. I can't go home," she says before snatching the envelope from my hand.

The gigantic boulder that's been threatening me falls off the cliff. It misses my head and crushes my heart. I am dead.

She bursts into a sob and runs to her car, leaving me standing motherless on the curb.

With my brain on autopilot, I do the only thing I can at the moment; I drive home. As I pull up our gravel driveway, I think about how I sided with my mother over Elisi. I've got to undo the damage I've done.

But how?

Safe inside the house, I close my eyes and breathe deeply, evenly. When I open my eyes, Elisi stands before me. "She's gone," I say.

I brace myself for Elisi's wrath, but instead she reaches up and touches my cheek. Her lower lip trembles. "All her life she dreamed of being a mother, but when your father died, she broke. It's not you. Remember that. Okay, John?"

I crumble into Elisi's arms. The strength of her embrace is more than I can handle. A tear rolls down my cheek, followed by another, and another. She holds me and pats my back, while I cry like a baby.

****

Susan returns alone, much to my delight. Cameron supposedly took some aspirin and crashed on the couch. Poor baby.

When we finish dinner, Mom asks me to give Zack his meds. He has to take a pill to calm down at night because the medicine he takes in the morning for hyperactivity disturbs his sleep. I hate that he has to take anything at all, but when he goes without his medicine, his meltdowns are way worse.

Zack and I play Monopoly. Midway through our game, his meds kick in. He can barely keep his eyes open, so I tuck him into bed then curl up in front of the TV for some R&R.

Five minutes into this cool retro '80s movie, Mom approaches me with a plate full of food. "Take this to Cameron. I'll bet he's starving."

In one calculated move, she robs me of a great flick and much needed free time. I should have known she wouldn't rest until she was sure I was back in Cameron's good graces. She can't have her insolent daughter insulting her friend's son.

I push myself off the couch and take the plate.

Susan smiles. "Cameron is going to be happy to see you."

I find the strength to return a weak smile.

Outside Cameron's room, John's words play in my head. *He's not good enough for you.* Whether it's true or not, the words come at me like an eighteen-wheeler, and I stop. A room service cart outside a nearby door catches my eye. I leave the plate meant for Cameron on top of the dirty dishes and double step down the hall. I can always tell Mom and Susan he didn't answer. My heart races, and I fight the overwhelming urge to giggle.

I stroll the first floor, admiring the Cherokee artifacts that adorn the hallways. People pass by in twos and threes. Some are in a hurry, others lag about, chatting. I seem to be the only one without a companion, but I don't mind one bit, because right now I'm walking on air.

The faint thrum of dance music drives me in a different direction. It doesn't matter. I'm on me time.

Near the Casino entrance is an elaborate light display. Two massive mushroom-shaped structures with varying shades of gold and silver panels twinkle from floor to ceiling. Behind them, the long hallway stretches into a ritzy game room, packed with people hovering over rows of slot machines, yanking on the levers as if they believe they'll soon be millionaires.

I hear my father's voice and turn as he enters an adjacent hallway with his arm around a woman in a blue, sparkly dress, sporting bleached blonde hair, platinum like a pinup model. What the heck is he doing? I dart behind one of the light structures so he won't see me.

Why I'm hiding escapes me. I'm not doing anything I'm not supposed to.

But him?

I follow them for a few paces and move behind a Roman-shaped pillar near a large glass window that overlooks a stream running through the resort grounds. When I get up the nerve to peek around the column, Dad and the blonde are near the end of the hall in front of a hotel room. My father brushes her hair behind her ear and kisses her neck. The woman lazily swings her head to the side and leans into him. Mom was right. He *is* having an affair. I'll bet he bought her the wine, so she'd get drunk and wouldn't come looking for him. He swipes a keycard through the lock and opens the door. If he goes in with that woman, he's going to ruin everything.

I dart out into the center of the hall and shout, "Dad!"

Both his feet practically leave the floor. The woman spins around and stares at me, her mouth wide.

He places his hand over his heart, key card cinched between two fingers. "Ace, you scared me." He glances at the open door and then at me. "What are you doing here?"

"The question is, what are *you* doing there?" I take a few cautious steps toward him.

He straightens his suit jacket and smiles like a used car salesman, cunning, yet a bit aloof. "Oh, this must look bad, but it's not what you think. Come here. I want you to meet my business partner, Holly."

My feet grow roots and anchor me in place.

Holly clears her throat and her mouth twitches up in the corners, simulating a smile. "Hello, darlin'," she says in a consolatory Southern accent.

Dad passes her the key card. “Excuse me a minute, will you?”

The blonde’s fake smile flat-lines. “Sure. Tell you what, I’m going to use the powder room. I’ll see you back in the casino.” She wiggles her fingers at me. “Nice to meet you,” she says before disappearing into the room.

Dad approaches in his usual easy gait. “You shouldn’t be roaming around the hotel alone this late in the evening. Let me walk you back to the room.”

My heart catches in my throat. He thinks he can act like nothing happened and I’ll go along with it. “How can you do this?”

“Do what, Ace?”

I press my lips together, while I blink at the tears filling my eyes.

“Stop acting like your mother,” he says. “I told you, she’s a business partner. We were stopping by her room to get a contract.”

No need to blink any longer. The anger brewing inside me boils the tears away. He might fool Mom, but not me. For the first time in my life, I truly hate him. “If it was her room, why’d you have the key? Why’d you kiss her?”

“I didn’t—” Dad turns beet red and slices his hand through the air. “No more foolish questions. I’m taking you back to our room.” Not only is my father betraying my mother, he’s trying to gaslight me. He places a hand on my shoulder and steers me forward.

Repulsed, I step sideways, escaping his touch.

We don’t speak a word, and when the elevator opens on our floor, I step into the hallway. He doesn’t get out.

“Good night, honey,” he says, in a voice more forced than pleasant.

“Have a nice night, Dad.” I make my voice saccharin, even though I long to crumple to the ground and die.

Dad catches the elevator door before it closes. “Ah, Ace, wait a minute.”

My heart pumps hope through my veins. Maybe he’s realized what he’s doing is wrong. Maybe he’s going to apologize for being a jerk and come with me to our suite where he belongs. “Go ahead. I’m listening.”

He holds a fist over his mouth and clears his throat. “I wouldn’t mention you saw me, if I were you. You know how your mom always reads everything the wrong way? If you say something she doesn’t like, she’s likely to go off the deep end again.”

If he’d slapped me I wouldn’t be more stunned. I never thought he’d gamble with my life. But he’s played the trump card and won. He’s placed my mother’s mental health in my hands. He knows I’ll do anything to protect her. So once again, I hear nothing. I see nothing.

And now, I feel nothing. As much as I want to rant and rave and scream and tear the wallpaper from the wall, I am silenced by the fact he’s right. If I open my mouth, Mom will crash and burn, and the social workers will get involved again. What will happen to Zack if they take him?

So with no other alternative, I leave my Dad behind and enter our suite, carrying his horrible secret.

Another secret I can never tell. Another secret guaranteed to burden me for the rest of my life.

## Chapter 5
## John Spears

The smell of breakfast floats into my room, making my stomach rumble. Dealing with my mom yesterday made eating impossible, but after mulling over my situation last night, and making the decision to concentrate on all the people in my life who love me, I find I'm hungry. Really hungry. Colossally hungry.

I run sock-footed down the hallway and slide into the kitchen, snagging the doorframe to stop myself. Elisi hovers over the stove with my sister Rae by her side. My brother Victor, cousin Lenny, and Aunt June are already seated at the table.

Lenny clutches his fork and spoon, pounds them on the table and chants, "We want food. We want food."

Elisi does a slow turn. A death stare masks her face. "June, teach that boy some manners before I get my wooden spoon."

Her wooden spoon was retired some time after I hit middle school. If I concentrate hard enough I can still feel the sting. Luckily for Lenny, she likes to threaten, but she never uses it anymore.

Aunt June grabs the silverware out of Lenny's hands and shushes him.

During the commotion, I sneak up behind Elisi and steal a piece of bacon from the platter.

She tries to grab it out of my hand. Before she gets

anywhere close, I have it over my head, far out of her reach. Elisi takes a dishtowel and playfully swats my stomach. "No eating until everyone is seated."

"Why, Grandma, what a big mouth you have," I tease.

Rae jabs me between the ribs. My body contracts and she steals the bacon out of my hand. I'm left with a tiny bit pinched between my fingertips.

Rae opens her mouth wide and shows me the stolen, chewed-up food. "Want it now, John?"

"That's gross." I scarf down the remaining morsel and reach for another piece.

"Oh no, you don't." Elisi snatches the tray. She ducks under my arm and runs for the table. Rae and I chase after her. Everyone is laughing.

I shimmy between Victor and Lenny on the bench and rub my hands together.

Victor punches me in the arm. "You're hogging all the space, bro."

I massage the sore spot. "If we weren't at the table you'd be a goner, punk."

Having a brother can be a pain, especially when he's three years younger and shows no respect for his elders. Namely me. I haven't decided whether I'm going to miss him when I go to college this fall.

"Boys, settle down." Aunt June frowns. "You're going to knock Lenny onto the floor."

Lenny jumps to attention and grabs the edge of the table. "I don't want to fall."

He was nowhere near taking a dive. Aunt June was nearly forty-six when she finally had Lenny. She didn't think she'd ever have children, so she babies him way too much. Maybe fussing over Lenny keeps her mind off her husband, George, who's always away working at the forest station.

Elisi places the food in the center of the table. Along with bacon, we have potatoes, scrambled eggs, and fry bread—a flatbread that's fried in oil. My mouth is watering like one of Pavlov's dogs. Just as I reach for the bread, the doorbell rings.

"Wonder who that is?" I rise to answer it.

"Sit down," Elisi says. "I didn't cook this food for my health. Eat while it's still warm."

I obey her for two reasons. One, if I challenge her, she'll gladly show me who's the boss, and two, I'm starving.

Elisi disappears into the hallway. The door creaks open and seconds later she sings, "Come on in."

By the bright tone of her voice I'd hazard to guess it's one of her sisters. I crane my neck, curious which one. Instead of an aunt, my ex-girlfriend, Jasmine, pops into the kitchen.

What's she doing here? I thought I was clear this time when I told her we were through.

"Hi, John," she says. "Sorry to interrupt your breakfast, but I haven't heard from you in a while, and I wanted to make sure you were okay. I can leave if you want." She bites her lower lip.

Over the last three years, I've learned a few things about Jasmine. One of them is she doesn't stop until she gets what she wants, and the thing she wants, at least for this moment, is me. Why else would she be here?

Elisi hooks her arm through Jasmine's and escorts her to the table. "You're not going anywhere until you eat. We have plenty."

I'm suddenly reminded of something else. My

grandmother loves Jasmine. I start to object but change my mind. Elisi thinks Jasmine walks on water because she's staying on the reservation and working at her father's business rather than going away to college. Elisi figures if we get back together I might stay, too. Well, she's dead wrong. Even if Jasmine were still my girlfriend, I wouldn't change my plans.

Maybe having my ex hang around for breakfast is a good idea. Then I can prove to Elisi there's nothing she or Jasmine can do to change my mind. Besides, Jasmine and I went together for three years. I owe her some respect.

Elisi lifts Lenny off the bench and places him in her chair. "Here, Jasmine, sit by John."

Her blatant attempt to push us together isn't going to work. "Grandmother," I say. She hates when I call her that. "You sit in my place. I'll pull a stool up to the counter."

Before I can move, Rae pushes her chair from the table. "Sit here, Elisi. My ride to work will be here any minute."

I glare at Rae. She tosses me a smug smile.

Damn it. She told me she'd get even with me for using her fancy hair shampoo as body wash, and I guess this is it. With both Rae and Elisi against me, I don't stand a chance. I'm stuck where I'm at for now, but as soon as breakfast is over I'm flying solo.

"Bye, all," Rae says. She looks at me and winks. "Call me later, okay?"

*What a traitor. She's dreaming if she thinks I'd phone her now*. I shake my head as I watch her flit from the room.

Jasmine inches behind the bench in her skyscraper

heels and scrunches in beside me. She's wearing white shorts and her bare leg rests warm against mine. I breathe through my mouth as the heavy scent of roses consumes me. Her body has a nice natural scent, but for some reason she's covering it up with smelly perfume today.

She takes my plate and fills it with food before preparing her own. Funny, I don't remember her waiting on me when we were together. All we ever did was fight.

When I'm all served, she unfolds a napkin and places it on her lap. "I've got something to tell you, John. I think you're going to like it."

Victor catches my gaze and wags his eyebrows.

I ignore him.

Jasmine rests her hand on my forearm. "Daddy has a job for you at his construction company. It's behind a desk, so you won't be busting your rear all day. It's only twenty-five hours a week for now, but he says it will eventually turn into full time. You can start tomorrow if you want."

I let out a little laugh under my breath. "That's real nice of you, but I already have a job."

Elisi's chair scrapes the floor as she scoots closer to the table. "You can't just ignore this offer. Marty Kingfisher is an important man."

Aunt June nods. "At least talk to him. He's offering you a wonderful opportunity. I wish George could work for him." She looks at Jasmine and raises a brow.

Jasmine pushes food around her plate and plays dumb.

Elisi slaps her palms on the table. "Stop it, June. This is about John, not George."

I do the football signal for time out. "Sorry, guys, but I'm going to finish the summer where I'm at. No point in starting something new. I'm leaving in the fall. Remember?"

Jasmine makes a pouty face. "Why don't you at least give it a try? Daddy said he'd pay you well."

"Listen to her, John," Elisi says. "Not only will you make a good living, you'll be with *yohvstianadvni*." She sweeps her arm out, gesturing to my "kinfolk" at the table.

If I didn't know better, I'd swear Elisi and Jasmine masterminded the whole deal. My insides burn. "I don't need a job. What I need is for you all to stop butting in to my life."

My words come out spoiled-brat-harsh and the room goes silent.

Aunt June, Lenny, and Victor stare at their plates. Elisi's face collapses into a complex set of wrinkles, and she drops her fork on the table. Jasmine takes a tiny bite of the potatoes that looked so good a few minutes ago, but no longer appeal to me.

I've got to get out of here before I blow my lid.

Grabbing a piece of flatbread off the table, I storm outside and plop down under the oak tree in the front yard. Too mad to swallow, I toss my bread to a squirrel hanging out nearby and rest my back against the tree's massive trunk, thumping my head repeatedly on the bark. It's sharp and hurts a little, but I don't care.

Why do I let them rile me up? My life is on the right track. I have a plan. And now, because of my stupid temper, I'm starving, my food's getting cold, and most importantly, I owe my grandmother an apology. Boy, did I teach them a lesson.

The front door opens. Jasmine steps outside and stops on the porch. "Is it safe to come out?"

She's balancing a plate of food on her palm. Hell, confronting her with my conspiracy theory is pointless. She'll lie. Besides I'm dying of hunger.

"Come on. I'm over it."

She struts across the lawn, somehow managing to hang on to my plate, despite navigating holes and clumps of grass in her nightclub shoes. As much as I'm sure we're not right for each other, I can't help but notice her long, lean legs and the way her chest bounces with every step. She is a beauty. She's have been a shoo-in for the Miss Cherokee contest last fall if she'd studied up on our government and been able to speak more of our native tongue.

She bends to hand me my plate. "Here, I didn't mean to ruin your breakfast."

"You didn't."

"You know, John, it doesn't have to be over between us, just because you're going away. I know we've been fighting a lot but…"

"Listen, Jasmine, I like you, and I'll always remember our time together, but the constant fighting was too much to handle. It wasn't working between us. Even you said as much. I think it's best if we move on. You're a great girl. You'll find someone else. Maybe even someone better." I wink.

For a second, her normally confident face withers, and I'm hit by a pang of guilt.

She sits beside me. "I get it. You haven't changed your mind, but since I'm here, can't we spend one last day together?"

I shake my head. "I don't know."

"As friends?"

I am feeling kind of lonely.

"So what do you say?" she asks.

I rub the back of my neck. "One last day would be okay. I guess."

## Chapter 6
## Ace McAllister and John Spears

Dad comes out of the bedroom, scratching the dark shroud of stubble on his face. I wonder when he got home?

He plops down at the breakfast table, obviously thinking he still has a right to be part of our family. “Morning,” he grumbles.

Zack and I pretty much ignore him, but Mom gives him a cup of coffee. We’re supposed to take a family trip to the Biltmore Estates today, but I don’t want to go. The sting of seeing him with the blonde is too raw.

Zack takes a handful of dry cereal from his bowl and shoves it into his mouth. Mom thumps her coffee cup on the table. “Oh no, you don’t, mister.” She waves a spoon in front of his face. “Use this.”

“I don’t like it,” Zack whines.

“Let me.” I take the spoon, dip it in his cereal and feed him a bite. “You’re big now. You need to do this on your own, Zackie.”

“I don’t want to grow up. I want to be a kid.” Zack puffs out his lower lip.

I stare at my father. “We all have to grow up, no matter how much it sucks.”

Dad steeples his fingers and rests his forehead on them. I’ll bet he’s praying I’ll keep quiet.

Zack reluctantly takes the spoon, scoops one

Cheerio, and picks it off the end with his teeth as if he's avoiding germs. He finishes chewing, and picks up another single O.

"Please hurry," Mom groans. "We need to get on the road."

Dad frowns. "You're always micromanaging everyone. Let the kid enjoy his breakfast."

Dad's attitude makes it clear this trip isn't a priority for him either, but after what he's done, he deserves to suffer. The thing is, being around him will make me miserable, too. I can't handle an entire day with him, much of it trapped inside the car.

I rub the back of my neck and scrunch my cheeks. "Mom, I'm feeling sick. Would you mind if I stay home and rest?"

My mother braces her hands on her hips. "Ace, you know this is supposed to be a family day."

"I know, but I couldn't sleep last night, and I have a migraine." I cut my eyes at my father.

Mom grabs her purse from the counter, roots around inside, and hands me a tiny white bottle. "Take one of these. You'll be fine by the time we get there."

"Mom, I'm not going to take your prescription pain killers. It's not legal."

Dad looks at me as he speaks, "Honey, if Ace is not feeling well, why not let her stay here?"

"But, Bradley—"

"We'll miss her, but there will be plenty other family outings."

She sighs. "Well, I suppose it will be okay."

He raises his eyebrows at me, as if seeking approval for his good deed. I turn my head. Sucking up to me won't make me forgive or forget.

Mom sighs. "I suppose you can hang out with Cameron. Susan says he's too blistered from sunburn to leave the room. I'm sure he'd love your company."

"Maybe later," I say. "If I'm feeling better."

Dad takes his wallet from his pocket. He pulls out a crisp one-hundred-dollar bill and lays it on the table if front of me. "This ought to cover dinner if you and Cameron want to go out."

He thinks he can buy my silence? Inside, hot metal courses through my veins. It takes all I have not to call him out. I speak though clenched teeth. "I have my own money."

"Ace," Mom says. "Your father's doing something nice for you. You need to thank him."

I sniff. She wouldn't say that if she knew it was hush money. My dad is lucky my instinct to protect her is greater than my disdain for his nasty secret.

"Thanks, Dad." I say as I push away from the table, leaving the money to rot.

Once the family is gone, I swap my pajamas for jean shorts and a tank top, which I cover with my favorite vest. The back has a beadwork scene of a sunrise over the ocean, colored in oranges, yellows, browns and blues. I created the design and hand-stitched it myself. Some say I'm talented and ought to sell my creations, but they are my heart and soul, my escape from the madness of my life. Turning my art into a job might take the fun out of it.

At the last second, I trade my flip-flops for my suede ankle boots and head for the lobby. I board the shuttle that goes to the center of the Cherokee Indian Reservation.

When the bus reaches a place where shops are

abundant, I ask the driver to stop. The town is not rustic like I thought it would be. People are everywhere. A steady stream of bikers zoom past, their loud engines vibrating against the pavement. Behind them is a line of cars. It takes a while for the traffic to clear enough for me to cross the street.

There are many stores Mom would call tourist traps, as well as outside exhibits. I pass a small platform where Cherokee street dancers perform a hoop dance for donations from the crowd, and a fenced area where guy with a megaphone dares people to ride a mechanical bull. For a price, of course. In the center of the shopping area, a large fountain spouts streams of water from the ground. Young children squeal as they run through the spray. Zack would love it.

I visit a few of the souvenir stores. They are filled with everything from shot glasses to jewelry. I'm dizzy from looking at so many items, and about to give up my shopping expedition, when I come across a small, unassuming place with a sign that reads Crafts and Things. Inside I find bolts of leather and colorful fabrics, racks of beaded clothing, and an entire display case of every shape and color bead imaginable. I'm in heaven.

A girl with a name-tag reading "Stella Rae" approaches me. She's about my age, with silky dark hair shaped in a shoulder length bob and deep brown eyes. "Good morning. Can I help you?"

She also looks really familiar, and I can't figure out why.

Her brows furrow. She shifts and checks the buttons on her shirt. "Is there something in particular you're looking for?"

"Sorry. I didn't mean to stare. It's just I feel like I know you from somewhere. Have you ever been to New Jersey?"

"No. I've lived here all my life." Her slight southern twang confirms her statement.

"Oh, okay. I must be mistaken."

"If you'd met me before, you wouldn't have forgotten. I promise." She laughs with both her mouth and her eyes. She does seem like she'd be a lot of fun to get to know.

The wall phone dingalings. It's black with push buttons, and the receiver jiggles with each unanswered ring.

Stella turns. "I've got to get that. Look around. Let me know if there's anything I can help you with."

I browse through the racks of clothing—first the vests, then the shirts, jeans, and dresses. They are all beautiful, adorned with hand-sewn bead patterns. I fall in love with a jean shirt with beaded elk above both pockets.

After she hangs up the phone, I approach the counter. "Can I try this on over my shirt?"

"Sure. Let me help you." She sashays to my side of the counter and helps me remove my vest. Holding it on the palm of her hand, she runs the tip of her finger over the beadwork on the back. "Say, where did you buy this?"

"The vest came from a department store. I stitched the sunset on the back myself."

"You did the beadwork by hand?"

I nod.

"That's incredible…ah…ah…what's your name?"

"Ace. Ace McAllister."

“Ace? How cool. Where’d you get a name like that?”

“My dad thought it up. He said it would bring me luck.” I don’t tell her he’s a professional gambler and truly believes in stuff like that. Most people get weirded-out when they find out his occupation.

She wiggles her nametag. “My name’s Stella. Do you live around here?”

I shake my head. “We’re staying for the summer. Why?”

“No reason. Actually, I’m glad you’re a visitor. For a moment I thought we had some major competition.” She dangles my vest off her finger. “Has anyone ever told you you’re good?”

“My friends, but you know what they say about friends and family judging your talent.”

“I sure do.” She snickers. “Seriously though, I meant what I said.”

“Thanks. I’d love to learn about Native American beadwork. Do you have any books or patterns for sale?”

“Typically, no, but if you tell me how you made that sunrise, I’ll gladly share a secret or two with you.”

“You got a deal.” We shake on it.

In between customers, she shows me one of her patterns, and I draw mine out for her, carefully color-coding the tiny boxes on the graph paper. Then I sift through the many beads in the store and select several different types. I put them in plastic bags and set them on the counter along with the elk shirt.

Stella and I chat some more. Before I know it, we’ve moved on from beadwork to high school stuff. Something about her makes me trust her enough to tell her about my brother and some of my family problems, and how alone I feel at times.

Her cell phone rings, and I pick up my bag. “I guess I better get going. Thanks for the patterns. I can’t wait to get home and start sewing.”

“Wait. Don’t leave yet. I’ll only be a moment.”

She picks up her phone and I wander to the other side of the store and scan the rack of clothing once more.

When she’s done talking, she motions me over to the counter. “When I get off, some friends and I are going to Sliding Rock. Do you want to come?”

“What’s Sliding Rock?”

“It’s a large boulder in the middle of the river. It’s slick. You sit on your butt at the top and rushing water carries you into a pool of water at the bottom. It’s sort of a natural fun park.”

“That sounds fun.”

“Good. Then grab a swimsuit and meet me back here at two-thirty. It’ll be a blast. I promise.”

I’ve never gone off with someone I just met, but after spending most of the morning with Stella, she doesn’t feel like a stranger. My gut tells me she’s a good person. “Okay. I’ll see you then.”

I pull out my phone to call the shuttle. Multiple texts from Cameron fill the screen. I barely know him and he’s acting like we’re best friends. If I go back to the hotel and he finds out what I’m doing, he might tell my Mom I’m not sick. I can buy flipflops, a swimsuit, and a towel from one of the local stores.

I text Mom and tell her I’ve silenced my phone so I can sleep, not bothering to wait for a response. Then I delete every text from Cameron just because it feels good.

A little ways down the road, I find a store that sells swimsuits. Most of the bikinis are neon and skimpy. Very skimpy. A lone black one catches my eye. It's bedazzled with sparkly studs and has a strand of fringe across the top—not something Mom would want me to wear. In fact, she would hate it. I snatch it off the rack, and as if fate's at play, it's exactly my size. I ask the clerk's permission to use the fitting room.

After I put it on, I examine myself in the mirror. The fringe on the top wiggles when I turn from side to side. I throw my shoulders back. Not bad. Not bad at all. It's even kind of sexy. I stick my head out the door and wave at the clerk. "Can I wear this out of here?"

"Sure. Bring the tag to the register."

I stuff my spare clothes in my bag from the craft store and leave the fitting room with only my cutoffs and sunrise vest covering my new suit. I've never felt happier with a purchase.

I meet Stella outside her shop at two-thirty on the nose. She texts her friend and a few minutes later a blue pickup truck pulls up to the curb.

"Come on," Stella says. "I'll introduce you to everyone."

We stop at the bed of the truck. Stella points out her friends in the back. "This is Jack, Simon, and Chloe. They live here on the Rez, too." She rests her hand on my shoulder. "This is Ace. I met her today at the shop. She's cool. You'll like her."

I wave and we exchange hellos.

"You're not from around here," says a husky boy with shaggy black hair.

"My family is visiting for the summer."

He winks. "New friends are always welcome—as

long as they're female."

Stella slaps the back of his head. "Don't worry about Jack. He's harmless. Trust me. I know."

The other two in the bed laugh.

Jack waves her off. "You don't know nothing."

Stella grabs my elbow and tugs me to the cab. Inside, a guy with two long braids appears to be arguing with a girl with long purple nails and matching lipstick.

Stella pounds on the roof. "Hello."

The guy swings around and sticks his head out the open window. "Give me a minute, will—"

Before he finishes his last word, our eyes meet. My entire body jolts from shock. We stare at each other, mouths agape.

"Ace," Stella says, "this hothead is my brother, John."

****

What the…. It's her. Ace is standing outside my truck. With Rae?

Jasmine pokes me in the ribs. "Close your mouth."

I lean out the window to get a better look. Damn, she's hotter than I remember. I swallow to kick-start my breathing, and try to think of something suave to say, but all that comes out is, "How do *you* two know each other?"

"I met her at the shop," Rae says. "She can stitch a mean vest." She grabs Ace by the shoulder and twists. "Take a look at that sunrise."

The beadwork on her back is definitely fine, but it's the black bikini top underneath flaunting two of her best assets that grabs my attention. "Yeah, that is nice."

Ace turns a shade pinker if that's possible but doesn't say anything. She seems to be in shock. I pick my brain to find the right words to ease her nerves—and my own.

"So, how's your boyfriend?" I finally say—the second stupid thing I've blurted out in less than a minute.

She frowns. "Sunburned, but alive. No thanks to you."

*Ouch.* This time, I feel *my* cheeks redden. I suppose I deserve it. I must have made her mad yesterday, too.

"Wait." Rae wrinkles her nose. "You two know each other?" She flicks her pointer finger back and forth between Ace and me.

Both Ace and I speak at the same time. I stop and gesture for her to go first.

"No, you go ahead." She waves her hand around like she's trying to be nonchalant, but it comes off more like she's swatting a fly.

I clear my throat. "We met yesterday at the Adventure Center. She was one of my passengers."

Rae grins. "No way! You mean the trip that almost got you canned?"

When will my sister ever learn to keep her big mouth shut? Getting in trouble makes me look like a total jerk. Ace is staring at me with her honest blue eyes, so I lie. "No. I left work early because there weren't enough customers to go around."

Rae gives me a quit-your-bull look and turns back to Ace. "Wow. It's a small world. John's my younger brother. I'm older by two minutes."

There she goes with the younger brother bit again. At least she didn't call me out.

Ace's eyes ricochet between Rae and me. She

blinks a few times. “You’re twins. Now I know why you looked familiar,” she says to Rae.

Hot damn. Ace must have remembered me, if she made some sort of connection when she met my sister. Rae’s six inches shorter, but we do look an awful lot alike. I swear I can feel my head swelling.

Jasmine slides close and rests her arm on the seat back behind me. “Hi, Rae. Why don’t you two climb in the back?”

Crud, I forgot she was in the cab.

Ace’s expression flat-lines, and I think about moving, but no matter which way I lean, Jasmine will only move closer, so I hop out of my truck and gesture to the cab. “There’s room for one more. Want to sit in the front?” I ask Ace.

She waves at Jasmine, then takes a step back as if I have cooties. “I’ll get in the back with your friends. Stella can ride up front with you.”

“Stella?” I look at my sister questioningly.

Rae rolls her eyes. “I introduced myself by my real name.” She turns to Ace. “My friends and family call me Rae.”

“Oh, I get it.” Ace says.

She looks at me again, then hustles to the back of the truck as if I’m some sort of girl repellant.

I rub my head. For some reason, I don’t quite understand, it feels like I’m losing her for a second time.

Simon rises to his knees and extends a hand to help her climb in. They touch and, for the first time, I’m jealous of my best friend.

Ace situates herself on the rear wheel housing and glances at me. I wink at her and she gives me a dirty look.

I'm a jerk. Why did I wink? I totally lose my cool when she's around. Why do I even care? I barely know her. Besides, I like my hard-earned single status.

Everyone is staring at me.

"What are you looking at?" I say to my friends in the bed. They make themselves suddenly busy, but my sister's shaking her head like I'm a pathetic fool.

"Get in," I snap at her.

She beats on her chest like an ape. She doesn't take orders well, especially from me.

"Please?" I groan.

"Okay, but let me get in on the other side. I wouldn't want to come between you and Jasmine," Rae says, her voice sounding way too innocent.

Why should I expect any help from her? She's still hell bent on getting even with me. I'll pay for using half her bottle of pricy shampoo for the rest of my life. I shoot her my most pathetic look, hoping she'll pity me enough to help me out. She ignores me and rounds the truck to the passenger side.

When everyone is seated, Jasmine folds her hands in her lap and smiles. At least someone is happy with the arrangement.

I put the truck in gear and we take off. From the rearview mirror, I watch Ace. Simon has positioned himself awfully close to her. What a player. Old tricks die hard. Great, now I'm going to have to spend the rest of the day guarding her virtue. I mean, it's not really my job to protect her, but she seems clueless where guys are concerned. Just look at the idiot she chose for a boyfriend.

We come to a light and I ease on the brakes,

careful not to jar my passengers—especially the one with the blue eyes sitting on the wheel well. Jasmine is blabbing to Rae about how stupid I am for turning down her father's job offer. She jabs me with her elbow and asks me something, but I'm too concerned with what's going on in the back of my truck to answer.

"Earth to John." Her eyes lock on mine in the rearview mirror. She glances over her shoulder. "What are you looking at?"

"Nothing. How about moving over a little bit, huh? I can't shift." She's got to get over the idea she has a claim on me.

Rae huffs and moves closer to the door. Jasmine clucks her tongue and gives me an inch of breathing room. It's not much but it's better than nothing.

When we reach the edge of town, I lower the sun visor to block out the glare and turn onto the Blue Ridge Parkway.

With one eye on the rearview mirror, I keep a vigilant watch over my passengers. Ace has her hair clamped in her fist, but loose strands are flying every which way. She's laughing like a kid on a merry-go-round. I'd give anything to take Simon's place in the back of the truck. If I didn't love Old Blue so much, I'd pull over and make him drive.

We hit a bump in the road. Ace grabs the side of the truck and eases herself off the wheel hub onto the bed. Simon leans into her and whispers something in her ear. His lips are inches from her cheek.

*Oh, hell to the no.* Not happening.

A tourist's milepost is a stone's throw away. I'm going to stop. I'll figure out what to do once I get there.

The drive up the half-mile stretch of highway to the

post is the longest of my life, but eventually we reach the sign reading Cowee Overlook. I swing into the parking area.

Jack and Chloe pound on the cab window and shrug.

“Why are we stopping?” Jasmine moans.

“We’ve been driving a while. I thought Rae’s friend might want to get out and have a look.”

Rae raises an eyebrow. “You hate tourist stops.”

I frown. “Everybody out.”

Rae listens to me for once, but Jasmine doesn’t. She takes out her phone and taps out a text, which is okay by me. The busier she is, the less trouble she’ll cause.

Jack stands in the bed of the truck. “Do you need to take a whiz?”

I give him the evil eye. “No.”

“Then what are you doing?” he pries.

Simon and Chloe chime in with questions of their own.

If I don’t answer them, they’ll never quit. “Being an out-of-towner, I thought Ace might want to see one of the most photographed spots on the Blue Ridge Parkway.”

“Whatever,” Chloe says.

Ace purses her lips. “It’s beautiful here, but I don’t want to hold everyone up.”

“Come on,” Rae says. “When my brother gets a crazy idea there’s no changing his mind. If you don’t get out and look, we’ll never make it to Sliding Rock.”

Ace and Rae walk to the overlook. Ace cups her hands around her mouth and shouts, “Hello.” Her voice echoes across the valley like a song.

I drag Simon to a spot out of earshot of the others. “Hey, man, I got a favor to ask.”

“What’s that?”

“Do you think you can drive the rest of the way?”

“Yeah, I’ll drive, but why are you whispering?”

“Just take the keys, okay?”

He shrugs and I toss them to him, then jog across the lot to join Ace and Rae on the overlook.

****

How could I have not wanted to spend the summer in Cherokee, North Carolina? Everything is gorgeous. From the overlook, the air smells of green foliage mixed with a hint of sweetness from the purple and white wildflowers that dot the terrain below. Fluffy clouds drift in the heron-blue sky, skirting the tops of the rounded mountain peaks. I cup my hands around my mouth and shout “hello” once more. My voice echoes until it fades to nothing.

John trots up behind us. He’s wearing a black wife-beater tee beneath a white one with the word Brave written in gold script across the front. His jeans are faded and hang low, and a thick silver bracelet decorates his wrist. He’s definitely hot. Too bad he’s a jerk.

“Well,” he says. “What do you think?”

The wind shifts and a whiff of his spicy cologne shoots up my nose, and, for a second, jumbles my senses. I’m unable to speak. What is the matter with me? He’s only a guy—a guy with a big enough ego to flirt with me in front of his beautiful girlfriend.

“The view is spectacular,” I croak.

“Thanks.” He hooks his thumbs in his underarms and the corners of his mouth twitch.

What in the world is so funny?

Then it dawns on me. I'm staring at him and not the view. "I meant the mountains. Conceited."

Rae bursts out laughing. "Well, she told you."

"It was a joke," he says. "Girls never know how to take a joke." He reaches over his head, clasps his hands, and stretches. His muscles twist and flex in all the right places. "If you think the mountains are something now, you should come here in the fall when the colors change."

"I won't be here."

His arms drop to his sides. "That makes two of us."

"What do you mean?" I ask. "I thought you lived here."

Rae gives him a playful shove. "My little bro's been accepted at Duke. The Rez isn't good enough for him anymore."

"It's not that and you know it," John shoots back.

"Don't lose your cool, fool." Rae says. "I was only kidding." She elbows me. "Guys never know how to take a joke."

John shakes his head.

All joking aside, he must be smart to have gotten into Duke. I'd love to go away to college after I graduate, but I'll have to do the community thing. There's no way I can leave Zack alone with my mom. My parents' bright idea to hold me back a year when I was five so my SAT's would be ivy-league-high was all for naught.

"Hey," Jack shouts from the parking lot. "We've got to hurry if we're going to get there before summer's over."

"He's right." Rae loops her arm through mine and

marches me to the truck, prompting John to follow.

Chloe and Jack are already seated when I climb into the bed. John nods at Simon.

Simon hops in the cab with Jasmine and Rae, then John hops in the back of the truck and settles near me. Monster-like butterflies attack my stomach and my neck itches.

Jasmine bangs on the rear window and glares at John. “What are you doing?”

He ignores her and arranges himself cross-legged. One of his knees touches mine.

A meteor shower of heat explodes inside me. Why is this happening? I don’t like him. I can’t like him. The way he treats Jasmine makes him the epitome of loser boyfriends. Why does she put up with it?

Maybe he’s a good kisser. His lower lip is full and looks awfully soft. I wonder if his kisses are tender and smooth, the kind you feel in your knees, or wet and yucky like some guys.

Ugh. What am I thinking? He’s taken, and I’m no boyfriend thief.

I inch over toward the sidewall until we’re no longer touching and frown at him.

Jack slaps John on the back and snickers. “With the way the girls are looking at you today, you’d better watch your back.”

John laughs, furthering my belief that he’s nothing but a Lothario.

The truck takes off with a jerk. I sway sideways and lose my balance. My hand lands smack on John’s upper thigh. I snatch it back. “Sorry.”

He grins. “Don’t worry about it. I kind of liked it.”

My face flushes, and I adjust my positioning so I’m

not facing him, though I feel the slow burn of his stare on the back of my neck.

"So, Ace," he says, "are you having fun?"

I want to say I'm having a blast, but as I stare at the back of Jasmine's head, I'm reminded that only a horndog would sit next to me when his girlfriend is in the cab.

I shrug instead.

He nudges me. "Did I do something to make you mad?"

I've never been in the back of a pickup. In the open air, I'm as free as the wind whipping past. I won't let anything spoil this day. Not John. Not his girlfriend. And especially not this stupid attraction I have to him. "Let's not go there right now. I'm trying to enjoy myself."

He continues bating me with questions, but after I give him a few more one-word answers, he stops trying to talk to me. I'm more than happy to zone in my own world where I'm safe from guys who have nothing better to do than treat girls badly and break their hearts. And I'll bet breaking hearts is what John does best.

A considerable drive later, we reach an area where the tree limbs blanket the road. The sun peeks through the thickened leaves, casting shimmering rays of light on the earth. Out of the corner of my eye, I catch a glimpse of John. He seems to be miles away, his dreamy dark eyes gazing off into the distance. He's really good looking, but that only makes him doubly dangerous.

With a yank of the wheel, Simon pulls off the road. He parks in a small lot marked with a wooden sign reading Sliding Rock.

Everyone strips off their shirts, and shoes. I do the same. When I go to remove my shorts, Rae tells me to leave them on so I don't get rock burns on my butt.

John peels off his T-shirts and nearly blinds me with his rock-hard abs. Looks and a hot body. It's not fair to the rest of the male population for one guy to be so blessed. It's a good thing I'm immune to him.

We stow our belongings in the cab of the truck and head up the trail that leads to Sliding Rock. The background hums with the sound of rushing water, and birds chitter in the trees above. Little purple butterflies flit around us without fear. One lands in Rae's silky, bobbed hair. She gently shakes it free.

We cross a wooden bridge and to the right is sixty feet of sloping rock. Water rushes over its surface and pools at the bottom. It looks a bit dangerous and my skin tingles with excitement. People are lined up behind a single rail that's drilled into the outer edges of the rock where it meets the woods. Screams and hoots from the sliders are firing off all around us.

We descend a long wooden staircase to the bottom of the rock and stop on a large deck where spectators are watching.

Jasmine perches herself on the railing. "I'm going to wait here."

Everybody pretty much ignores her and continues on.

"John," she says. "Could you come here? I want to talk to you."

Rae looks at Chloe and rolls her eyes.

John crosses his arms. "I didn't drive all the way out here to sit and talk."

The rest of us leave him to duke it out with Jasmine

and head for the other side of the deck. We wade through a foot of cold water over slimy river rocks to get to the path that leads to the top of Sliding Rock. Within seconds, John, apparently done with fighting, is by my side.

He offers me his arm. “The rocks are slippery.”

I glance over my shoulder. Jasmine frowns at me. The last thing I want to do is come between them. “I can walk by myself. I’m not completely helpless.”

No sooner have the words left my mouth when I slip on a slimy rock and fall on my buns into the water. It’s cold, and I squeal. Really loud.

Now people are staring. I scurry to get up and slip again. This time I’m on all fours with a small rock digging into my kneecap. John stands over me with his fists propped on his hips. His eyes are twinkling and I suspect he’s holding back a laugh.

I could just die. Instead, I blow a strand of hair out of my mouth and say, “Don’t just stand there, help me up.”

He gets behind me, slips his hands into my armpits and lifts. *Thank god I didn’t forget my deodorant.* When I’m on my feet, he takes hold of my elbow and escorts me to the place where the ground is solid rock and mostly dry. I brush the sand off the back of my shorts, grab the railing, and begin my ascent.

Once the heat of embarrassment passes, I realize I’m shivering, and hug myself to stop the tremors.

“I can go get a towel from the truck,” John offers.

We’re already behind the rest of his friends. I don’t want to squash his fun.

“I don’t need one,” I stutter through chattering teeth.

Next thing I know, John is rubbing my arms with his large, warm hands. My body temperature soars.

Rae turns around and waves, then does a double take. Her eyes don't blink for a full thirty seconds, at least.

I shimmy out of John's clutches. "Shouldn't we catch up with the others?"

"Uh-uh." He shakes his head.

"Why?" I foolishly ask, certain he's looking for a reason for us to be alone.

"If you try to cut in line, I'm going to get beat to a pulp defending you."

Well, he told me. Still, uneasy with our much-to-close proximity, I move forward until I'm nearly touching the person in front of me.

"Why are you trying to avoid me?" he asks. "Is it because of that stupid boyfriend of yours? He's not even here."

"First off, he's not my boyfriend—not that that's any of your business.

John's eyes brighten. "He's not?"

"No. He's a family friend."

"That's great. I could have sworn—"

I give him the hand. "Let me finish."

"Go on."

"And secondly," I take a deep breath, "your girlfriend is over there watching you put your hands all over me." I nod in Jasmine's direction. "That makes you a bigger dummy than Cameron ever was."

"Is that what you think?" John lips press together in a tense line.

"Yes."

"Well, I might be dumb, but you're wrong about

Jasmine. She's not my girlfriend."

Oh, brother. I'd like to believe him, but everything about this situation screams he's lying. "Do you think I'm daft?"

He puffs. "Okay. She *was* my girlfriend. Once. We broke up two months ago."

"Then why is she here?"

"She asked if she could come along and I didn't want to hurt her feelings. But I made it clear she's only here as a friend."

"Oh." Maybe he isn't as much of a Lothario as I thought. At least I hope not. Still, I'd better keep my guard up.

The line moves and we move with it, until John and I are standing together at the top of Sliding Rock. We're so high, and the water moves so fast, I'm seriously thinking about turning back.

"What's the matter?" John asks when I hesitate.

"I don't know about this. It looks scary from up here."

"Let me go first and I'll help you. We can go down together." He steps into the rushing water then offers me his hand.

My pulse is racing, and I don't know if I'm afraid because I'm about to take the plunge of my life down a rock immersed in rushing water, or because I'm about to do it with John.

"Come on," he says. "I've got this."

I reach out and his fingers lock around mine. He takes a slow step forward, and I follow. Somehow we make it to the center of the rock, and I'm looking down, while icy water rushes over my ankles.

"Are you ready?" he shouts over the roar of the

falls.

"I don't know."

"You'll be fine. I promise."

My whole body shakes as I sit on the rock, and the frigid water rolls up my back. John lowers himself beside me.

He squeezes my hand. "One." I close my eyes. "Two." I open them and he grins. "Three."

He pushes off, dragging me with him. The water whooshes us down the rock. I slide faster and faster. I have no control, and I love it.

"Wheeeeee," I scream into the rushing wind.

Momentum stretches us apart. A little at first, but then the force grows stronger. His hand slips, and we are holding onto each other by the fingertips. A strong jerk breaks our tether.

The plunge into the frigid water takes my breath. For a few seconds, my mind goes numb. Then something in my brain sparks and my adrenaline kicks in. I paddle like crazy until I break through to the surface. I'm happy. I'm brave. I've done something on a to-do list that I didn't know existed. Until this moment.

John pops up beside me. We are both safe and laughing like crazy.

"It's freezing," I shout between giggles.

"What? It's warm today. The water has to be at least fifty-two degrees."

"Omigod." I swim with fervor toward the shore. John beats me there and helps me climb the river rocks to the deck.

"So, what do you think?" He sweeps his arm out, gesturing to the surroundings.

"I think this is the coolest thing I've ever done. I'll never forget it." I clamp my teeth to stop the chattering.

"Now will you let me get that towel?"

Too cold to object this time, I nod.

He takes the stairs two at a time and runs onto the trail, while I jog in place. Across the way, Rae and the crew are already going for a second round.

Jasmine slides off the railing and walks over. "So you're having fun, huh?"

"Yeah, a great time," I say.

"You like John, don't you?"

"What do you mean?"

"Don't play innocent with me. Your eyes practically pop out of the sockets when you look at him."

I don't respond. My instincts tell me sharing my personal feelings with Jasmine might not be a good idea. Besides, how can she be so sure how I feel when I don't know myself?

She picks at the back of her long, purple fingernail. "John comes from a traditional Cherokee family—one strong with cultural values. Did you know that?"

"No, we've just met."

"Well, I've known him and his family forever. He and I have been dating for three years. Did he tell you?"

"Yes. He also mentioned you two had broken up."

She smirks. "You're pretty, you've got an okay body, and, you're, well, you're white. Sort of a different flavor. Not better by any means, but different if you get my drift. Unfortunately, you're not too smart."

"What are you trying to say?"

She sighs. "You're nothing but a plaything for him. As soon as he gets what he wants, he'll leave you in the dust. John and me, we're two of a kind. We understand each other. Every now and then we take time off from our relationship, but we never ever break up for long. If you were one of us you'd know that."

I do my best not to let distress show on my face. John sounded like he was telling the truth, but Mom says guys will lie to get what they want from a girl. Just look at my father.

Rae emerges from the water, and I hurry to meet her.

"What's the matter," she asks. "You look pale. Did Jasmine sink her fangs into you and suck out all your blood?"

As much as I trust Rae, I'm new to the group. The last thing I want to do is cause drama. "No. She was nice. I'm just cold."

"O-kay. Just so you know, she can be a real witch with a capital B when she wants."

John comes bounding down the stairs with a towel around his neck, waving another in his hand.

"Looks like your towel's here." Rae says.

"Yeah." I shiver. It's here all right, but at whose expense?

# Chapter 7
# John Spears

Ace avoids me for the rest of the day. When we're ready to leave, I invite her to sit in the front of Old Blue. Even though she's shivering, she refuses, opting to sit with Chloe, Simon, and Jack in the back.

I grab a sweatshirt from behind the seat. "If you won't sit in the cab, at least wear this."

She holds the sweatshirt out in front of her and reads the logo out loud, "Native Americans discovered Christopher Columbus."

Uh-oh. I forgot that was written on the front. Hope she's not too offended.

Oddly, she smiles at me for the first time in an hour. "That's interesting," she says. "I suppose it's true, depending on which side of the world you came from." She takes the sweatshirt and slips it over her head. "Thanks. It's really warm."

Phew. Made it past that bit of cultural awkwardness without crashing and burning. Ace won't ride in the front of the truck, so I'm stuck with Jasmine and Rae again, but at least she's speaking with me. Maybe with a little strategic planning, I can find a way to talk to her alone and figure out what made her change from lukewarm to cold so quickly.

Once we reach the reservation, I take the back way rather than the shorter route through town. Rae reminds me by reaching behind Jasmine and yanking on my braid. I make a face at her, hoping she'll get my drift and keep quiet. Thankfully, Jasmine's too busy texting to notice what's going on.

I drop off Simon, Jack, and Chloe, then head for Jasmine's place.

When I turn onto the road that leads to her house, she stops texting and cranes her neck from side to side. "What are you doing?"

"Taking you home."

She glances into the back of the truck, where Ace sits alone. "I get it. You're trying to get rid of me because you have your sights set on the *yonega*."

Of course, the one word Jasmine knows in Tsalagi is derogatory. "Cut it out, Jasmine."

"You're wasting your time chasing her, boyfriend. She's not *Aniyunwiva*. You're just a plaything to her."

*Aniyunwiya*—the name our ancestors used to refer to the Cherokee people. I'm impressed. Jasmine's pulling out the big guns, but I've got on my bulletproof vest. "It doesn't matter Ace or no Ace, you and me are not getting back together."

The only sound in the truck is the roar of the engine and a pop song on the radio. Jasmine sniffles and huge crocodile tears roll down her cheeks. I hate it when she cries. Now I feel obligated to say something nice. But what? I don't want her to think she can control me.

"Listen, Jasmine, I'm sorry for being rough on you, but I thought we'd moved past this. We agreed to be friends. Remember?"

"Keep your apology. I'm glad we broke up. You're a jerk and dating you was the biggest mistake I've ever made in my life."

Rae shifts abruptly and scowls. "I've kept my cool so far, but enough is enough. Lay off my brother."

"Last thing I want to do is lay him. He's a loser." Jasmine makes an L with her thumb and index finger.

Rae braces her hand on the dash and gets in Jasmine's face. "Nobody talks about him like that. Get it?"

Great. Now my sister's involved, and she's really loud, too. I glance in the rear-view mirror to check if Ace is taking any of this in. I can't tell if she's listening, but she doesn't look happy. "Could you two tone it down a notch?"

Both Jasmine and Rae glare at me. I can't win. I've had enough dirty looks from women today to last a lifetime.

Jasmine crosses her arms. "Don't worry, I'm done talking. Oh, and that job offer with Daddy's company has been rescinded. I'll make sure of it."

I throw up my hands for a second, then white-knuckle grip the wheel. Maybe she has her father wrapped around her finger, but she doesn't have me—not any longer.

The remainder of the ride takes forever, but we finally make it. I stop at the foot of the drive. Rae's pouting and doesn't open the door, leaving the three of us crammed in the cab like a bunch of ticked-off sardines.

I put the shifter into neutral, smash down the emergency brake, run around the truck, and open the passenger door myself. Rae climbs out and stands with her back to me. Jasmine shoulder checks me on the way past, not forgetting to turn and sneer one last time before she marches inside her house.

Ace is frowning at me from the bed of the truck. Glutton for punishment that I am, I gesture for her to get in the cab. She shakes her head. Why am I surprised? She hates me, too.

I get in Old Blue and drum my fingers on the steering wheel.

Rae hops in the passenger seat and slams the door. The dash rattles.

I cringe. "What did my truck do to you?"

She side-punches me. "I stick up for you, and you tell me to shut up? What's your problem?"

"Sorry, I didn't mean to. I guess you got caught in the crossfire."

She folds her arms over her chest and huffs.

I squeeze her shoulder. "Come on, Sis. You know I love you."

"Yeah. I know" Her posture softens. "But if you're acting a fool to impress her"—she hooks a thumb in Ace's direction—"it's not working."

I grab her wrist. "Put your hand down, she'll see you."

"Oh, man, you are smitten."

"No way. I'm enjoying my life as it is. Free and single is the only way to fly. I think she's cool, that's all."

Rae rolls her eyes.

"No, really—but can I drop you off first? I want to talk to her alone."

"She's not interested."

"How can you be so sure?"

"She's freezing to death and chooses to ride in the back of the truck."

"That doesn't prove anything."

"Boy, are you asking for it."

"I want to be friends, that's all."

"Sure, sure. Drop me off by the road so Elisi doesn't see. I don't need her on my back. And whatever you do, don't screw up *my* friendship with Ace."

"Of course not." I stop on the road near our driveway.

"You owe me one," Rae says before she hops out.

Ace's eyes go wide. "Where are you going?"

"John's dropping me off first. He said he'd like to get to know you better."

Oh no, she didn't just say that? I can't trust my sister to do anything right.

Ace shakes her head emphatically. "I don't think that's a good idea."

"You'll be fine," Rae says. "If he tries anything funny, just give me a call. I'll make sure he's miserable for the rest of his life."

Ace purses her lips, wraps her hands around her knees, and draws them into her chest. "Well…I suppose."

"Okay, see you later." Rae shoots me a warning glance before heading up the gravel drive.

I get out of the truck and lean on the bedrail. "If you sit up front, I promise I won't bite."

Ace blushes but doesn't budge. The bubblegum color of her cheeks melts my heart, and I try another angle. "I'm going to look foolish driving up front all alone with you in the back. Would you get in the cab, please?"

Ace's face twists. "I suppose."

I offer her a hand, but she vaults out the other side

and sucks in a deep breath before getting in the cab. I settle behind the wheel and smile at her.

She stares straight ahead and says, "Take me to the shopping area. I can catch the shuttle back to the casino from there."

"I can drive you home. It's not that much further."

"No thanks." Ace bites her lip and speed-dials a number on her phone. She talks to someone at the shuttle company and arranges a lift. When she's done, she busies herself on the Internet.

I should probably leave it alone for both our sakes, but I can't stand to be ignored. Plus I've got to know why she went cold. "If you're mad at me, could you at least tell me why?"

She frowns. "If you must know, I don't like what you did in front of Jasmine."

I wrinkle my nose. "Huh?"

"Don't play dumb. Jasmine told me everything. I can't believe I held hands with you. I would never have done it if I'd have known."

"Known what? What did she tell you?"

"She says you break up all the time and get right back together. Wherever we were going with this thing just isn't right…"

"Jasmine and I are over for good and she knows it. She's not the kind of girl I want in my life."

"Tell me. What kind of girl is she, John?"

"She cuts me down. Every day is a new fight. Plus she parties a lot."

Ace cocks an eyebrow. "What's the saying: Birds of a feather flock together."

"You're right. I'm not completely innocent. I was into partying for a little while, but not anymore. My mother is an alcoholic. She left when I was four. I've lived with my grandmother ever since. I don't want to go down that road myself, so I've vowed not to be around people who travel on it." I take a deep breath. "There. Now you know everything. Are you happy?" My words come out harsher than I meant, but this is one subject I hate to talk about.

Ace's brow wrinkles and her lower lip quivers.

Oh, no. I've upset her. I shouldn't have yelled. "Look, I keep screwing up. I'm sorry."

"Don't be. I understand completely. My mother's an alcoholic, too—a bad one. It's a family secret. She'd kill me if she knew I was talking about it. Sometimes she stays drunk for days, and I pray she'll leave so I don't have to deal with it anymore."

I don't think Ace realizes how bad it is to not have a mom, but I nod and keep my thoughts to myself. She's entitled to her feelings.

She wrings her hands. "Jeez, I thought it would feel good to tell someone, but I think I feel worse."

I struggle to find the right thing to say, but nothing comes to mind, so I offer her my hand.

She unwinds her fingers and slips her little hand into mine. Her soft skin is warm against my calloused palm. Neither of us says another word as we cruise along the winding mountain road, but the silence doesn't bother me, it seems right.

All too soon, the town comes into view, and I have to shift. I wait to the very last minute to let go of her hand. When I do, I'm suddenly filled with an unsettling emptiness.

She points in the direction of Rae and Elisi's store. "I can catch the shuttle from there."

I find parking on the street nearby. If I don't say something now, I may never get a chance. "So what's up with this Cameron guy? I hope you're not thinking of hooking up with him. because you deserve better. Someone like me, for instance."

*Damn. Open mouth. Insert foot. The story of my life.*

She freezes seemingly processing my asinine words, then bursts out laughing.

*There's no recovering from this one so I might as well go with it. Maybe she'll think I was joking.* "Don't laugh. I bet you've never kissed a Cherokee guy before?"

"Can't say I have."

"We're good. Really good." I wiggle my eyebrows.

"What about you? Have you ever kissed a white girl?"

My heart jumps. I didn't think she'd bite.

She pokes my arm. "Well, have you?"

"No. Can't say that I have."

"Do you want to kiss me, John?"

She's flirting, but with a face like mine, why not? "Sure, that would be cool. And by the way, you won't be disappointed. I promise."

"I don't know if I'd be a good judge. I've only kissed two guys—a slobberer and a great kisser with a personality so rotten it spoiled the kiss."

*Here's where she backs out. I'll make it easy for her.* "If you don't think you're qualified…"

"I'm probably not, but it couldn't hurt to try."

I swallow. "Are you serious?"

"Absolutely, but for curiosity sake and nothing more. The kiss means absolutely nothing. Deal?"

"Deal. For curiosity's sake only."

She holds out her hands and we shake. Then she sweeps her tongue over her lower lip and puckers up. I wrap my hand around the back of her neck and we both lean forward until our lips touch. I start off slow, keeping the pressure to a minimum. Her mouth is soft and warm and tastes sweet, like fruity gum. I stroke the tender skin behind her ear with the pad of my thumb. She sighs, then opens her mouth, inviting me in.

*Holy freaking wow.*

Our tongues meet in the middle and slide all over the place. My head pounds against my ribs so hard I wholly expect one to crack. She tastes so fine. I can't breathe, but I don't care. Oxygen is something we need on earth, and I'm clearly somewhere else. I brace my knee beneath the steering wheel to keep the lack of gravity from pulling me out of my seat. After all, this kiss doesn't mean anything.

I feel a slight hesitation on her part. In the next instant, she breaks away and wrestles with the door handle. "I have to go."

"Not before you give me my rating. You can't tell me that kiss wasn't great."

"I'll have to think about it. But don't worry too much. It was okay."

"With the way you were kissing me back, it had to be better than okay."

"Nope, just okay."

The door pops open, she leaps out and shuts it behind her. She offers me a second of toothy smile, then bolts across the street. By the time I can get my brain working enough to get out of the truck and go after her, she's disappeared into the crowd.

## Chapter 8
## Ace McAllister

I collapse on to the hard vinyl seat in the back of the shuttle and bury my face in my hands.

*John Spears. Omigod. JOHN SPEARS.*

I hoped that if we kissed, my infatuation with him would pass. I'd been so counting on him screwing it up. But it's been less than a minute since I left his truck, and I already miss him.

I squeeze my head, trying to stop my racing thoughts. But how can I stop anything when my lips still tingle from his kiss and shimmers of flesh bumps cover my body at just the thought of him?

The shuttle comes to a stop in front of the hotel, and my breath hitches. I'm a mess. My hair is tangled and all the makeup is washed from my face.

And—OMIGOD—I'm wearing John's sweatshirt.

I tug it over my head, turn it inside out to hide the logo, and tie it around my waist. Then I pull my tank top and vest out of my backpack and cover up my new swimsuit top. The fringe shows through the fabric, but there's nothing I can do about it now.

"Are you getting off here, miss?" the driver asks.

"Oh, yes. Thank you."

As I exit the shuttle, I pan the area. Luckily no one familiar comes into view. I hurry through the lobby and take the stairs, too nervous to wait for the elevator.

Outside the suite, I hold an ear to the door. All's quiet inside. Maybe if I shower and climb into bed, no one will know I was gone. I open the door and drop my bag beside it.

Three steps in, I stop dead in my tracks. Mom, Cameron, and Susan, are in the living area, frowning at me. Zack, who's on the floor in front of the TV, is the only one to offer a smile.

"Ace." Mom stands and crosses her arms. "You told me you were sick. Would you like to tell us where you've been?"

Before I can respond, Cameron jumps in. "I texted you, and you never answered."

Susan eyes me suspiciously.

A lump lodges in my throat, nearly choking me. "After a nap, my headache was gone, so I went shopping."

Zack leans back and cranes his neck. "Your hair is messy."

I run my fingers through the stringy tendrils to smooth them down. They get stuck in a knot. Zack is dead right about me being a mess, but why does he have to be so honest?

Cameron looks me up and down. "Do they have a swimming pool in the shopping area?"

Idiot. He's trying to get me in trouble.

"Actually, there are fountains. They're a blast to run through. You ought to go sometime."

Almost in unison, my three persecutors drop their chins and stare at me with narrowed eyes. They don't believe me, and I could care less. The only person I owe an explanation to is my mother. And that's debatable.

Mom props her fists on her hips. "That doesn't explain why you disappeared without a word. We've all been worried sick."

I shrug. "Sorry, but I needed some me-time."

"That's not an excuse not to call." Mom frowns. "I'm grounding you for a week. You're not to step out of the suite. Maybe that will teach you to be considerate of your family."

Which reminds me. "Where's Dad?"

Mom's face sags like a death mask. Instantly I'm sorry I brought him up.

"Quit trying to change the subject." She plucks her glass of wine from the end table and swishes a sip around in her mouth before swallowing. "You're grounded. Now go to your room."

"Don't treat me like a child."

"Quit acting like one." She takes another sip.

"It's funny you feel that way since I'll be the one taking care of you later tonight when you pass out."

Her cheeks turn the color of the wine in her glass. "Not only is my daughter disobedient, she's a lying, vengeful little brat."

I try to convince myself it's the wine talking, but it still hurts.

"Quiet," Zack shouts. "I can't hear my program." He turns up the volume on the TV.

Mom marches over and snatches the remote out of his hands. "We've got enough going on here without all your ruckus, mister."

"The arguing is bothering me." Zack covers his ears.

Poor kid doesn't need the stress. I head for the bedroom.

“Ace,” Cameron says, “wait a minute.”

I turn around.

“Where did you get the sweatshirt?”

Great, in all the commotion, I forgot about it. My adrenaline rises as I tighten the sleeves around my waist. “I’ve had it for a while.”

His brows furrow. “I’ve never seen it before?”

“I don’t remember allowing you to take inventory of my clothes.”

“You don’t have to. I know everything about you.”

“That’s creepy, Cameron. You’re creepy. Stay away from my stuff.” I push open the bedroom door and lock it behind me. Then I collapse on the bed.

Someone’s knocking. I rub my eyes and check the alarm clock by the bed stand. The green florescent numbers read ten o’clock. I must have fallen asleep.

“Zack?” Where’s Zack?

“Ace, let me in,” he says.

I get up, unlock the door, and peek into the hallway. All the lights are on, the TV’s blaring, and Zack is still in his T-shirt and underwear. He has chocolate cake all over his face. “What happened? Where is everyone?”

“Cameron and Miss Susan went home. Mom’s sleeping.”

“Come on, let’s get you cleaned up.” I lead him into the bathroom and wash his face. Then I hand him a toothbrush and tell him to get busy. When he’s done, I help him out of his dirty shirt and into clean pajamas.

“My stomach hurts,” he moans.

“Get in bed, and I’ll see if I can find something to make you feel better.”

I tuck him in and make my way to the kitchen. A

half-eaten chocolate cake sits on the table, and my mother is lying flat on her back in the middle of the living room floor. I nudge her with my toe. "Wake up. Zack's sick."

She groans and her eyes open for a second, then roll back in her head. She must have started early today. My stomach roils. I want to slap her. Slap her hard. I draw back my hand, but stop midair, my entire body trembling. I've never been a violent person, and she's not going to turn me into one. She can lie there until Dad comes home. Let him deal with the mess he's caused.

I dig through the kitchen cabinets and find some antacids. The label says they are safe for children twelve and older. Zack's twelve, so I take one from the pack and hurry to the bedroom.

I sit on the bed beside him. "Here take this. It will make you feel better."

He opens his mouth, and I pop the tablet inside. "You shouldn't have eaten all that cake. It's no wonder you're sick."

"But it was good."

"I know, Zack, but next time ask me. I'll cut a big slice, but not so big that you get indigestion."

Zack sits up and leans toward me until our noses almost touch—his way of showing affection. "I didn't want to ask you because I'm mad at you, Ace."

"At me? Why?" I ask, wondering what I've done to anger him.

"Everyone was yelling and saying bad things about you today. I thought you were gone forever."

"Oh, Zack, I'm sorry you were worried. I'll never go away for long without taking you with me."

He takes a quick bite on his wrist, another one of his stims.

"Are you still mad?"

His brows scrunch together. "No. I'm fine now because you're back."

"Remember, even when I'm not with you, you're with me right here." I pat my heart.

He nods and settles into his pillow.

I turn out the light.

"Ace," Zack says, "do you think Dad will come home soon?"

He's breaking my heart. "Everything's going to be fine. I promise. I'll make sure of it."

"'Kay. Goodnight, Ace."

"Night, Zack," I say, kicking myself for having promised the sweetest boy in the world the impossible.

# Chapter 9
John Spears

After a long ride on the trails, I lead Billy to the barn behind our house to brush him down. I speak gently to him, but he doesn't want to settle. Can't say that I blame him for being keyed up. Nighttime riding is not something we do often, but I needed time by myself to sort through my thoughts. Even though Billy is the best listener in the world, I'm no better off than I was when I started. I don't care what type of deal Ace and I made about the kiss meaning nothing. It wasn't nothing. She kissed me back, damn it.

Why do I even care? There will be plenty of girls at college. Besides, I'm not looking to hook up with anyone. Or wasn't.

Closing my eyes, I try to fantasize about what the Duke girls will be like, but all I see is one girl and she's staying at a casino right here in Cherokee. What the hell? I thump my head with the heel of my hand. Ace is even messing with my thoughts about other girls?

By the time I get Billy hunkered down into his stall, it's almost midnight. Inside the house, Elisi, Rae, Victor, Aunt June and Uncle George are gathered around the TV watching a movie. The only one missing is Lenny, and he's probably in bed, where I'd hoped everyone would be by now. I wave as I pass through the living room.

"Come join us," Elisi says.

I stop and do a quarter-turn. Somehow the idea of sitting with my happy family is depressing me right now. "Can't. I've got to be up early in the morning."

"George is home, and I'd like us all to spend some time together," Elisi all but orders.

Here she goes again, using the situation to get me to bend to her will. Uncle George works at a forest station, and he's only home once or twice a month. When he is here, he and Elisi don't get along well. They're in a continual power struggle over who is the boss of Aunt June. Without some sort of hidden agenda, Elisi would only celebrate Uncle George's presence when it was time for him to go back to work.

Uncle George sits on the opposite end of the couch with his arm around his wife who serves as a hefty barrier between him and Elisi. His eyes are glued to the television. I don't think he knows I'm here.

"Come on, John. Have a seat." My kid brother, Victor, pats the spot next to him on the floor. "Don't you like us anymore?"

I make a mental note to kick him in the butt next time no one's looking.

Rae shifts and dangles her leg over the arm of her overstuffed-chair. Her lips are pressed together. She looks like she's trying not to laugh. Leave it to my dear sister and brother to get off on my misery.

"Don't any of you people sleep?" I ask.

Everyone but Uncle George stares at me with a you're-not-getting-out-of-this-one look. My family bonds together tighter than the cap to a tube of superglue, and I'm one of them, so there's no escaping it. "Okay, but let me change first. I smell like horse sweat."

Now that the family is assured they'll get their way, they turn back to the movie as if I don't exist. I go to my room, purposely leaving the light off. I don't want to wake Lenny. I drop my jeans in a puddle on the floor, snag some sweats from my closet, and slip them on. Sensing something behind me, I spin around. A figure looms in the doorway, leaning on the jam.

Startled, I blink my eyes till they come into focus. "Holy hell, Rae, you look like the grim reaper lurking there in the dark."

She snickers.

I kick my jeans into the corner. "Did you enjoy the show?"

"You in your tighty-whities is anything but entertaining."

"Ha, ha. Why are you spying on me?"

"I wasn't spying. I want to talk to you."

"About what?"

She holds a finger to her lips and points at Lenny, then motions for me to join her in the hallway. I step outside the door and ease it shut behind me.

"Don't play dumb with me," she says. "How'd it go with Ace?"

I know my sister well. She'll dig and pry and follow me to the ends of the earth until she gets an answer—a trait she inherited from Elisi—so there's no use putting off the inevitable. "That girl is the most frustrating person I've ever met."

"You bombed, huh?"

Why does Rae always assume I'm a loser with girls? "No. She kissed me."

Rae's eyes go wide. "Willingly?"

I glare at her. "Just forget it."

"Don't be a baby." She smiles. "I was only kidding."

"If you're not here to help, I'm done talking."

"She kissed you, so why are you acting like you hate the world?"

I explain how our kiss was an experiment, but I felt something, and was pretty sure Ace did, too. Until she took off without so much as a goodbye. Rae hangs onto every word, like she really cares. That's the great thing about having a girl twin. She's sarcastic at times, but when I'm seriously down, she gets it. By the time I'm done telling my tale, she's rubbing her temples.

"Sounds like Ace doesn't know what she wants," she says. "I can't help you with that one."

"She gave you her phone number. Can I have it?"

"It wouldn't be right. If she wanted you to have it, she'd have given it to you."

"Come on, Rae. I want to talk to her. If I offended her, I want a chance to apologize."

"I think the best thing you can do is give her space. Face it, John, she might not want that kind of relationship with you."

I conk the back of my skull on the wall.

Rae shakes her head. "Well, don't break the wall. You're going to Duke. Do you really want to start a new relationship?"

I straighten. I'd never really thought that through. "It would be nice to have a girl to hang out with the rest of the summer, then when school starts…you know. I think it would be a win-win situation for both of us."

"Oh, brother, what you don't know about women is a lot."

“Then teach me.”

“Rae! John!” Elisi shouts. “You’re missing the zombie attack. Get in here.”

Rae rolls her eyes. “Girl 101 will have to wait. We better go now or she’ll make us watch the sequel as punishment.”

I take a deep breath and ready myself to do some hard family time.

# Chapter 10
## Ace McAllister

I awake and shoot to a sitting position. It's early morning, and my dad is screaming at my mom. She wails something, but the words are garbled. Leaving her on the floor last night seemed like a good idea at the time, but now my parents are fighting and it's all my fault.

Thankfully, Zack is sleeping soundly in the bed next to mine. He's been exposed to enough bad stuff. He doesn't need to hear this. I climb out of bed and crack the door open. Dad's standing over Mom, who is still lying in the place I left her.

"Get up." He pulls her to her feet.

"Where were you?" she blubbers. "With some whore?"

I figured she was too drunk to notice he was gone last night. Obviously she's not as clueless as I thought.

"The condition you're in has nothing to do with me not being here." Dad sneers. "You're a sloppy drunk."

Mom's knees buckle and if Dad didn't have a firm grip on her, she'd crumple to the ground. He shakes her hard—too violently for my liking.

I burst through the door, run to Mom, and wrestle her away from him. "Dad! Look what you're doing! Leave her alone."

Dad lets go and looks at his hands as if they belong

to some evil stranger. “Sorry, but she made me do it. Someone has got to straighten her out.”

“You think screaming at her and shaking her is going to fix this?”

Mom totters and uses my shoulder to anchor herself. “That’s right. You tell him, Ace.”

Dad frowns. “I’m not going to stick around while you two team up on me.”

“Wait, don’t leave.” I say. “I’m not taking sides. You have to stay and help. This is a family problem. We can fix this.” A tear leaks out of the corner of my eye and trickles down my cheek.

His face crumples. “I can’t do it anymore. Not when the sight of her makes me sick to my stomach.”

I clutch my chest and wait for the burn to pass. “Please don’t give up.”

He shakes his head, goes to the door, and flings it open. A breeze from the hallway blows a tuft of his hair and it falls in the center of his forehead. He looks young again.

Mom staggers after him. “Go on and leave. And don’t come back. See if I care.”

I catch up and stop her. “Shhh, Mom. You don’t mean that.”

Dad stares at the floor, then without making eye contact, crosses the threshold and shuts us out of his life.

I force myself to breathe.

Mom’s pretty face bends and twists in torment. She latches on to me and sobs. “I really do love him, Ace. You have to believe me.”

I pat her back while we both cry. I don’t know if I’m the one comforting her or if her unrelenting hug is comforting me in some convoluted way. When I finally peel her off, my shirt is tear-soaked. "Come on. Let's get you to bed for a nap. He'll be back."

"You think so?" Mom sniffles.

I nod, though I can't help worrying this could be the time he leaves for good.

Once my mother is tucked in, I fetch a glass of water and put it on her bedside table. If I hadn't taken off yesterday, maybe she wouldn't have gotten drunk. And, if I hadn't left her on the floor, Dad would be here now. I'm a total failure as a daughter.

My phone buzzes. It's a text.

Rae: *We're going to a party at the river tonight. Want to come along?*

Sure I want to go. More than I've ever wanted anything. But I no longer have a choice. Not when my family is falling apart. I have to stay here and figure out how to fix the mess I've caused.

# Chapter 11
John Spears

The next day after work, I head straight home. "Rae," I holler as I enter the house.

She doesn't answer.

The living room and kitchen are empty. Poor Rae lost her room when Aunt June, Uncle George, and Lenny moved in. She keeps her stuff in Elisi's room, so I check in there. The door's wide open and there is no sign of her.

Across the hall, my brother, Victor, is sitting on the floor in our bedroom, playing a game of solitaire. He snaps a card down, peeks under the pile next to it, then swaps out cards. Who does he think he's cheating?

Simon is stretched out on our bed with my headphones, listening to music, nodding to a beat only he can hear.

"Ya'll seen Rae?" I ask.

Victor looks up from his deck of cards. "She called and said she'd be a little late."

"Didn't you hear me yelling for her?"

"Yeah, but…" He shrugs.

Kid brothers suck. So do best friends. I glare at Simon, but he doesn't notice.

My phone is burning a hole in my pocket, so I text Rae, asking for the third time if she invited Ace to the river tonight. I wait, but she doesn't respond. What's her problem?

My eyes wander from one corner of the room to the next. Junk covers every surface and clothes spill out onto the floor, like the closet threw up. "How can you two stand to wallow in this pigsty?"

Simon still doesn't look at me, and Victor goes back to cheating at solitaire.

It's clear I'm on my own. I sift through the mess, hanging what looks clean and tossing the dirty stuff into a pile. When I'm done, I pick up Lenny's toys and toss them in his toy box, then go to the dresser and dust the top with one of Victor's dirty socks.

A pillow hits me from behind, and I spin around. "What the hell?"

Simon's propped up on my bed with the headphones hanging around his neck. His grubby elbows are digging ruts into my mattress. "Slow down man, you're making me tired."

I smack the toe of his black Converse sneaker. "How about getting your smelly shoes off my bed?"

"You never cared before. Hey, Victor?"

My brother looks up from the cards. "What?"

"Do you care if my shoes are on your bed?"

"Nope," he says.

I shake my head. Simon is acting more and more like my annoying brother every day. We've been best friends since we were two, so the line between friendship and family has definitely been muddied. Still there's no excuse. "Well, I mind, so move."

Simon rolls to a sitting position and plants his dogs on the floor. "What's wrong with you? I've never seen you so tense."

Victor tilts his head back to look at Simon. "He's

all hung up on a girl."

Simon wrinkles his nose. "I thought it was your idea to break up with Jasmine."

"Not her, stupid," Victor groans. "Ace."

"You mean the white girl from yesterday?" Simon asks. "That was quick. She must have done something awful good when you drove her home last night." He wiggles his zipper.

"Let it go," I warn.

A dopey grin stretches across his face. "Ohhhh…John found a tourist with a Native fetish. How many balls were hit before you got to fourth base?"

His disrespect makes me want to spit fire. I make fists and take a step toward him. "Cut it out. She's not that kind of girl."

Simon throws his hands up in a "don't hit me" position. "Geez, sorry. I didn't know you actually liked-her-liked-her."

"Who said I do?" I reply, hoping to maintain a scrap of privacy.

Victor pokes Simon in the leg. "Don't let him fool you. I heard him begging Rae to call her." He slaps his cheeks. "Please give me her number?" He says in a girly voice.

I bop him with a knuckle to the skull.

Victor tosses his cards, grabs my knees, and next thing I know, I'm on the floor face down with him on top of me. I struggle until I'm on my back, then twist him into a headlock. His spiky hair pokes me in the eye.

"Don't just lay there," he barks at Simon. "Give me a hand."

Simon dives on top of us and pries my arms from

Victor's neck. The three of us go at it—them against me. They pin me to the carpet, and I arch my back and thrust my legs. The dresser thumps against the wall and a lamp crashes down on us.

Almost simultaneously, a loud whistle pierces the hallway, then a shout, *"Ha-le,"* which means "cut it out" in Tsalagi. The three of us freeze.

"Uh-oh. Elisi. We're dead," Victor mutters under his breath.

Rae stomps into the room. "Are you guys totally cray?"

We stare at her for a moment, then each other. A second or two of silence follows before we burst out laughing.

"What's so funny?" she asks.

"You sounded just like Elisi," I say.

She kicks me in the rear with the side of her foot, then picks up the lamp from the floor and pushes a dent out of the shade. "You guys better cut it out before she gets home and grounds you for life."

I use the distraction to break free from Simon and Victor's clutches and jump to my feet. "They attacked me."

Victor's eyes narrow. "You started it."

Rae huffs. "It doesn't matter who started it. You have to stop."

"What's up, Rae?" Simon asks. "A year ago, you'd have been down here on the floor with us. Since when did you become such a…a girl?"

Rae's face goes all red and she glares at me. "Eighteen years old and you and Simon are still acting like children. Fine role models you are for Victor."

Victor and Simon laugh. I think about joining them

but change my mind. It's probably not a good idea to tick off my lifeline to Ace. "She's right. Ya'll get off the floor and finish cleaning up this mess. I've got to talk to Rae."

Victor rolls his eyes. "I sure hope you have some good news. I can't stand much more of him bossing me around."

I ignore him and tug Rae into the hallway. She drags her feet the whole way.

Once I'm sure we're out of earshot, I ask, "So? Is she coming?"

Lines form at the bridge of Rae's nose. I haven't seen her this serious since our mother left. My pulse races, like when I'm running the football with a tackle hot on my heels. "Come on, Rae. Spill it."

"She got into trouble when she went home last night. Her parents won't let her hang with us anymore."

My face stings like I've been slapped. "Is it because we're from the Rez?"

"She didn't say. It has to do with her mom. She thinks if she disobeys her, the whole family will fall apart. Something like that."

"That's the stupidest thing I've ever heard."

"I agree, but you can't change the way she is. Besides, she's not the only one with mother issues." She shoots me an accusatory look.

"I want to talk to her. Let me have her number."

"She specifically told me not to give it to you."

It takes a moment to process what Rae has said. When I do, not only my face, but my entire body stings. Below the burn, anger brews with such fury, I spew, "I don't know why I'm surprised. I'm not rich enough. I'm not preppy enough. I'm not white enough, and I never will be."

"You need to cool down. I don't get those kind of vibes, at least not from her."

"Yeah, well, what else could it be?"

Rae shrugs, and I stomp back to my room.

Simon stands when he sees me. "So what's up?"

Even though he's my best friend, I don't want to talk about it. I want to get Ace off my mind once and for all. "Nothing. I'm tired of sitting around the house wasting away."

"Okay, but I'm hungry. Let's grab a bite to eat before we head to the river."

"Elisi left some fried chicken in the fridge," I say. "We'll eat, then go."

A little later on, Simon and I climb into my truck. I'm just about to fire the ignition when Rae darts out of the house, wearing a pink hoodie with sparkles on it. I haven't seen her dress in girly-pink since she was three.

She pulls open the passenger door. "Simon, either get out and let me in or move over. My ride bailed on me. I'm going with you guys."

She has dark eyeliner covering her upper and lower eyelids and three tiny red dots that look like wings jutting out from the outside corners. Rae hardly ever wears makeup. She looks pretty in a freaky sort of way.

"What's up?" I ask. "You look like a fashion doll. We're going to the river, not the prom."

"Ha, ha, very funny." Rae muscles her way over Simon to the middle seat.

His jaw drops and he gawks at her like she's an unknown organism under a microscope in a science class. "I think you look really nice," he finally says.

Rae's face turns a shade of red I didn't think was

humanly possible.

"Thanks," she says, "but close your mouth. Your tonsils are ugly."

Good old Rae. It's nice to know she still exists under all that glam.

Once we're all buckled in, I pull onto the road and take the route to the river. Even the idea of going to a party can't get the thought of Ace's diss out of my head. Simon and Rae laughing and joking can't drown out the memory of her soft lips or her candy-cane taste. Three mental replays later, I still can't figure how I got it so wrong.

Damn, I thought she was kidding when she said she'd kiss me only for curiosity sake. What does it matter anyway? I'm a fool for letting myself get all worked up over her. Flying single is the only way to go.

Just past the road that leads to old man Swimmer's property, I slow down near a break in the treeline. After a sharp right, we're on the dirt road that opens into a small clearing. I navigate over a few bumps and around multiple vehicles before I find a level place to park. We get out and follow the foot-worn path down to the river. About twenty people have already gathered. Most are recent high school grads like myself, but some are underclassmen.

Jasmine stands in the middle of the crowd. I can't miss her. She's dressed in short-shorts and a croptop, displaying a jeweled belly button ring. She's got a beer in her hand and is hanging on Yarrow—who's name ironically rhymes with sorrow—but is otherwise known as the local go-to guy. If you want to get high, he's your guy. He's shirtless and his shorts are hanging so low, they barely cover his junk.

Good thing Jasmine is no longer my girlfriend or I'd have to knock his lights out.

Jasmine's radar blips, and she waves. "Hey, guys. Glad you could make it."

"Yeah. Good to see you," Yarrow says, though his tone suggests otherwise.

Rae grabs me by the crook of the arm and tugs me in the opposite direction. "Nova's over there by the oak tree," she says. "Why don't you go talk to her? Word has it she's crushing on you."

Nova is pretty with long black hair and large, doe eyes. She looks older, and she's really cool, but she's only going to be a junior in high school next year and I'm leaving. A hook-up with her seems like a heartbreak if not trouble for both of us.

"Go on and have fun," I say. "I'm going to hang with some of the guys."

"Whatever," Rae says. "Come on, Simon. Let's mingle."

My traitor best friend doesn't think twice before following my sister into the crowd like a trained seal, leaving me standing here alone. He's sure been acting strange lately.

A bunch of my buddies are sitting around a fire, so I join them. I kick a stray log into the pit and settle on a large river rock. The embers pop and fizz as the flames stretch toward the sky. Eddie passes me a can of beer.

I nod, not sure whether to thank him. I made a promise to myself that if I got accepted to Duke, I wouldn't drink or do anything that could mess up my life. I stare at the aluminum tab and turn the can around a few times. Alcohol may have ruined my mom, but she never learned moderation. Besides, she drinks whiskey.

There's nothing wrong with having a beer. I've never had a problem with it. With what's happened over the last few days, I deserve a little R&R. I pop the top and down the whole thing on purpose. Since I'm only having one, the faster I drink, the better the buzz.

Sudden laughter from the guys around me pulls me in and I laugh with them, at what I don't know. I raise my beer can in a salute, then polish off the backwash. I wonder if Ace drinks. If she were here, would she join me or would she make like horse dung and hit the trail.

Oh wait. Stupid me. She's already done that—and for no good reason.

"Hey brother, want another brew?" Eddie calls from across the pit. He opens a small cooler resting between his feet.

"I don't think so, man," I say.

"Ah, come on. It's not going to kill you."

I'm feeling so much better after one beer, could one more hurt? He tosses me another. I drink this one slower, savoring the flavor, and before I know it, I've got three empty cans at my feet, and a full one in my hand. With each swallow, what happened with Ace bothers me less. I'm definitely still into her. Or am I? It's probably only my horndog-hormones playing tricks on me. Everyone knows love at first sight is friggin' bull.

Oh well, things happen for a reason. She's a tourist, and a fickle one, and come September I'll be gone and on to my new life.

My head is fuzzy, so I slide into the sand and use my rock-perch as a backrest. I pop open my beer. It fizzes, spurts and sprays all over the place. Someone comes from behind and wipes my cheek with a

Kleenex, and the scent of roses clogs my nostrils.

"Jasmine?" I say.

"I thought you quit drinking, John," she says.

"Yeah, well, even I have to cut loose sometimes."

"Move over," she says, pushing me off my rock pillow. She squeezes in next to me. She's not all bad. It would be so easy to travel down the Jasmine highway again for a night or two. Granted, she's a pain in the place the sun don't shine, and definitely a narcissist, but she's here and she does know how to love me.

She bumps my shoulder with hers. "I think we made a huge mistake breaking up, but I'm willing to forgive and forget if you are."

I turn and stroke her cheek. She strums her fingers lightly down my chest and stops at the waist of my jeans.

"John, let's give it another try?" she asks. "I won't bug you about leaving in the fall or working for Daddy. You won't regret it this time. I promise."

I'm sure I will, but there's no reason to stress that point. Not now. Not tonight. I turn toward her with the idea to pull her into a kiss, but before I do, she plucks a joint out of the middle of her cleavage. She holds it between her lips and fires it up. "You're not going to smoke that, are you?" I say.

"Why not?"

"Can't you refrain from getting high for one night?"

She ignores me and lights the joint. Mossy-smelling smoke circles my head and burns my nostrils. I cough and fan the air. "Get that thing away from me."

She sucks in a huge toke and speaks while holding her breath, "Come on, John. Take a hit. For me?"

What could it hurt if it gets me what I want?

I reach for the joint, but as she exhales, an image I keep in my head of Duke University disappears into the cloud of smoke. I know it's only my mind playing tricks on me; still I want to puke. Not only am I downing beers like a jerk, I'm seriously thinking of tricking a girl into hooking up with me. I don't want to be this kind of guy. No matter what's happened between us, she doesn't deserve that. Not now. Not ever. I wing my beer can, and I crawl out of the trap she's made with her presence. Once on my feet, I stagger a few steps before recovering my balance. "Sorry, Jasmine, but this is a bad idea."

"What's your problem?" she snips.

"I can't be around you because it always leads to this."

"To what, John?"

"You deserve better. Trust me."

Her eyes fill with tears, but I can't think about that now. I have to leave before I make the biggest mistake of my life.

I rummage through the crowd in search of Rae, but she's nowhere in sight. It takes forever, but I finally find her down by the river, talking with Simon.

"Rae, have you been drinking?"

She scrunches her cheek. "No, why?"

"Take my keys and drive me home." I practically shove them into her hands. "You can use my truck to come back if you want, but I have to go. Now."

"Are you okay?"

"Don't worry about that, let's go. I'll explain later."

She looks at Simon. "I've got to go."

"I'll come with you," he says.

The three of us make our way up the riverbank to my truck. Rae drives to the road and we leave the lake, the beer, and the party behind. A place I vow to never visit metaphorically or physically again.

# Chapter 12
## Ace McAllister and John Spears

Someone knocks on the door to our suite. I don't bother to get up because Mom's already on the way to open it. Since my mutiny a week ago, I've devoted my time to taking care of Zack, and doing whatever my mother asks. It's paid off. Mom quit drinking, leaving Dad no excuse to stay away. So he's back, at least physically. And thus the cycle of my family life goes on.

Tonight, Cameron and I will go to the Powwow on the Reservation held over the Fourth of July where tribes from across North America compete in authentic traditional dance competitions to authentic Native American music. Not that I want to go with him. It was my mother's idea. Little does she know Rae and John will be there. Rae says John's really upset that I won't speak with him. I can't see him anymore, but it's not the kind of thing I can explain in a text or even a phone call. If I'm lucky, I can find him and make him understand why things have to be this way.

"Cameron's here," Mom calls. She turns her back to him and mouths the word, "Hurry."

I walk slowly nonetheless. He comes in with a smile and has flowers in his hand. Undoubtedly, he thinks this is a date. I'll set him straight later.

I take the bouquet.

"Aren't they beautiful?" Mom says. "Put them in some water."

Out of habit, I obey and rifle through the kitchen cabinets until I uncover a vase behind some plastic containers.

"Cameron," Mom says. "Stay close to Ace. I've heard it's not safe for women on Indian reservations."

What the heck? Mom and her prejudice. She hasn't even been to a reservation. She doesn't, however, have an issue sending me with a guy who might have gone through my belongings without permission.

"You know I'll take good care of her, Miss Dawn," Cameron says.

They're speaking about me as if I'm a child. I slap the flowers on the table hard enough for some petals to fall off. No one seems to notice.

"You two go have fun," Mom says. "I'll take care of the flowers." She gives me a sideways glance. Then she takes them from the table and examines them for damage. I'm sure she'll lecture me later about beating up the bouquet.

I grab my backpack from the hall closet, but before we can get out the door, Zack tears into the hallway in his underwear.

"I want to go to the Powwow," he says.

Cameron frowns. "Not this time, bud. You're too little to go out with us."

Zack scowls and his breathing becomes labored.

"Listen, Zackie," I say, "if we were going during the day, we'd take you. How about I bring you back a surprise instead."

"No!" He hops around on his toes, his arms flailing. "I want to go. I'm not little anymore. You think

I'm little."

Mom's eyes widen and she blushes. "I'm sorry, Cameron." She stomps her foot. "Zack, stop it. Right now."

"Mom," I say, curtly. "I'll handle it."

I get in front of Zack and bend to his level, taking care not to get too close. When he feels threatened, he lashes out. Not in anger, but fear. The trick is to stay calm. "You're right Zack. You are big," I say, "but there's going to be fireworks, and you hate loud noises."

Zack stops hopping around and tilts his head. "They're going to be really, really loud?"

"Yes, they will."

He tugs at his earlobes, and flashes a frown at Cameron, then holds rare eye contact with me. "Will you buy me a tomahawk? One made of stone like in the books—not plastic."

I choke back a laugh, guessing whom he intends to use it on and guiltily hoping I'm right. "I'll do my best."

As if a switch flipped off in his brain, his shoulders relax and his face brightens. "Okay, I'll stay here and watch a movie."

Mom smiles and mouths a "thank you" to me. I wish she were as proud of me all the time and not only when I'm taking care of Zack.

A short drive later, Cameron pulls into the Acquoni Expo Center parking lot. He makes it there without directions or one wrong turn. It's as if he knows the reservation well, but when I ask, he claims he simply followed the traffic. I suspect he's lying, but it's not worth debate, so I let it go. If he wants to sneak off to the reservation, who am I to judge?

Inside the gates, among the explosion of spectators, the area blossoms with people dressed in colorful regalia stitched with intricate bead patterns. Many are adorned with feather accessories and jewelry made from turquoise and other natural stones. Bells jingle from the pants legs of a man wearing a large headdress of feathers as he strides past.

We pass the vendor tents and enter an area where several canvas sun-tents create a half-circle on one end of the field, sheltering groups of musicians from various tribes. An emcee booth is positioned in the arc.

People, some dressed in regalia, who appear to be friends and family of the dancers, finish the circle with lawn chairs and umbrellas. I scan the crowd for John or Rae, but with all the people moving about, finding them seems next to impossible.

The bleachers on the outskirts of the field quickly fill up, mostly with tourists. Cameron goes to save us seats, and I head for the vendors' tents. The vendors sell every craft and artifact imaginable. I buy traditional Indigenous clothing for Zack and a rubber tomahawk. He'll be disappointed it's not real, but it's much safer this way.

In another tent, I admire a pair of long earrings shaped like wings. A horn-like end locks them on the front of the earlobe, making them look like ear gages. The vendor tells me they are hand-carved from bone. I run my finger over the small wing and decide I must have them. After I pay the vender, I use a mirror on the display table and put them on. I pull out my phone to text Rae when anxiety gets the best of me. What if John is angry and doesn't want to see me? What if he's with another girl? That would hurt. If he were alone, with Cameron waiting, I wouldn't have more than a minute to say hello and would probably piss him off even more, so I chicken out.

I tuck my phone away and return to the bleachers. Cameron is sitting in the top row. I squeeze through the people already seated and slide in next to him.

Cameron flips one of my new earrings with the tip of his finger. "Where did you get these?"

"In one of the booths when I was buying Zack a present." I open the bag and show him the regalia and the tomahawk.

"I leave you alone for a moment and you turn into an Indian Princess wannabe."

"That's racist, Cameron. Shut up, you're not funny." I glance around. Thankfully no one seems to be paying attention to us.

"Let your brother look like a dork if he wants to, but you need to take those things off."

Almost on command, obedient little me starts to remove the earrings like the perfect people-pleaser I've become. Why am I always trying to make everyone else happy? I hate conflict, but just where the hell does he get off telling me what to do?

"No. I like them," I say in a voice less powerful than I wanted, but inside, the tension releases a bit.

"Okay, Ace. If you want to play Indian, go ahead. But you should be nicer to me. I'm your ride. If I leave, so do you."

"That's true, but it doesn't give you a right to be rude." I fold Zack's regalia and place it inside my backpack. There's something hard in one of the zipper flaps, and I open it. Oh, no. Mom's vodka. I forgot I'd hidden it there. I drop the tomahawk and it clanks against the foot rail. “Damn it.”

“What’s the matter?” Cameron asks. “Did you lose your wampum at the trading post?” He grins.

“Quit being stupid.” I lower my voice and cinch my backpack closed. “There’s something in here that shouldn’t be.”

“Let me see.” He snatches my backpack and peeks inside. “Whoa, you’ve been holding out on me. Were you going to keep it all for yourself?”

“I didn’t bring it on purpose. My parents must have borrowed my bag.” Lies, lies, and more lies.

“They’ve probably forgotten all about it by now. They’ll never miss it.”

“I’m not worried about that. Didn’t you see the sign out front that said, ALCOHOL PROHIBITED? I’ve got to throw it away before we get arrested.”

Cameron takes my backpack and crunches it closed. “Calm down. You’re not going to get into trouble. Give me a minute and I’ll take care of everything.”

He takes off down the bleachers and disappears into the crowd. Hiding the booze in my bag seemed like a good idea at the time. Not so much now. Maybe I am only with Cameron because of Mom, but he isn’t all bad. He’s sure being a friend now.

The emcee announces over the loudspeaker the Powwow is about to begin. Drums sound, poom, poom, poom, and singer’s voices undulate long heart-felt words I don’t understand, but they sound as if they are drawn from emotions from deep within. My heart takes on the rhythm of the drumbeats and the tiny hairs on the back of my neck tingle.

Native American veterans march into the circle on the field first, leading a procession of dancers adorned in regalia, many with dance bells attached to their knees and ankles, that jingle with each syncopated step.

Men, women, and children dance onto the field until there is almost no room for more. Through feathers, colors, and ornate scarves, I catch a glimpse of a guy with a simple spiky headdress.

John Spears.

Though I'm watching from afar, I'm sure it's him, dressed in a red shirt wrapped with a tan belt, dancing freely, uninhibitedly. He's more handsome than I remember.

Just then, Cameron crosses in front of me. He's holding drinks and food in a cardboard box and totally blocking my view. I lean to the side and try to see around him.

"Who you looking at?" he asks.

My cheeks combust. "The dancers. Could you move, please?"

He takes his time sitting down, and by the time I have a clear view of field, John is nowhere in sight.

"Here. I bought this for you." He hands me a blue crushed-ice drink.

"Thanks," I mutter.

"Why don't you say it like you mean it?"

"I'm sorry. It was very nice of you."

"Well, drink up."

It tastes sour, but I'm really thirsty so I drink it anyway. I watch dance after dance, studying each person and passerby in search of John, only to be disappointed every time. Soon one dance bleeds into the next, and I can no longer keep up. Cameron buys me another drink, and I'm so hot, I suck it down quicker than the first. He leaves to buy me another.

The Powwow continues into the night as the sun fades into the horizon and darkness encroaches. The cool air meets my sweaty skin and chills me to the bone.

"You're shivering," Cameron says. "Come here and I'll warm you up."

I move closer and he wraps his arm around my shoulder.

"I want you to know this isn't a date."

"Then what is it?"

My mind is foggy and I have trouble forming my words. "I'm not sure, but we're definitely not on a date."

Cameron laughs and squeezes me tighter, which I'd never allow if I weren't so cold.

Next thing I know, the dancers are gone, and the sky is alight with sparkles and colors. Loud booms vibrate down my spine and jostle my internal organs. The flashes make me dizzy, and I rest my head on Cameron's shoulder and close my eyes to escape the flashing-color-overload. Everything goes black.

I awake to the sound of Cameron's voice.

"Ace, get up. It's time to leave." He tugs on my arm.

It takes every bit of my strength to stand. When I do, I teeter a bit and plop back down. "What happened?"

"You fell asleep."

People are leaving the bleachers and heading toward the exit.

"Where's my backpack?" I ask.

“I’ve got it here.” He turns sideways to reveal it slung over his shoulder. He grabs my upper arm and pulls me to my feet, then steadies me as we navigate the stairs.

My head’s foggy and aches a little. I blink a few times to be sure I’m not dreaming. We walk to a dumpster behind a vendor’s truck. Cameron opens my backpack and pulls out my mother’s bottle of vodka. It’s empty.

My heart beats rapid fire. “You were supposed to throw that out.”

“Come on, Ace. Did you actually think I’d waste a free high?” He tosses the bottle into the bin.

Now I know why I feel like hell. I don’t want to know, but I do. “You put vodka in my drinks.”

Cameron smirks. “You’re too uptight. You needed something to loosen you up.”

My muscles twitch beneath my skin. My hand balls into a fist, and I swing at him.

He catches my wrist right before my knuckles reach his nose.

I struggle to break free, and he twists my arm behind my back.

“Let go of me or I’ll scream. I swear, I will.”

“You think you’re tough, don’t you?”

A guy on his way toward the gates stops. “Hey man, you better let her go.”

Cameron looks from side to side at a small crowd that’s gathered and loosens his grip. I spin around and yank my backpack off his shoulder. “Give it to me. It’s mine.”

He lets go with a push. I stumble backward and fall on my tailbone. Pain shoots up my spine.

Someone gasps.

Cameron's head jerks like his brain just switched on. "Ace, I'm sorry…." He offers me a hand.

"Go to hell." I scramble to my feet, and take off running, pushing through clumps of people on the way out.

The world is coming at me rapid fire as I sprint across the parking lot. Car brakes squeal and a fender stops inches from me. I push off the hood and dash for the road. I swore I'd never drink. Now because of Cameron and his stupidity, I'm going to turn into an alcoholic like my mother. Tears stream down my cheeks and I let out a gut-wrenching sob.

A few horns honk. People are staring at me as they drive by. I'm alone on the road at night, and it's scary, but anything is better than being with Cameron.

I need to call my dad. I slow my pace to a walk and pull myself together. When I finally call him, rather than a concerned hello, I'm greeted by voice mail.

I text him next, but he doesn't respond. Either he's in the middle of a high-stakes game of poker or he's with his girlfriend. What am I going to do? I can't call my mother. If she's drinking she might drive drunk with Zack. The Casino is only five miles away. I can walk.

****

When the Powwow's over, the guys and I head for Simon's Cavalier. Elisi smiled broader tonight than she has in a long time. She's never prouder than when I embrace our culture.

"Where's your sister?" Simon asks. "Isn't she going to ride with us?"

"Naw, she's driving Elisi home."

His expression flattens. "Oh."

I'm about to ask him what's up when Jack shouts, "Shotgun!"

I push him out of the way and vault into the prized seat.

"Hey, man, I called the front," he says.

"Get over yourself. We haven't been in middle school in years. Besides, my legs are longer than yours."

"But I'm bigger." He pats his stomach.

I tilt my seat forward and laugh as he squeezes in the back.

He thumps my head.

I make a grab for his arm and miss. "Listen, fat boy, you better not turn your back if you know what's good for you." Even though I totally deserved the slap, it's fun to rile him up.

"There he goes, Simon," Jack says. "Acting like the Godfather." He pushes my shoulder. "Stick to law school if you know what's good for you. Leave the tough-guy stuff to me. You're no good at it."

Jack's had a few minor skirmishes with the law and he believes he's the baddest dude in Cherokee. But everyone here knows he has too much heart to be a real criminal. Not only would I trust him with my wallet, I'd trust him with my sister.

I smile. He wouldn't stand a chance against her.

Simon cranks the car. "Roll down the windows, it's hot in here."

Jack and I do what he says and cool air fills the car as we creep through the jammed parking lot. When we reach the road, the traveling speed is not much better, but at least we're moving. I busy myself playing a game on my phone.

"Wow, look ahead." Simon whistles.

I don't bother. "The traffic will clear once we hit the main drag."

"Not the traffic, doofus. There's a hot girl, and she's walking all alone."

I'm not going to look at another girl until I get to college. I've had enough girl trouble to last me for a while.

Jack sticks his head out the window. "I wonder what's she's doing out this late all alone? Maybe she's looking for someone like me?"

"I doubt that," I say.

"Slow down," Jack insists. "You're going to pass her."

Simon hits the brakes hard. My head jerks and I rub the back of my neck. "Are you trying to give me whiplash?"

"Hey, baby," Jack shouts at the girl. "Want a ride?"

She doesn't respond. When will he learn he's not the super-stud he thinks he is? He pokes me in the shoulder. "Hey? Isn't that the girl who came with us to Sliding Rock?"

I look once. Then do a double take. "Hell, yeah. It's her. Simon, stop!"

Simon pulls onto the shoulder. "Oh, boy, here we go again."

Ace keeps her eyes on the ground. She moves off the easement onto the grass and takes off running.

"Ace," I shout. "It's me, John."

She keeps running.

I practically fly out of the car and sprint to catch up with her. For a split second I worry I've got the wrong girl. But when I reach her side, she stops.

It's really her.

"What are you doing out here all alone?" I ask.

Her hair is forward, covering her face and she shakes her head.

"If I scared you, I'm really sorry. I won't do anything to hurt you."

"I know. I'm not scared. It's just, I don't want you to see me like this." She hides her face with her hands.

"Like what?" I ask, gently prying them loose.

Her cheeks are wet and blotchy. Black mascara streaks her cheeks and she smells of alcohol. I didn't think she was into drinking. At least I hoped she wasn't.

"Why don't you get into the car?" I gesture toward the Cavalier. "We can talk there."

She glances over. Simon and Jack have stupid grins and are waving like they are miles away and we can't see them.

"I don't want your friends to see me either. Just go, I'll be okay." She begins walking again. Fast.

I run back to the car and toss Simon my keys. "I'm walking with Ace. Go to my house and get my truck. Park it up the road a bit, near the river by the bridge and leave the keys under the mat."

"Why don't ya'll ride with me?"

He looks puzzled, but I don't have time to explain. "How about be a friend and do what I ask for once, okay?"

Jack leans forward. "There he goes playing the Godfather again."

I don't have time for senseless banter. Ace is getting farther away. I'll never forgive myself if something happens to her. I ditch my friends, trusting they'll follow my instructions, and catch up with her. "If you're not going to take a ride, at least let me walk with you."

"I told you I'm okay. Besides, if you hang around me, I'll only ruin your life."

"Huh? How is walking with you going to ruin my life?"

She stops and looks at me. Her eyes are sad. So sad, I almost taste her misery. "It's okay. We don't have to talk."

She nods, and we continue on in silence for a long while, and this time it doesn't feel right. When I can't stand it anymore I say, "So where are we going?"

"The casino." Her response is so curt it stings.

"If you don't want me around, just tell me. Once you're home safe, I won't bother you again."

"That's not it, John. I want you to bother me, okay? But my life is a mess. My dad's cheating on my mom. My mom's a drunk. I thought I could make everything right. But tonight I had a huge epiphany. I can't."

"Is that why you're drinking?"

Her face flatlines. "How did you know?"

"I can smell it."

Tears pour from her eyes. "I didn't do it on purpose. Someone spiked my drink."

"Who?" I ask, though I'd lay bets it was that creep Cameron. Good thing he's nowhere near or his eyes would be black and blue within a minute.

She dabs at her nose with the back of her hand. "It's not important. It's too late to change anything. All my life I've avoided alcohol because of what it did to my mother. Now I'm doomed to become a drunk just like her."

My life isn't always easy, but I suspect hers is worse. I place my hand on her shoulder. "Ace, look at me." She lifts her head and captures me with her big blue eyes. "I don't know what happened tonight, but if you don't want to have a problem with alcohol, don't drink. One time won't change you forever. You have the power to be who you want to be."

"You make it sound so easy."

"I don't mean to. My family has some bad stuff, too. Everyone's does. Bad things won't happen to you just because it happened to someone else. You have control of your destiny."

"I sure hope so."

We reach the area where the river meets the road. The traffic sucks.

She looks both ways and shakes her head. "We'll never make it alive."

I offer her my hand. "Let's cross over. We can do it together."

She bites her lower lip and stares at my open palm. Then, without a word, she slips her little hand into mine.

Bang. Zoom.

No way should my heart be beating out of my chest from just her touch. No way should my scalp be tingling, but it is. It doesn't make sense. I feel like a middle schooler, orbiting 'round Planet Love, trying to decide whether or not to land. Holy hell, this girl is extra. She affects me like no other. I've got to get my feet on the ground before it's too late.

A few cars stop and with me leading her, we make it across without any physical damage. Staying next to the road might be quicker, but I want more time with her. “Want to walk by the river?”

She glances at our hands, still locked together, and says, “Yeah, I do.”

Her breathy words seep under my skin to my innermost being and make me buzz all over. I nudge her forward and we sidle down the embankment where the rocks meet the rushing water. The wind blows her hair into my face, and the scent of rosemary consumes me. I’d recognize the scent anywhere. Elisi grows the herb in our garden. I’ve read that in the Middle Ages it was often used as a love charm. It must work because in this very moment, I feel like I’m in a fairy tale.

Ace lets go of my hand and kneels on the rocks. She washes her face in the river, scrubbing the streaks of black mascara from her cheeks.

I squat down beside her. “What happened tonight? The truth please?”

“Cameron put vodka in my drink, and we got into a horrible fight. I never liked him before, but now… I was only with him because Mom wouldn’t let me go to the Reservation alone, and I wanted to see you.”

I knew that guy was no good. I fling a stone across the river.

She doesn’t stop with Cameron and what happened at the Powwow. She tells me about her mother’s blackouts, and how she covers for her so her dad won’t find out. She’s afraid if she leaves her mother’s side her entire life will come crashing down. She can’t take care of Zack on her own—at least not yet. I always thought having no mother was worse than a drunken mother, but after listening to what Ace goes through, I’m not so sure anymore.

I wipe a tear from her cheek with the pad of my

thumb.

The corners of her mouth carve a slight smile. “Thanks for listening.” She leans toward me, her lips parted. She’s so sad, and she’s been drinking. The last thing I want is to violate her trust.

I turn away and dig at the ground with a stick, killing the potential kiss, and we linger in uncomfortable silence with only the sound of the rushing water to fill the empty airspace.

She rises, then hugs herself and shivers.

“Are you cold?”

“Sort of.”

I think to give her my shirt, then I realize I’m still in my traditional clothing, including a porcupine roach on my head. I remove my headdress and carefully lay it on a large river rock. I stand behind her and open my arms. “May I?”

She sets her backpack on the ground and nods.

I invite her into the circle of my arms. She leans against me and rests her head on my shoulder. Above us, the moon is nearly full, casting bluish light across the river. The sky is a starry mess. “Look.” I point to the sky. “There’s Ursa Major.”

“What?” she asks.

“The bear constellation.”

“Where is it? Show me.”

I raise her hand and trace the starry image like I’m doing a dot-to-dot picture. “There’s the head.” I swoop her hand left. “And there’s the tail.” I finish by pointing out the bear’s front and rear legs.

“The way you do it makes it look like a skinny, headless dog,” she says.

I laugh. “Where’s your imagination?”

"Let me try." She lifts my hand and traces a detailed shape of a bear, describing the air-drawing from ear to toe. "Is that better?"

"Perfect," I say. "Like you."

She laces her fingers through mine.

I rub tiny circles on her palm with my thumb as I speak. "When I was a kid, I used to fear the bear would swoop down from the sky and eat me alive."

"That's horrible." She presses her lips together, and her ribs shake in suppressed mirth.

"I wouldn't laugh if I were you," I say. "Elisi says that bear is pretty bad."

"Don't worry. I'll protect you from Starbear." She makes a muscle, flexing and releasing her cute bicep.

"You will, huh?" I tickle her side.

She squeals, wiggles around, and digs her fingers into my ribs. We engage in a full out tickle-war. In the middle of our battle, the wind shifts and the earth rotates, and soon we're on the ground with her straddling me, both of us panting.

Our eyes lock, and I brush a strand of hair behind her ear. She leans over inch at a time until her nose touches mine. She kisses me, only a peck, then runs the tip of her tongue around lightly around my lips. Unable to resist any longer, I pull her to me and crush my mouth into hers. Our tongues collide in a slippery duel as her hands roam up the back of my shirt, leaving ruts of pleasure wherever her fingers graze my skin. She raises my shirt, then does the same with her own and presses her warm belly onto mine. Our bodies melt together, and I grab her rear and grind my hips into hers.

If I don't stop now, I'm going to lose control and

there will be no turning back. I can't let that happen. Not while I taste alcohol on her breath. It's not right to go any further unless she wants me as much as I want her. And tonight I can't be sure.

"Ace," I whisper, "we need to stop. This isn't the time or place."

She freezes. Her chest rises and falls as quickly as my own, and she struggles to speak. "Oh, yeah, right. Maybe we can go somewhere more private."

I lift her off me and help her into a sitting position. "That's not what I meant. We're moving too fast, and I don't think this is a good idea—especially after what happened to you tonight."

Her chin falls to her chest. "I'm sorry, I don't know what came over me."

"You have nothing to apologize for. Let me take you home." I jump to my feet and help her up."

Sometimes doing the right thing really, really sucks. I snatch my porcupine roach off the rock and brush it off.

She stares at the heavens for the longest time and then says, "You're right, John. Take me home. We better get out of here before the bear falls from the sky and devours us both."

## Chapter 13
## Ace McAllister and John Spears

As we leave the river, my stomach is an achy mess. Maybe John needs some time to think. Maybe he doesn't like me the way I like him. Even if he doesn't want to see me again, I don't regret one moment of tonight.

With a firm hand on my lower back, John leads me across the street and on to a parking lot a little ways down the road. A blue truck, his truck, is parked ahead in an empty dirt lot, waiting for us. "How did this get here?"

"Let's just say I have good friends."

"You mean you planned to drive me home all along? What if I refused to go back?"

"Ace, I'd never leave you. It's a long walk to the casino and it's dark."

A gritty lump forms in the back of my throat. I'm so used to taking care of people, I don't know how to respond when someone wants to take care of me.

He opens the passenger door and places my backpack on the floorboard. I settle onto the cracked vinyl seat. The scent of honeysuckle, lots and lots of honeysuckle, burns my nostrils and my sinuses, too. I plug my nose.

John opens the driver's door and a breeze stirs the already overwhelming scent. "What the hell?" He digs around the floorboard, then under the seat, and pulls out four metal tins. "Air freshener?" He tosses the cans in the bed. "Simon must like you."

I can't help but giggle.

John hops in and positions himself behind the wheel, then rolls down his window. "Sorry about the smell."

"It's not that bad," I lie, holding my breath until I can get my window open, too.

Once we're on the road, fresh air replaces the stinky, man-made floral scent. The traffic has died off and it takes no time to reach the highway that leads to the casino. John stops at the light and puts on his blinker. This is it. I'm a few minutes from home, and if I don't speak now we may never see each other again.

"Wait," I say.

"Did you forget something?" He glances at me, then back at the light.

"Sort of." My mind's cloudy, making it difficult to think. Finally, I blurt, "I had a great time tonight."

He raises a brow. "So did I."

Heat rises from my neck and spreads across my cheeks. "I mean, I'm glad I got to see you again."

"Sounds like you think I'm going away."

Enormous and extremely excited butterflies attack my stomach. "You're not?"

"Only if you want me to."

I wiggle a heat vent on the dash while I collect my thoughts. "No, never. I've been thinking about you since Sliding Rock. Maybe even before."

"Before? That leaves only the first time you met me?"

Damn it. I go from words practically dying in my

throat to a blabbering idiot in sixty seconds. My emotions are all over the place. It has to be the booze. Maybe that's why Mom acts crazy all the time.

He clears his throat. "So when *will* I see you again? I need an answer because I don't want to rely on fate this time. Fate is not always friendly."

The light turns green and he pulls onto the highway.

Mom will ground me for life if she finds out I'm with John tonight. Other people can date who they please, but not me. My dates are hand-selected.

When I don't answer, he continues. "I don't have to work tomorrow, and I planned to do something special. There's no reason you can't come with me. How about I pick you up in the morning. Say around ten." His eyes twinkle.

Oh, brother, I'm in trouble. Not only does he look good enough to be on a magazine cover, he has twinkly eyes. How can I possibly say no?

"Okay, but where are we going?"

"I'm not telling, but I'll give you a hint. You have to wear sneakers and jeans, not shorts." He turns toward me and grins. The truck swerves and he compensates to guide it back into the lane.

"Will anyone else be there?"

He clears his throat. "Not this time?"

"So we'll be all alone?"

"Yes, but I'll be a perfect gentleman. I promise."

Well, that's disappointing. But if this special place is anything like Sliding Rock, it's bound to be fun.

We pull into the casino parking lot, and my moment of bliss is squelched by hardcore reality. I point at a secluded spot on the far back. "Quick. Park over there."

He frowns and hits the brakes hard. "What's the matter? Are you embarrassed to be seen with me?"

"No. My mother doesn't know about you. I want to tell her before someone else does, and I'm not ready."

"All, right, but do you think I can at least get your phone number this time?"

I dig in my backpack for my phone and discover something missing. "Darn, I must have left Zack's tomahawk at the Powwow. I promised I'd bring him one. He's going to be so disappointed."

"It's no big deal. We can get him another one tomorrow."

"Don't let me forget." I wake up my phone. Multiple texts from Cameron pop up on the screen. I quickly swipe the lock to hide them from view.

John plucks his phone from a hidden pocket in his shirt and we exchange texts. He glances at the screen and smiles. "Finally."

"I better go."

"Will you be okay? I mean with your Mom?"

"Don't worry. I can handle her."

He flashes me a crooked grin. "I'll see you tomorrow."

Tomorrow cannot come soon enough.

****

Once Ace is safe inside the hotel, I head home. I can't believe I have a date with her. When I left the Powwow, finding her was the furthest thing from my mind. It's almost as if some invisible force is drawing us together, making things happen. All the coincidences of our chance meetings have to have some meaning, so how can this thing between us possibly be wrong?

I toss my phone onto the passenger seat still warm with her presence. I'm itching to call her just to hear her voice, but she made it clear she wants to keep me a secret for now. While it feels sort of funny, I don't blame her. I'm thinking about doing the same. Telling Elisi about Ace will cause something close to the Apocalypse in my world. If I can only get Elisi past the fact that Ace is not Jasmine, or Cherokee, I know she'll like her.

Jasmine and I were together for a long time and I thought I loved her, but my feelings for Ace are way stronger. Ace is beautiful, and her real-girl curves are sexy, but there's more to her than her looks. She's smart and kind, and I love the glints of silver in her eyes when she smiles and the sun-freckles that dust her cheeks. The more I'm around her, the more I want to be. I'm dying to know everything about her. Like, what's her favorite color? What does she do on rainy afternoons? Where does she see herself in the future? Hopefully, she'll give me the time to learn the answers.

****

My heartbeat double-times as I stop in the casino lobby to scan the text messages. The ones I ignored moments ago. But now they seem important. Knowledge of what trouble lies ahead will give me time to plan a defense. Not a single message belongs to my mother. Good sign. They all belong to Cameron most begging me to call him. One particular message catches my eye.

Cameron: *Ace, I'm sorry. Please don't tell your parents what happened tonight.*

Someone's hand clamps down on my shoulders.

I twist around.

It’s him.

I swallow a breath and can’t release it. For several seconds I’m suffocating…five, six, seven. “Don’t touch me,” I growl, as the air leaves my lungs.

He holds up his hands, palms open, and glances from side to side. “Shhh…what’s wrong with you?”

“Wrong with me?”

“You took off like a mad-woman. I’ve been driving all over the place searching for you.”

“You’re lucky I didn’t call the police.”

“I’m sorry. I shouldn’t have pushed you, but I can’t change it now. Besides, you caused the whole mess. You were the one who brought the booze. If you try to tell anyone, I’ll say you got wasted and wandered off.”

He’s got me there. I smell like I’ve been drinking. I have no witnesses. If my mother believes him, I’ll be grounded for the rest of the trip. I can’t take that chance. Cameron left me in one piece. He didn’t hurt me that bad. Besides he’s dumb. I can handle him. “I won’t tell on you, as long as you stay away from me from now on.”

“You don’t mean that. You’re just mad.”

The muscles in my cheek twitch and it takes all my concentration to keep my voice below a roar. “I mean every stinking word, and I’d be happy to tell the entire lobby if you don’t believe me.”

He shrugs. “Whatever you say Ace, whatever you say.”

I’ll take it for now, but something tells me he doesn’t mean a word of what he says.

****

When I get home, Simon’s Cavalier is parked out front. His parents are probably fighting again. When his

’rents get along they act like two turtledoves, but when they go at it, things at the house start flying, so he comes here to stay. When we were kids, we spent hours in a tree behind his house waiting for the storm to blow over. Now we hang out mostly at my house. It’s quieter even with a gazillion people living here.

I wiggle my key in the lock and ease the door open. The house is dark except for the glare of the TV. Simon and Rae are on the couch in the living room. He’s on one end, practically sitting on the arm, and she’s on the other, smoothing her hair, mouth hanging open as if she thinks I’m a stranger about to rob the place.

“Oh, John,” Rae says. “You’re home.”

“Yeah, hi,” Simon practically screeches, his eyes wide.

If I didn’t know better, I’d think I interrupted something. That’s a stupid thought, though. Up until a year or two ago, Rae scrapped with him more than she did me. I’ve had to pull her off him on more than a one occasion.

“How’d it go with Ace?” Simon asks.

“It went fine. In fact, it went better than fine.” I plop down on the couch between them and drape my arms over their shoulders. “We’re getting together tomorrow.”

“That’s great,” Rae says. “I didn’t think you had a chance.”

I mess up her hair. “Oh, ye of little faith. When are you going to realize your twin brother is a stud?”

“Get off my hair.” Rae smacks my hand away, and I high-five Simon on the rebound.

Rae clucks her tongue. “Don’t get too full of yourself, tomorrow isn’t here yet.”

"But it will be in…" I glance up at the clock, and it hits me. "Damn, I have to be up in six hours."

Rae bursts out laughing. "Now I've seen everything. John's worried about getting beauty sleep." Simon joins her, braying like a donkey.

"Shh…keep it down. You'll wake the whole house," I say. "Where's Elisi anyway?"

"In bed," Rae says.

"Do me a favor and don't say anything about Ace. I want to break the news gently."

Rae puffs. "Good luck. A thousand down pillows wouldn't be enough to cushion the blow from this news. You know how Elisi feels about us dating outsiders."

"She's just going to have to get over it 'cause I'm not bending."

Rae shakes her head. "John, John, John, you're a magnet for punishment."

"You'll see. Everything will be fine." I pat her knee.

Rae looks at me as if she thinks I'm pathetic.

I know telling Elisi won't be a picnic, but I'm willing to go through whatever I have to for Ace.

I stand and stretch. "You coming, Simon? I'll throw out the sleeping bag for you."

Simon looks at Rae and she gives him a nod.

"Uh, yeah, sure," he mumbles, sounding like I asked him to shovel manure.

The two of them are acting awful strange tonight.

"Night Rae," Simon says before following me down the hall.

## Chapter 14
## Ace McAllister and John Spears

I dress in a pair of jeans, then slip on the pink silk blouse my mother bought me, and a pair of delicate sandals, knowing she'll be happy with my choice of feminine-looking clothes. I roll a t-shirt into a ball and stuff it in the bottom of my backpack along with a pair of sneakers.

Staying calm is a necessity in this situation, but it won't be easy. I put on my best doe-eyed look and glide into the kitchen.

Mom smiles. "You look nice. Are you and Cameron going somewhere?"

"Um, no. I thought I'd catch the shuttle to the mall in Concord."

"By yourself?"

"Yes, if you don't mind? No one likes to shop as hard and as long as me. You know that." I hate lying to her, but I don't have any other choice—not if I want to go with John without a major blow up.

"Well, I suppose it will be okay. I have plans with Susan later tonight. Be home early around dinnertime. I'll need you to watch Zack."

"Sure, Mom, no problem," I say politely, even though I'm royally ticked off. While I love Zack with all my heart, he's her son, not mine. She needs to quit acting as if I'm on call.

The shuttle stops in the center of town, and I exit with the other passengers, thanking the driver before I leave. I find a bench in the plaza and sit, crossing and uncrossing my legs until I find a pose that doesn't make my thighs look fat. Then I text John. Minutes pass and he doesn't answer.

Maybe he's having second thoughts.

My mind runs in all sorts of wild directions, working out scenario after scenario of everything that could possibly be wrong. What if I misunderstood him? What if he meant another day? I hop off the bench and pace, staring at my phone.

The longer I wait for him to respond, the more I worry. What if he stands me up? That would be the ultimate insult. I need to leave. I need to get out of here before someone sees me.

John's blue truck pulls up.

My heart takes off like a racehorse, and my head spins. Thankfully, I haven't moved too far from the bench, and grab onto the backrest for support.

He gets out of his truck, and when he notices me, a huge smile lights up his face.

Gone are the braids. His hair hangs in silky strands almost to his elbows. He's wearing a black v-neck t-shirt, blue jeans with white decorative stitching, and black high-top sneakers. Everything about him is perfect. His face. His hair. Even his body moves in perfect symmetry as he approaches.

"Wow. You look beautiful," he says. "I might need to change our plans or you'll ruin your clothes."

"No," I say. "I brought a T-shirt and sneakers to change into. I can use the bathroom in one of the stores."

"Don't bother. There's a place to change where we're going."

*I hope it's not behind some bushes somewhere*. I drop my phone. It crashes face down onto the pavement. "Oops."

John picks it up, examines the glass, and wipes it on the bottom of his shirt. "Looks like it survived."

He hands me my phone, and I thank him. I want to say more, but my throat is dry and I can't speak.

A little while later, we pull off a mountain road and onto a steep, gravel driveway. John stops the truck in front of a small wooden house. A garden of pink, white, yellow, and purple wildflowers decorate either side of the steps leading to the white porch.

"This is home," John says.

We climb out of the truck. Wind chimes hanging on the corner of the porch make a high-pitched jangle, like pixies laughing.

"It's really nice," I say, not because I'm supposed to, but because I've always pictured living in a cozy house nestled on the side of a mountain.

He flashes a heart-melting smile. "It's okay. The house is screaming for a fresh coat of paint, and it's a little crowded inside, but it will do."

"Are we going in?"

"Nope. We are going someplace much better." He motions for me to follow around the side. A small weathered barn sits in the very back of the yard, behind it are rounded North Carolina mountain tops and wild nature as far as the eye can see.

"What's in there?" I ask.

"I have someone I want you to meet," he says.

As we near the barn, snorts and whinnies sound

from within. John swings open the door and across the dirt floor is a single stall, housing a beautiful gray and white Appaloosa with brown markings on its face. The horse raises and dips his head as we approach.

Joy radiates inside me. “You have a horse?” I practically squeal.

“Ace, meet Billy,” he says.

I reach out to stroke Billy’s face. He backs up at first, but then succumbs to his curiosity and steps forward to meet my hand. I rub my cheek against his and stroke the other side of his head. “Oh Billy, you are a sweet one.”

“I see I have some competition here,” John says, interrupting our horsey love fest.

Poor John doesn’t know how stiff his competition is. I’ve been riding since before I could walk. My horse, Amaretto, lives in the stables on my grandparents’ estate. “He is awfully cute,” I say, kissing Billy’s nose.

“All right, enough of the lovey-dovey stuff. Want to go for a ride?”

“Yeah, that sounds great,” I squeak, unable to contain my glee.

John straps a bridle on Billy. “Have you ever ridden before?”

“Yes, a bit,” I say, pressing my lips together to stop a smile.

“Hope you don’t mind riding double-bareback. Billy’s gentle, and I’ll make sure you don’t fall off.”

“I trust you.”

John grabs a small knapsack off the ground. “Do you have anything you want to bring along?”

“Just my phone.” I hand it to him and he places in a pocket of the sack.

He runs his fingers lightly over the collar of my pink blouse. “You better change. I’ll wait outside.” He leads Billy out of the barn and shuts the door behind him.

John is outside the door, and for a split second, I’ll be shirtless. I’m wearing a see-through nylon bra. The thought of it nearly takes my breath. I turn my back to the door and change quickly. Then I hang my pink shirt on the hook on the wall and slip on my sneakers. I wipe the thick layer of sweat from my forehead and walk outside.

John’s smiling. “You look great.”

I tug at the bottom of my T-shirt. “Thanks.”

“Come here, I’ll give you a foot up.”

I place my foot into the cup of his hands, grab onto Billy’s mane, and swing my leg over his back. Billy sidles. I lunge forward and wrap my arms around his neck. John steadies him with the reins.

“Are you okay?” he asks.

“I’m fine,” I say, but I’m better than fine; I’m ecstatic. Nothing makes me feel more alive than the power of a horse beneath me. Except maybe riding with John double bareback.

John tosses me the reins. “Hold these tight and grab his sides tight with your knees. I’m getting on.”

In a swift move, he mounts Billy’s back behind me. Our bodies are spooned, and his breath tickles my ear. Every nerve in my body pings as he reaches his arms around me and takes the reins.

“Where are we going?” I ask.

“It’s a surprise,” is all he says.

Then he taps Billy’s haunches and we ride off into the early morning sun.

****

Billy's pawing at the ground with his hoofs, but I rein him in. He's not used to two riders, and I don't want to tire him out. I ease him onto the trail that leads to my escape from the world. With each clomp of his hooves, Ace's body settles deeper against mine. It ought to be illegal for her nudges and bumps to feel this good. If I don't chill, we'll never make it to our destination.

I concentrate on what Elisi will say when she finds out about Ace, and how many days or weeks I'll have to live with the scowling face only my grandmother can make. That helps a little. Now if I can only forget about the rosemary scent of Ace's hair, tempting me to bury my nose into her neck, I'll be fine.

"What's the matter?" Ace asks.

"Nothing, why?" My cheeks burn. I hope she can't feel how happy I am to be near her.

"You're so quiet and your arms are tense. Doesn't it hurt to hold them out stiff like that?"

I hadn't realized in my lame attempt at self-control, I'd positioned my arms out in a giant u-formation, barely touching her. I must look like a jerk. "Um, I didn't want to make you uncomfortable."

"I'm uncomfortable imagining the pain you're in. It's okay to relax." She pulls my arms around her waist and finagles the reins from my hands. "Is that better?"

"Yeah, a lot." So much for taming my urges. "Think you can handle Billy?"

"Just relax and tell me where to go." She holds the reins in one hand and leads him away from loose rocks on the edge of the path and out of the line of a low hanging branch.

"I get the feeling you've ridden horses a lot."

"What makes you say that?" There's a hint of exaggerated innocence in her voice. She's toying with me.

"You handle Billy like it's second nature to you. Come on, 'fess up."

"If you must know, I started riding when I was a tot. My grandparents have stables on their property."

Could this girl be any more perfect? "Ha, I knew it. You are full of surprises." I tickle her side.

She wiggles. "Stop. No fair messing with the driver."

"Okay, but you need to take a right at the Y in the trail up ahead." I tickle her once more.

She clamps down on my hand with her elbow and guides Billy around the bend.

As we climb further into the mountains, we talk about our favorite childhood memories, what we like to watch on TV, and how much high school sucks. My life in North Carolina seems a lot more laid back than hers in New Jersey. Still, talking with her is easy. Despite coming from different places, and her Northern accent and my Southern twang, Ace and I have more in common than Simon and me. It feels like I've known her forever. Wonder how Simon will feel when I tell him I'm considering replacing him as a best friend? When it comes down to it, Ace is tons hotter.

After a few more turns, we reach an open area where the sun shines bright on the trail. The sky is clear blue with only a few clouds kissing the tops of the mountain peaks. I suck in a breath and fill my lungs with the cool, clear air.

Ace pulls Billy to a halt.

"The view is awesome," she says. "I can see for miles."

Her eyes are wide and her lips are parted. She turns her head and takes in the view panoramic-style. Her awe reminds me not to take these mountains for granted like I do sometimes because I've lived here all my life.

I point to a peak ahead of us. "Do you see the tall pine growing at an angle on the overlook?" Her eyes follow the line of my arm. "That's where we're going."

"Do you mean the tree over there with a hawk peeking through the branches?"

I squint. "Yeah, that one. Geez, Ace, not only can you ride horses, you have the eyes of an eagle. What else are you going to wow me with today?"

"I'll never tell. A girl's got to have some secrets." She leans her head back so it's resting against my shoulder.

"Well, I intend to stick around until I know them all."

She stiffens.

"Did I say something wrong?"

She raises her head and stares straight ahead. "No, John. I don't know. It's crazy. Everything about the day is so perfect. I'm afraid if I enjoy myself too much it will all disappear."

I wasn't expecting that answer, though I'm happy she gave it. I squeeze her tighter. "Well, there's more perfect to come. Think you can handle it?"

She nods and she relaxes against me once again. I tap Billy in the haunches and we move forward.

Not long after, we reach my family's property. The fire pit is just how I left it, with a few half-burned logs. Toward the back of the clearing is my *asi*, a lodge

Simon and I built on a whim using branches and cane woven together and covered in clay like our ancestors did back in the day.

I hop off Billy and hold out my arms in order to help Ace down. She accepts graciously, though I have no doubt she could make it down on her own.

Once her feet are planted on the ground, Ace reaches over her head and stretches. Her long hair kisses the bottom of her shoulder blades and her skin glistens like a goddess under the strong summer sun.

Wow. Just wow!

I take my eyes off her but only long enough to tie Billy's reins to the tree.

"What is that giant beehive-looking thing over there?" she asks, pointing at my *asi*.

I laugh. "Watch it. That's my home when I come hunting or when I feel like getting away from the world."

"That's a home?"

"Sure is. It started out as a fort, but Simon and I took it a step further. It's old time Cherokee-style. You didn't think all Indigenous people lived in teepees, did you?"

Ace shrugs. "I assumed…and you know what they say about people who assume."

"Hey, don't be so hard on yourself. You can't help it if they teach bogus history in your schools. Come on, I'll show you."

There is only a small opening and no windows, so I pull a flashlight from my bag and remove the board covering the entryway. "Be careful. It's a long step down."

Ace grabs onto my elbow, and we duck inside. The

floor is dug deep enough and the ceiling is high enough that I can stand tall, but only in the middle. Ace takes the flashlight from me and turns around, examining every inch of the place. She points the light on the small fire pit. "No wonder it smells smoky in here. Is it safe to burn wood inside?"

"There's a smoke hole in the roof."

She looks upward. "I don't see any light."

"I keep it covered in the summer."

She sighs. "Seems kind of dangerous."

"Don't look so worried. I keep a large bucket of water nearby, just in case."

She shines the light on the parameter, pointing to each pallet of blankets as she passes, then raises an eyebrow. "Who are all the beds for?"

"Usually Simon and Jack come with me. Occasionally Rae and Victor."

"Oh." She smiles. "It is cozy in here."

"One day I want to build a home for my family—when I have one. Getting into town might be rough. Maybe I could clear some trees. Make a gravel road. I don't know. That's too far away to worry about."

"At least you're thinking about your future. I can't seem to plan beyond the next day, sometimes beyond the next hour."

"Don't you see yourself anywhere beyond today? What are you going to do after high school?"

"I'm thinking about going to a community college near home next year. Zack needs me. My mom isn't always in the best shape to care for him." Ace's voice cracks.

"I'm sorry. I didn't mean to bum you out."

She rubs her temples. "It's just, right now, I'm so

happy, I don't want to think about anything else."

The sparkle has left her eyes. She must be holding back a lot, but it's probably better not to pry. She'll tell me when she's ready. If she's anything like me, she needs breathing room to figure stuff out for herself.

She points the flashlight at my bow and arrow.

"I use that for hunting. I like the challenge of a bow. It takes more skill and it's fairer to the animals."

"I've never hunted with a bow or gun or anything for that matter," she says. "I do all my hunting in the meat section of the grocery store."

I chuckle. "We never get meat there. Elisi relies on Victor and me. She grows the rest of our food in a garden behind our house."

Ace picks up the bow, holds it by the grip, and draws back the string.

"Want me to show you how to use it?"

"Sure." She climbs out of the *asi* with my bow slung over her shoulder.

I grab the quiver of arrows and follow. Without waiting for my help, she stops in the middle of the field, lifts the bow, and scans for targets. I hand her an arrow. "Why don't you aim for that oak tree over there?"

The tree trunk is huge. At least that will give her a slim chance of hitting it on her first try.

"What about that tree over there? The one with the knothole about eye level."

The tree is narrow and from this distance, the knothole she's talking about is the size of a silver dollar. "You might have an easier time if you aim at the bigger one."

She shrugs and blows a piece of hair out of her face.

I place my hand over hers and draw back the bowstring, wondering how I'll ever help her achieve this nearly impossible goal. The warmth of her body messes with my head, making me want to hold her tighter. She'll never hit anything that way. Her success is important to me, so I shift my thoughts back to our task, and explain about compensating for distance and wind thrust. When I'm done instructing, I take a step back.

She remains still, appearing to be taking aim. I hope she's not too disappointed when she misses. I'll be here to cheer her on in any case.

With a quick pivot, she shifts toward the small tree. The arrow sails through the air and meets the thin trunk with a thunk—boing, boing, boing. I stare at her gape-mouthed for a moment, then jog to the target.

I yank the arrow from the tree. There is a scar to the left of the knothole. "If you tell me that's luck, I won't believe you."

"Okay, it wasn't. I'm on the archery team at school."

I shake my head. "How could you let me stand there like a fool, trying to teach you?"

She fights a smile. "Sorry, but once you put your arms around me, it felt too good to say anything."

I pause a moment, trying to figure out if she's being serious. Elisi always says there is truth in jest. I jog back and kiss her cheek. "You are so perfect, I can't even stay mad at you." I snatch the bow from her hands. "My turn."

We strike up a friendly competition and take turns hitting targets. I lose track of time until my belly grumbles, reminding me I'm near starving to death.

"Are you hungry?" I ask.

She rubs her stomach. "Sure am."

"I brought lunch." I run into the *asi* and grab one of the blankets and spread it out near the edge of the clearing where we have a good view of the scenery.

Ace plops down without reservation. Not only can she ride a horse and handle a bow, she's not afraid of a little dirt. Jasmine always complained about eating on the ground.

As soon as I sit next to Ace, Billy whinnies.

"Wait a minute, buddy, I didn't forget you." I hand Ace our bagged lunch and retrieve an apple from the side pocket of my backpack.

Ace peels back the lid of her sandwich. "Hmm…peanut butter and jelly. I thought you grew all your own food."

"Okay, maybe I exaggerated a little bit. We do buy some stuff from the grocery store."

Ace giggles. "Good choice."

During lunch, I learn that Ace's favorite color is blue, that she loves animals and children, and hopes to become a special education teacher. We're a year apart in school, but not in age. I turned eighteen on April fifteenth and she turned eighteen on May eleventh. That makes me an Aries and her a Taurus—two compatible signs. She'd be graduating this year like me if her parents hadn't held her back before kindergarten.

We reminisce about the rafting trip where we first met, and she confesses she felt a connection to me from the beginning just like I did to her. Ace thinks we may have subconsciously willed ourselves together. It doesn't matter how we got here, only that she's here with me now.

"Hold still," she says. "You've got jelly on your lip." She leans over and wipes it away with the pad of her thumb.

Her blue eyes capture mine and everything around me blurs. The only thing in focus is the two of us.

She wets her lips and her eyelids drop to half-mast, exposing her blue-tinted eyelashes. I'm one-hundred percent sure I've never wanted to kiss any girl as much as I want to kiss her right now.

I brush her hair to the side and stroke her neck. Then I press my lips to hers. Her breathing stops momentarily, but then she opens her mouth, inviting me in. I grip on to a handful of grass to hold myself back, then let go almost as quickly. It's no use. I want her close. I want to feel her skin against mine. My hands roam her perfect body. She makes little groaning noises into my mouth. "You are the best thing that's happened to me," I whisper.

"I'm the lucky one," she whispers back.

My heart smiles.

Just then, a raindrop hits the back of my head—then another and another.

*Damn it.*

I tear myself away from her and stare at the sky. A large drop plops between my eyes and rolls down the side of my nose. I wipe it away, and a rumble of thunder sounds in the distance. The drops fall quicker and grow larger. In the blink of an eye, both of us are nearly soaked.

We hop to our feet, stumbling over each other, laughing. I gather up the blanket, take Ace's hand, and we run into the *asi.*

The sun hasn't budged. It's still shining hard on the

earth. We sit in the doorway, my arm around her shoulder, watching the world's largest sun-shower. Even the rain can't ruin a day when she's around.

She wipes drips from her face. "This is the most magical place I've ever been."

It's the same place it's always been. If there is any magic here, she brought it with her. I rest my head against hers and dream.

Eventually, the rain slows, and Ace's expression falls. She pulls on a strand of her hair and examines it. "I was supposed to be at the mall. I can't go home looking like a drowned rat."

"Just say you got caught in the rain? It's not a lie."

She gestures toward her wet jeans and sighs. They are covered with dirt. Even her fingernails are dirty.

"You can tell your mom that when you were done shopping, you went horseback riding with me. Maybe she won't be as mad as you think." I say this to make her feel better, but if her mom is anything like Elisi, my words are of no comfort.

"You don't understand. My mother runs my life. She always has. When she's not drinking, she micro-manages everything I do, including choosing my friends."

I'm afraid I know what that means. A dull ache in my stomach grows stronger and burns all the way to my brain where it bursts in to flames. "Sometimes you have to say screw off and do what you want."

Ace frowns. "You speak like you're an expert on the subject. Who have you ever told to screw off?"

Ashamed, I hesitate. "My mother. I'm a disrespectful creep, okay?" I draw my knees to my chest and rest my forehead on my forearms.

She places a hand on my shoulder. “I’m sorry. It’s none of my business.”

“No. It’s fine. I don’t want to keep secrets from you.” I lift my head and turn slightly so she won’t see the tears welling in my eyes. “I had to do it. It came to the point where it was too painful to be around her.”

“If it hurts really bad, I think it’s allowed, John,” she says softly.

“Thank you.”

“For what?”

“For not thinking I’m a jerk.”

She lifts my hand and laces her fingers though mine. “I’d never think that. Because you’re not.”

She’s so sweet, if I don’t change the subject, I’ll burst out crying. I glance at my watch. Elisi went to the shop with Rae to do the books. She won’t be home until dinner. “I know what we can do to keep you out of trouble.”

“I’m listening.”

“You can take a shower at my house. We can wash your jeans there, too.”

“My jeans won’t be done in time. I promised I’d be home before dinner.”

“Then you can borrow a pair of Rae’s.”

“Are you sure she won’t mind?”

“Don’t worry. Everything will be fine, but we better hurry if we’re going to get you back in time.”

I untie Billy and give Ace a foot up.

The three of us head down the mountain to the real world where families have problems, people struggle to survive, abuse is everywhere, and sun-showers have a scientific explanation.

## Chapter 15
## Ace McAllister

We reach John's place, and he reins Billy to a halt in front of the barn. As soon as my feet hit the ground, sadness washes over me. Maybe not sadness, something deeper—more like heart-wrenching melancholy. No matter how hard I wish for this day to go on forever, it's logically and philosophically impossible.

John leads Billy to his stall. I grab my bag and pink shirt off the hook on the wall and swap my shoes for my sandals. "Mind if I leave these here?" I use my toe to point to my mud-covered sneakers.

"Sure. I'll clean them for you later," John says. "Let's go into the house. I'll throw your T-shirt and stuff in the dryer. Billy can wait for his brush down until you're in the shower."

As we head to the back door, I realize I'm about to meet John's family. My feet grow roots and I freeze. "Are you sure this is okay?"

"Why wouldn't it be?"

He sounds so confident my concern subsides. Somewhat.

Inside, the house is quiet, except for the creak of the back door as John shuts it behind us. He'd told me he lived in a house full of people.

"Where is everyone?" I ask.

"Elisi and Rae are at the shop, and Victor and

Lenny went with Aunt June to the ranger station to visit Uncle George. I told you everything would be fine."

I swallow, eye-squintingly hard. "So, we're completely alone."

His cheeks redden. "I didn't think you'd mind?"

"Oh, I don't." I shrug like it's no big deal, though inside I'm light-headed in a cross between exhilaration and apprehension, like the time in middle school when a friend and I snuck into a second movie after ours ended and got away with it. Only much worse.

We cross the living room. It's small with gold shag carpeting and age-worn blue furniture. Real wood tables donning strategically placed coasters flank the sofa.

One wall is covered with a myriad of family pictures, many of John and Rae at various ages. Another wall hosts a fireplace. The mantel is covered with knickknacks and homemade decorations—the kind kids make in art class. The room is nothing like our large, stark living room at my home in New Jersey, where every item is selected specifically to add to the decor. This room screams family. My chest tightens as I'm reminded of the artwork Zack and I brought home from school, never to be seen again.

John runs a hand through his hair and scratches the back of his head. "Sorry. It's not much."

"What are you talking about? It's really nice." I walk to the wall filled with pictures. "Who are the people?"

John points to each one and tells me a little about them. Elisi looks as no-nonsense as he describes. Her hair is streaked with gray and tied tightly back. She doesn't smile in any of her pictures, but behind her stern expression, her dark eyes possess a sort of gentleness. His brother Victor, tall and lean, smiles broadly while posing with a long distance running trophy. In the next photo, his aunt June sits on a bench with Lenny propped on her ample lap while his uncle George stands behind them in a shot that appears to have been taken at a theme park.

John stops speaking when he reaches a picture of a young Cherokee woman. She has long, black hair, and dark, brooding eyes. With her perfectly symmetrical features, she bears an uncanny resemblance to John. If the photo wasn't faded with age, I'd suspect she, John, and Rae were triplets.

"Is that your mother?"

"That's her." John presses his lips together and frowns.

"She's pretty."

"I guess." He shrugs. "Want to see the rest of the house?"

I want to know more about his mother, but from his curt tone and hurriedness to change the subject, I think it's best to let him tell me when he's ready.

"Where to next?" I ask.

He finds my hand and tugs me forward. "There's not much more. The kitchen is to your left. The first bedroom used to be Rae's, but now Aunt June and Uncle George stay there, so Rae's stuck rooming with Elisi. Most nights she can be found on the couch." He chuckles.

"Where's your room?"

"I saved the best for last." He winks.

My stomach churns. "Elisi won't mind?"

"It's okay, I promise. Besides, she's not here to

care."

His little reminder of our aloneness does nothing to settle my stomach.

He kicks some athletic clothes out of the path as we enter. "I share this space with Victor and Lenny. They never put anything away."

The room is small and blue. A double bed butts against one wall and a single bed, with a toy box at the foot, lines the other. There is a graffiti-like mural, with many indigenous designs mingled with urban jargon, painted on the wall behind the double bed.

"Is that your handiwork?" I ask, admiring the art.

"No, Victor's. He wants to be an artist."

"Hmm…this wall belongs to Victor"—I lift the lid of the overstuffed toy box, peek in and close it—"and the toys must belong to Lenny. What in here belongs to you?"

He points at the dresser. "See the bumper sticker? That's mine."

I read it out loud. "Coolest Grandma Ever."

"Elisi gave it to me." He rolls his eyes. "I had to put it somewhere. Old Blue would throw a rod if I stuck that on the bumper." He presses his lips together and snorts.

As hard as I try, I can't hold it in. I burst out laughing. He joins in and we both double over. I hold my ribs, and struggle to regain my composure. "We've got to stop. It's impolite."

"You're right," he says, suppressing his laugh until he nearly chokes. "She gets on my nerves, but she's okay."

"I have no doubt," I say. "So there's nothing here that's yours other than that tiny sticker?"

"Just my clothes. Oh, and my side of the bed. I'd invite you to sit, but I share it with Victor, and I don't want you to get his cooties. Roommates suck. Especially when they're your kid brother."

I giggle at his humor, but also in relief. Most guys would have no qualms about pushing me into bed, even if the sheets hadn't been washed in a year.

John shows me to the bathroom. The tiles are pink and gray. Even the toilet and tub are pink—left over from the old days I'm sure, but still it's clean and has a "retro-cool" feel.

He reaches in a small closet, pulls out a towel, and rests it on the sink. "Be careful with the hot. There's no regulation on the water heater so you'll scald yourself if you turn the valve too far."

"I think I got it." I glance at the floor, then at him. My body's begging me to do all kinds of naughty things, but my mind is dizzy with panic.

He backs out into the hallway, ending my internal war, and I let out a slow breath.

"Hand me your wet clothes when…you know…" Before finishing his sentence, he shuts the door.

I strip off my clothes and roll them in a ball, underwear, bra and all. Then I cover my chest with one arm and open the door just wide enough to pass them through. Once my things are in his hand, I snap the door shut again.

It feels weird to be stark naked in a strange bathroom. I turn the lock on the knob and jump in the shower, pulling the curtain closed at the same time.

When I'm clean, I wrap in the towel and dry my hair using a blow dryer on the vanity and style it with the travel brush I keep in my backpack, then I peek out the door and call for John.

He doesn't answer so I shout a little louder.

A woman appears in the hallway.

I take in a quick, sharp breath. I recognize her from the pictures. It's Elisi.

"Who are you?" she asks.

She's not very big, but her scowl is humongous. Paralysis settles in my throat, and I can't speak.

She crosses her arms and taps her toe. "Well?"

It'll be okay. She'll chill once she knows I haven't done anything wrong. She has to. I find my voice. "I'm John's friend, Ace."

"Ace? What kind of name is that? And what are you doing in my bathroom?"

Rae comes up behind her, eyes wide and mouth open.

I break out in a cold sweat. "Um, John has my clothes."

Rae closes her eyes and shakes her head.

John comes running down the hall, brushes past Elisi, and hands me a wadded-up bundle. My underwear falls onto the floor. I bend at the knees to retrieve it between two fingers. My cheeks flame.

"You." Elisi points at me. "Put some clothes on." She spins around, grabs John by the ear, and pulls him down the hall, leaving me with Rae, whose face is still frozen in shock.

"Rae, I know it looks bad, but nothing happened. We were riding Billy and got caught in the rain. I couldn't go home all muddy."

Rae shakes her head. "John is in so much trouble."

"Can I borrow a pair of your jeans?"

Rae cocks a brow.

"Please?"

"What happened to your…no don't tell me," she says before disappearing down the hallway.

From inside the bathroom, I hear bits and pieces of John trying to explain the situation to his grandmother. I don't know if he's getting through to her because she keeps shouting over him, saying something about him disgracing her house.

Someone knocks. I crack the door open.

Rae shoves a pair of jeans in my hand. "I'll wait and make sure you get out of here alive."

"What?" I grab my throat.

"I'm kidding. But hurry."

When I'm fully clothed, I open the bathroom door. Rae whisks me past Elisi, who is still shouting at John.

Once we reach the middle of the front yard, I peek over my shoulder at the white house with the tiny porch. "I guess I've blown it. She'll never like me now."

"Don't worry about it. You never stood a chance anyway," Rae says.

"What do you mean?"

"It's a long story."

"I didn't mean to cause any trouble. Honest."

"Don't blame yourself. Blame John. If he had called me, we could have avoided the whole situation."

"I don't understand."

"Never mind." She shakes her head and her eyes lock on mine. "By the way, where have you been for the last week?"

"My mother grounded me because I went to Sliding Rock without permission."

"That sucks. I hope you got permission to go off

with John today."

I cringe, but don't say anything. By her pinched expression, I can tell she already knows the answer.

"You and John are a lot alike. You are both gluttons for punishment."

"I don't know when I'll be able to get away again but I'll return your jeans as soon as I can."

"Take your time. I'll wear yours until then."

"You can keep them."

"The wet ones, lying on the hamper? They're designer."

"I know, but I want you to have them."

She wraps her arms around me and squeezes. "Ace, you're the best."

John jumps off the porch and skids across the grass. His clothes are wet, and his hair hangs to his elbows in soggy strands. "I'd better take you home. You can meet Elisi another time."

I hustle to his truck, more than happy to escape. I need time to process what happened before I can conjure the nerve to face her again.

"I'll text you later," Rae says.

I flash her a thumbs up. Behind her, Elisi stands in the doorway, hands on her hips, glaring at me.

Boy, did I screw up.

Once I'm safe inside, John starts the truck. "Sorry you got caught in the crossfire," he says. "Are you okay?" He's trying hard to be calm, but the stress in his voice totally gives him away.

"I'm fine, but I wanted to make a good impression on your grandmother, and now she'll hate me forever."

John takes my hand. "It doesn't matter what she thinks. I like you a whole lot, and that's all that matters."

Though I'd love to believe he's right, I'm not sure liking me "a whole lot" is enough where Elisi is concerned.

When we reach the casino, he parks on the lot farthest from the building. "Come here." He opens his arm.

I slide over and position myself under the wing of his arm. He takes my hand. The fresh scent of the afternoon sun-shower radiates from his being, taking my mind back to the magical place.

He kisses the top of my head. "When will I get to see you again?"

"I don't know, but I'll figure something out."

"What about tomorrow? I can meet you after work."

I glance over my shoulder at the casino. "I'll try, but I have to make sure Mom's doesn't need me for anything first. I better go now or I'll be late."

"Wait, I have something for you." He reaches under the seat and retrieves a handmade tomahawk with an anvil made of gray stone. Two feathers attached to braided leather, hang from the handle. "This is to replace the one you lost the other night. I meant to give it to you earlier, but I forgot."

"Is this real?"

"I got it from an artisan on the Rez."

"It's so cool. It must be expensive. I can't take this."

"Yes, you can. He practically gave it to me for free."

"I don't believe you, but thank you anyway." I place the tomahawk in my backpack. It doesn't fit. I leave the zipper open so the handle can stick out the top. “Zack is going to love it.”

John smiles and cups the back of my head and we fall into a kiss. Our tongues dance together in sort of a slippery, erotic tango. I move closer to him and grasp his arm. I’m falling fast and hard and I don’t know how to stop myself. Not that I want to.

He pulls away first and holds my face between his hands. Then he kisses the tip of my nose. His lips travel to my cheek, my chin, and end at the nape of my neck, leaving me a hot, melting blob.

“Ace,” he whispers, we haven’t known each other long, and I know it might sound crazy, but I think I might be falling in love with you.”

Did I hear him right? My blob-self melts to a puddle on the floor. I pull it together long enough to say, “Thanks,” and pour myself out the door.

Heart fluttering from head to toe, I wave goodbye and run for the casino. I don’t stop until I’m outside my suite. There, it dawns on me what an idiot I am. At one of the most romantic moments of my life, rather than say “I think I love you, too” (because I’m almost positive I feel that way), I thank him and runaway like a ten-year-old. I take out my phone to text him, then stop. What if he didn’t really mean it? Grandma says sometimes guys tell you that to get what they want. But John’s not that way. At least I don’t think he is.

My hands shake so hard I’m unable to press send, so I redirect and open the door to face whatever is waiting for me inside. Mom and Susan are on the couch, watching some sort of reality show on TV about housewives. Both have a glass of wine. Mom’s slouching with her bare foot draped over the arm of the chair. I've seen her this way enough to know she's drunk.

"Ace, come on in and have a seat," she slurs. "How was shopping?"

I slide my backpack off my shoulder and sit in a chair in the corner of the room. "It was fun. I've got my eye on an outfit, but I wanted your opinion before I buy it since it's kind of expensive."

She smiles big like she believes me. This is going a lot better than I expected. Too bad it won't go this smoothly when I tell her about John. One day.

Zack comes running out the bedroom. "Did you bring me something?"

"Hmmm….I don't remember," I tease.

"You promised."

"Let me check my bag." I take out the tomahawk.

"Wow. Let me see. Give it to me." He tries to grab it out of my hand.

"Wait a minute, first you have to promise you won't hit anyone or anything with it. It's not a toy. It was made by a Cherokee artisan."

He bounces on his toes as he speaks. "I won't. I'll be good."

I hand him the tomahawk and he examines it closely, then dashes into the bedroom.

Mom pulls a face. "Where did you find that?"

I bite my lip while I drum up a lie. "After the mall, I walked around the town of Brevard. I bought it from a street vendor."

"You better watch Zack with that thing. If anything gets broken, I'm holding you accountable."

"I will."

Susan turns away from the TV. "You know, Ace, I

think Cameron would have enjoyed going with you. He moped around most of the day. Why don't you give him a call and let him know you're back?"

Cameron obviously hasn't told them a thing about what happened at the Powwow.

She hands me her cell phone with Cameron's number already on dial. *Please, please, please don't pick up*. After the fifth ring, voice mail kicks in.

"He's not answering," I give the phone back to Susan.

"He said he might go out. I bet you just missed him. I'll tell him you tried to call."

"Ace," Mom says. "Zack needs his bath. Oh, and bring me that club you gave him. I'll make it disappear." She winks at me.

Disappear like our childhood artwork. No way. I hurry to the bedroom and shut the door. "Zack, you're going to have to let me keep the tomahawk for you or Mom's going to get rid of it."

"No, it's mine," Zack whines, hugging it to his chest. "I want it."

I sit on the bed and pat the place beside me. "Come here. I want to tell you something. It's a secret so I have to whisper."

Zack flops down, still clutching the tomahawk.

"Mom said she's going to throw it out. Let me hide it for you."

"No. You gave it to me."

"Listen to me, Zack. Mom's afraid you might get hurt. Remember when you fell off your bike and she wouldn't let you ride it for a whole month?"

"I remember."

"Well, this is the same thing, only she'll take it

forever. Let's wrap it in a towel, and I'll put it somewhere Mom will never find it. I'll let you look at it every night before bed when we're alone." Mom's been drinking; I can only hope she forgets about it.

Zack releases his grip on the handle and holds it out in front of him. He runs his finger over the edge of the stone. "Okay, you can keep it safe for me."

I cradle it in my arms. "Thank you, Zackie. I'll help you protect it."

And I will. I'll guard his tomahawk with my life.

Once I get the nerve to tell my mother about John, if she thinks I'll throw him away too, she's in for a big surprise.

****

When I get home, Elisi has moved a living room chair so it faces the front door. She doesn't say a word, but there will be no peace in the house until we talk. That's okay. I have a few things I want to get off my chest anyway, so I say, "Thanks a lot for embarrassing me in front of Ace. Was all the yelling really necessary?"

"You disrespect me by bringing a whore in my house and you are questioning me?"

"She isn't a whore. She's a nice girl and I asked her to go with me. Like I told you, we got caught in a storm. She was cleaning up while her clothes dried."

"The fact you've been hiding her tells me all I need to know."

"I didn't tell you about her because I was afraid you'd act like this."

"She may fool you, but she doesn't fool me. No self-respecting girl would take a shower in a boy's house. Especially when no one else is home."

"What's with the sudden moral judgments? If it were Jasmine in the shower, we wouldn't be having this conversation. Ace is not going away, so you're going to have to get used to her."

"What is wrong with you?" Elisi slaps the arm of her chair. "You had a beautiful girlfriend whose father is an important part of our community and you toss her away for an outsider."

"Jasmine and I were over before I met Ace and you know it."

Elisi crosses her arms and frowns. "You disappoint me, John. All your life I've raised you to be proud of our heritage, and now you run around with a girl whose people slaughtered yours?"

"Your hypocrisy slays me. You go to meetings to support our civil rights, and demand we be respected and treated fairly, but then you look down on Ace only because she's white?"

Elisi rubs her arthritic knee, rises, and hobbles over to me. "You think you're smart, but you're young—too young to know the ways of the world. When this girl's done playing with you—the strong handsome Native—she's going to toss you away for one of her own kind. You'll be a distant memory for her—a memory to hide away so no one knows she bedded a poor, dark-skinned Indian boy. Is that what you want, John? Do you want your heart and your pride stomped on by her perfectly manicured white feet?"

I press my lips together to keep the foul words in my head from shooting out my mouth. "I'm going to try to forget you said that. This conversation is done. I'll be in my room."

"She'll betray you. She'll break your heart," Elisi

calls out behind me.

I twirl around. "No wonder Mom is messed up. She's had to deal with you all her life."

Elisi takes a few steps back as if she's been pushed. I stomp off in the opposite direction, totally disgusted with myself for insulting her, yet too mad to care.

Once in my room, I throw myself on the bed and stare at the ceiling. My butt sags in a low spot so I bounce over a bit. What I have with Ace is real. It's beyond color and heritage, and the sooner Elisi gets that through her thick skull the better off we'll all be.

Someone knocks on the frame of the door.

"Leave me alone," I groan.

"No. I won't," Rae says. "Not until I have my say." She comes in and swats my legs, then sits on the edge of the bed.

I squeeze my head with the heel of my hands. "I'm sick of it, Rae. I've got to get out of here before I go crazy."

"I know. I heard everything. But she's an old lady, John. She's set in her ways. Give her time to get used to the idea. She'll come around. She always does."

"Are you taking her side?"

"No. Actually, I'm on your side, but you're leaving for college soon and whether you want to believe it or not, it's going to be really hard on her. The least you can do is try to keep the peace until then."

"Are you suggesting I dump Ace?"

"Of course not. But try to understand where Elisi's coming from. I'll talk to her. I'll put in a good word for Ace. With two of us fighting for her, Elisi's got to bend."

"Thanks, Rae, but just so you know"—I grab her

wrist—"I'm not backing down this time. I'm not hiding Ace any longer, either. Elisi will have to accept her or I'm gone."

## Chapter 16
## Ace McAllister and John Spears

*Three days later*

After I read Zack an hour's worth of *The Adventures of Huckleberry Finn*, he's finally asleep. I kiss his forehead and tiptoe out of the bedroom. The dishes from dinner are still on the table, so I get busy. When the kitchen is clean, I check on Mom.

She's lying on the bed spread-eagle as if she fell from the sky, thanks to the bottle of merlot she polished off after dinner. Had Dad been here rather than cavorting with the bleached-blonde, this might not have happened. I have a good mind to march downstairs, pound on her door, and remind him marriage is supposed to be for better or for worse, and that it's not fair for him to check out whenever he feels like it.

Mom snorts, then gasps for air. I turn her on her side in case she gets sick and wait until the rasps subside. Then I leave her to sleep it off, and go to the living room, flop down on the couch, and text John. It's been three days since our trip to his property. I miss him so much I can hardly stand it.

ME: *Hey, what R U doing?*

Seconds later, my phone vibrates.

JOHN: *Missing you.*

A small ache pulses in the center of my chest.

ME: *Three days is too long. I want to see you.*

JOHN: *Then come on.*

ME: *I'm already dressed for bed.*

JOHN: *Excuses, excuses. Hey! What are you wearing?*

I laugh. I'm wearing sweats but write: *A pink flannel nightgown and granny panties.*

JOHN: *Sexy. I'd love to see that.*

ME: *Too bad you're so far away or I'd show you.*

JOHN: *I'm closer than you think. Can you sense my presence?*

I startle and scan the apartment.

ME: *Quit. You're freaking me out.*

JOHN: *LOL. I'm at a gas station near the Casino, on my way home.*

I know I shouldn't, but Zack's out for the night and Mom will never know.

ME: *Meet me on the back lot in five minutes.*

JOHN: *For real?*

ME: *Hurry. I'm on my way out.*

JOHN: *See you in a sec.*

I change into jeans and a T-shirt, brush my teeth, and rake a comb through my hair. My pillows make a pretty good body-double stuffed under my covers. Who knew a trick I learned from an old movie would work so well? After I'm through fluffing and molding pillow-me into a real sleeping beauty, I turn off all the lights in the suite. If it's dark enough when Dad comes home—if Dad comes home—maybe he won't notice I'm gone.

When I reach the back of the parking lot, headlights blind me. I shield my eyes to focus on the offending vehicle. It's John's truck.

My heart does a double-step.

He pulls up beside me and pops the door open. I launch myself into the passenger seat. He's inches from me now. Two tight braids hang down the front of his chest. He has a white headscarf, adorned with a stenciled black sun design, tied around his forehead and silver earrings with dime-sized symbols dangling from his ears. He's wearing a tight black T-shirt with the letters NDN stretched across his chest. Lampposts in the parking lot cast a dim light in the cab making him look even more surreal than he already does, and he's opening his arms to me.

Shimmering tingles run from my scalp to my toes as I fall into his embrace.

He pries me loose, holds my cheeks in his hands, and plants tiny kisses all over my face. "You changed," he says before giving me one more kiss on the lips.

"What do you mean? It's only been three days."

"No. I mean you changed your clothes. I was looking forward to seeing you in pink flannel and granny panties." He wags his eyebrows.

"I'm sorry, John, but you'll never get to see me wearing that. I'll go naked first." As soon as the words leave my mouth, I wish I could take them back.

His eyes glimmer and his mouth tips up in a wry smile.

An inferno burns beneath the fine layer of skin on my cheeks. "Don't look at me that way, that's not how I meant it."

"I know, but you can't fault a guy for using his imagination."

"You're not helping," I say, fanning my cheeks.

"All right, I'll stop." He draws an imaginary halo over his head. "But I'll sure miss the way your freckles darken when you blush."

I give him a look. "Ha, ha. Very funny."

"I'll stop for good this time." He runs his hand over his, face changing his jovial expression to semi-serious. "Where do you want to go?"

"I don't know. This is your town. You pick."

"Apart from the casino, everything pretty much shuts down at this hour. Want to go to the river?"

"Sure."

"The river it is, then."

A short drive later, we pull onto the same gravel lot John parked the night of the Powwow. He grabs a blanket from behind the seat. We cross the street and clamber down the bank to the rushing water. We walk until we come to a spot hidden from the road by trees and foliage.

John spreads the blanket, stretches out on his back, and motions for me to join him. We haven't talked much about what happened at his house the other day, but it's a subject we have to broach, if only to clear the air.

I sit cross-legged beside him. "Is your grandmother still mad?"

He rubs my back. "She's calmed down—a bit."

"Something Rae said has been bothering me."

"Oh man, Rae and her big mouth. Let's have it."

"She said I never stood a chance with your grandmother. What does that mean?"

"Elisi's from another generation and she's set in her ways."

"Does that mean she doesn't like me because I'm white?"

"Yes, but she'll have to get over it. You could be

purple with pink polka dots and I would still pick you."

"Pink and purple? Wow, you must really like me."

"I do."

The sincerity in his eyes makes my heart swell. "I know how it feels to have a difficult parent. My mom probably won't like you either, but I don't care."

"Are you saying your mother won't like me because I'm not white?"

"Yes, probably. And I haven't told you because I never want to say or do anything to hurt you. I'm so sorry."

"Ace. You don't have to apologize. I'm here with you, not her."

I nod and gaze at the sky. "Look. There's your bear." I point at Ursa Major. "Do you feel scared?"

"Not of the bear."

I stretch out next to him and rest my head on my fist. "So, what then?"

He brushes a strand of hair behind my ear. "I'm afraid you'll disappear again, like you did the night I said I might love you."

This time, I pause to work out what I'm going to say. "I know that was so immature of me. But I'm scared, too. Not of you. The thought of love terrifies me. I don't know how to tell if it's real." His mouth turns down, and the glint leaves his eyes. "However, if you were to say you love me again, right now for instance, and you really mean it, I'll say it back to you."

"I've been sorting out my feelings for the last few days, and Ace, I don't think I love you. I'm sure I love you."

Fireworks go off in my head. I can't move or speak.

He props himself on his elbow and places a hand on my hip. “Well?”

How can I not love a guy whose smile would dazzle Ebenezer Scrooge? I try, but still can’t form the words. I cover my face with my hands, then open them long enough to croak “Ditto,” before covering my face again.

“Ditto?”

I open my hands, peek out, and I say, “Uh-huh.”

Next thing I know, he’s straddling my stomach. The warmth of his thighs on my sides sends electric sparks racing through me. I can’t look him in the eye. He pries my hands away and pins them to the sides of my head, then leans down and captures my lower lip between his teeth and tugs gently. “Tell me you love me.”

A warm kernel of happiness sprouts inside my heart.

He nuzzles my neck and nips the tip of my ear. “Come on, you can do it.”

I run my fingers along the plaits of one of his long braids. “Okay, here goes. When I’m not near you, thoughts of you peck at my brain, like a little bird pecks at his own reflection in a window glass. I can’t sleep or eat or carry on a simple conversation without the click, click, click of your memory reminding me we’re apart.”

He rolls off me and snuggles me in his arms. “Wow. I do that to you? That sounds painful.”

“It is.” I sigh.

“You know what I think?”

“No, tell me.”

“I think that’s the best ‘I love you’ I’ve ever gotten. We’ll have to work on the pain part, though. I never want you to hurt. Ever."

A breeze blows off the river. I shiver and move closer to him. The only thing between us is a thin layer of clothing.

"Are you cold?" he asks.

I nod and he wraps the blanket around us until we're cocooned in a nest of warmth.

"So why do you think we found each other?" he whispers. "Do you think there's someone beyond the planets guiding us?"

"If there is someone, they certainly aren't very merciful because they took forever to lead me to you."

He hugs me tighter and kisses my forehead. I bury my face in his chest, inhaling the perfect cross of spicy cologne and boy smell. In his arms, I'm ecstatic. In his arms, I'm protected. In his arms, I'm loved.

****

"John?"

Someone kicks my foot, rousing me. Ace is in my arms, her soft breath pulsing against my neck. We must have fallen asleep. I blink a few times to clear my vision. Yarrow and Jasmine are standing over us, the full moon casting hazy shadows around their silhouettes. The scent of marijuana hangs thick in the air.

"Who you got under the blanket?" Yarrow asks.

I don't answer. He has no business getting in my business. Ace lifts her head. Her hair is matted and stuck to one side of her face, not the way she'd want anyone to see her.

"What's going on?" she mumbles.

Jasmine props her hands on her lower back, pushes out her chest, and smirks. "That's the *yonega* who's staying at the casino. I told you about her."

Yarrow gives me a long, snarky, look. "Oh yeah. I heard you went over to the other side."

The simmer of anger inside me heats up to a full-blown roil. I scramble to my knees. "You better back off, 'cause I don't like where you're coming from."

"Cool down, man. I'm only joking." He holds the blunt in front of me, too close for comfort. "Hit on this. It will mellow you out."

I push his hand out of my face. "Get that away from me."

Ace rises to a sitting position and pulls the blanket to her chin. I can tell she's uneasy.

Yarrow zeroes in on her and raises an eyebrow. "Aren't you going to introduce me to your lady?"

The emphasis he puts on the word *lady* pisses me off, and I remember a time when I was twelve. Yarrow was picking on Rae, and I beat the stuffing out of him even though he's two years older than me. I'd do it again tonight, but Ace is with me, and I don't want any trouble. I take a deep breath. "Ace, this is Yarrow. Yarrow, Ace."

Ace nods, and the corner of her lips work on a smile that doesn't meet her eyes.

"Enchanted," Yarrow returns.

Jerk. I don't know if I can hold my temper much longer. "What are you doing here, anyway?"

"We saw your truck, and Jasmine thought you might be interested in some of the goods I picked up tonight." He passes the blunt to Jasmine.

She looks at me, cocks an eyebrow, and takes a long drag. Without breaking eye contact, she rolls her tongue in a way she shouldn't and blows out three perfect smoke rings. I should have known she'd be behind our chance meeting. Her jealousy is becoming a major pain. But hanging with Yarrow? I think Jasmine is in over her head this time.

"If you don't want ganja," Yarrow continues, "maybe I can interest you in something else? I got Adderall, Oxy-C. Maybe you'd like some Ecstasy?" He winks at Ace.

I put myself between Yarrow and Ace. "She doesn't want any drugs. Neither do I. Find somewhere else to do your business."

Jasmine crosses her arms. "The college thing has gone to John's head. Don't you know he's too good for us now? "

Yarrow shrugs. "Whatever. If you change your mind, give me a call. We can talk about old times."

He makes me sound like a druggie. I used to smoke a little weed, but I haven't touched the stuff in over a year. "The good old days are long gone, Yarrow. So if you don't mind, we'd like to be alone."

"Your loss." He grabs Jasmine's hand and tugs her forward. "Let's go find a place where we're welcome, babe."

"See you, John," she says over her shoulder.

Finally they leave. And not a moment too soon. Now to repair the damage they left behind.

"I'm sorry," I say to Ace. "Yarrow and I grew up together. He used to be okay. Now he's nothing but bad news."

"You have nothing to apologize for." She combs her fingers through her tangled hair and glances at the sky. "Do you know what time it is?"

I take my phone from my pocket and click the

home button. She probably wants nothing to do with me now that she's met my druggie ex-friend. "It's a few hours to sunrise. Do you want me to take you home?"

She doesn't respond.

"Look, Ace, if this is about Yarrow and Jasmine, they were way out of line. Jasmine is having a tough time getting over our break-up, and well, Yarrow, he's… Look, I'd get it if you never want to see me again."

"John, I'm not upset. I know who you are. Besides, it's late enough now that getting home is no longer a concern. I want to stay."

My insides warm and happiness rises from within and shows itself with a smile that makes my cheeks hurt.

She places a hand on my shoulder and nudges me to lie back. Then she lays her head on my chest. A strand of her hair spreads across my face and the scent of rosemary consumes me. My body aches to be closer to her, to feel her warm alabaster skin against mine, but my mind tells me to wait—to savor every second I have with her, to know her soul first. She's the most important thing in the world, and I want to protect her from anything that could change her, even myself.

We cling to each other, while we talk about our lives, catching up on the last eighteen years. I share all I can remember, and I think she does too. We both understand the pain of having an addict in our lives and make a vow to each other to never go down that road. Every one of my emotions is brought to the surface. Pain, happiness, hurt, embarrassment, nothing goes untouched. There is nothing left to hide, I've exposed all of myself. I am stripped raw, free of all demons, for the first time in my life.

And then dawn approaches. Ace sits up and hugs her knees. “Zack will be waking soon, and I promised I wouldn’t leave without telling him.”

The weight of the lifting darkness pulls at my heart. Like a wounded warrior, I cling to the moment when all that will be left is faith in what is in the beyond. I rise and sit beside her, my knee resting on her thigh. “Can you stay until morning breaks?”

Ace looks at me and nods. Even in the hazy light of dawn, the features I love about her shine through—the bow of her full lips, the slight cleft in her chin, the way one eyelid dips a millimeter, hinting there’s more to her than she cares to reveal.

I pull her into my lap, and cling to her, while we wait together for the dreaded orange orb to peek over the horizon.

****

I wave one last goodbye to John as I head toward the casino. He’s smiling like I’m the most beautiful girl in the world. He’s the beautiful one. Inside and out.

“Ace, wait,” John shouts. He’s out of the truck motioning for me to come back. We meet halfway.

“I want to talk to you about something,” he says.

“Okay, but I’ve got to hurry. Zack will wake my Mom, and she’ll find out I’m not home. If she doesn’t already know.”

“I understand why you don’t want to tell her about me and that’s okay, but the thing is, my family is having a get-together this Saturday, and I want you to come.”

“I don’t know,” I stammer. “What will your grandmother say?”

"She'll respect you. I'll insist on it."

"Your *whole* family will be there?"

"Ace, this thing between us is real, isn't it?"

"Of course, but…"

"Then, I'm asking you to meet my family. It's important to me. Will you at least try to come?"

The thought of being face-to-face with Elisi terrifies me, but damn, the thought of disappointing John feels much worse. "Okay. I'll figure out a way."

His smile is so bright it could light up the heavens. We hug one last time before I tear myself away, and dart across the parking lot.

The lobby is nearly empty at this early hour. Only a few people are passing through. With my head down, I make my way to the elevator.

"Ace," my father shouts.

I let out a little chirp of surprise and turn to face him. He's coming at me fast. I wish for the floor to open up and swallow me whole. Unfortunately, it doesn't happen.

"What are you doing out at this time in the morning?" He gives me the once over and frowns. "Have you been out all night?"

A few lies flash through my mind, but none seem as good as the truth. "I went with a friend to the river on the Rez. It got late and we fell asleep."

"The Rez, Ace? You mean the reservation? Oh, come on." His eyes narrow.

"I have a bunch of friends there, guys and girls, but tonight I was with a guy named John."

"How long has this been going on?"

"Since shortly after we got here."

"Does your mother know about this?"

"No, and I'd appreciate you not mentioning it to her, if you know what I mean."

"You stay out all night with a guy we don't know, and you expect me not to tell your mother. I raised you better than that."

"Actually, Dad, you didn't." My voice oozes sarcasm.

Dad reddens. "If that barb is to punish me for being out late, it's not going to work. I'm a grown man and you're just a kid."

"Quit the bull. I'm a legal adult, and you are a liar and a cheater. If you want me to keep your secret, you have to keep mine. I'll tell Mom when I'm ready."

Dad kicks the carpet with the tip of his toe. He glances around as if he's worried someone might be listening and leans close to me. "Okay, Ace, you've never given me trouble before, so I'll trust you are making the right decision. Don't let me down. And don't get pregnant."

He doesn't deserve the satisfaction of knowing I'm still a virgin. "I'll try not to," I say.

We walk to our suite together, neither of us speaking a word.

Then, together, like two naughty teenagers, we sneak in. Dad stretches out on the couch, and I tiptoe to the bedroom I share with Zack. He's still sleeping, so I change in to my pajamas, remove the pillows posing as me, and slide into my bed, hoping to get a few minutes sleep before my day begins again.

## Chapter 17
## John Spears and Ace McAllister

Saturday morning, Victor and I get up early to cut the grass, clean the grill, and arrange chairs and tables for our guests. Elisi, Rae and Aunt June are busy in the kitchen, while Uncle George keeps tabs on Lenny.

As noon approaches, I go inside to face Elisi. We need to get a few things straight before I go to pick up Ace.

Aunt June stands over the stove stirring a pot. Rae chops vegetables on a cutting board nearby. When Elisi sees me, she kneads her shoulder, feigning pain.

"Elisi," I say. "I know you don't like the idea of Ace coming here today, but I want you to be nice to her."

Aunt June freezes, and Rae stops chopping. No one breathes as we wait for Elisi's response.

A vein swells in her forehead. "You defy me by bringing that girl into the house, and you have the nerve to tell me how to behave?"

"It's my house too. I help out around here."

"This house belonged to my mother, and it won't be yours until I die. Which is why I'm sure you are hell bent on sending me to my grave."

Guilting me into submission isn't going to work. Not this time. "She's coming or I won't."

Elisi unties her apron and flings it on the counter.

"Go ahead, bring the girl. Next thing you know, you'll get her in trouble and you'll have a blue-eyed child that you're never allowed to see to go along with your broken heart."

Aunt June slaps her ladle on the counter. "Pearl, enough. Just because she's white doesn't mean she'll do him dirty. Cousin Yolanda married a white man years ago and they're still happy. Besides, she's only coming for a cookout."

"That's right, Elisi," Rae chimes. "And Ace is really nice, too."

"Stay out of it. Both of you," Elisi spits. "This is not your business."

Rae's lips form a tight line and her shoulders stiffen.

Aunt June walks over to Elisi and rubs circles on her back. "What happened years ago…"

Elisi turns cherry-red and knocks June's hand away. "Enough. I don't want to talk about this anymore. If it will make you happy, I'll behave, but only if she does." She points a stiff finger at me. "You better keep her as far from me as you can."

"Thank you," I say.

She pushes me to the side and hobbles into the living room.

I turn to Aunt June. "What were you going to say to her? I've never seen her surrender so easily."

She goes back to stirring the pot on the stove. "Oh, nothing."

I look at Rae and raise a brow. She shakes her head and shrugs. I'll pump Aunt June later. Knowing how she shut Elisi down might come in handy in the future. But now I have to go.

Before I can get to my truck, my phone buzzes. It's a text from Ace.

Ace: *So sorry, John. Mom changed plans and I can't make it.*

What the hell? Kick me in the stomach, why don't you?

Me: *You're kidding, right?*

Ace: *No. She's with Susan. They decided to spend the night at the Biltmore Estate.*

Me: *And that's a problem?*

Ace: *She's left Zack with me. My dad's not around, so I have to watch him.*

Me: *If that's all, bring him. He'll have a good time.*

Ace: *Are you sure?*

Me: *Of course. He's a good kid.*

I stare at my phone while I wait for her response. After all I've done to make this happen she can't back out now. I almost start typing again, when her text comes through.

Ace: *Okay. We'll be waiting.*

Me: *See you soon.*

I exhale and crank Old Blue. Then I romp on the gas, driving faster than I should, with the idea to get to the casino before she can change her mind again. I weave around multiple cars on the mountain road, keeping an eye on the rearview mirror for cops. When I finally reach town, I'm forced to drive the speed limit. Darn tourists.

By the time I reach the parking lot, another text awaits me.

Ace: *This isn't going to work. Zack's dressed really inappropriately, and he won't change.*

Me: *Ace, you're making me crazy. Don't do this.*

*My whole family is expecting you. It doesn't matter what Zack wears. Just come.*

There is another pause. It takes all my strength not to march to their suite get down on my knees and beg them to come. Fortunately, my phone beeps with another text.

Ace: *We're on our way. But you'll be sorry.*

****

"Hurry up, Zack. It's time to go," I shout.

He struts out of the bedroom decked out in the regalia I bought him at the Powwow, and he's carrying the tomahawk John gave him.

"Wear your regular clothes, please?" I say. "You're going to embarrass me."

"You bought me these." He swoops his hands down, gesturing to his outfit.

"Yes, I did, but not to wear to a party at John's house. You'll insult everyone."

"No, I won't. They dress like this."

"Nowadays they only dress like that for celebrations or on special occasions."

"A party is a celebration."

"You need to change."

Zack's eyes fill with tears and he jumps around, shouting, "I want to wear them. I want to. I want to."

He's flailing the tomahawk around like a madman. He's going to break something, or worse, hurt himself.

"All right, Zack, you can wear the clothes, but only if you give me the tomahawk."

He stands still and stares at the floor. "I want to bring it."

"Zack, I've had enough. It's not a toy. If you don't give it to me, I'm going to call John and tell him we're not coming."

"You're mean." He pokes out his lower lip but surrenders the weapon. I take it to the bedroom and wrap it in the towel, then hide it under the mattress of my bed, where hopefully no one will find it. Including Zack.

As soon as Zack settles down, I retrieve a beaded jean shirt I designed myself and put it on over my tee, and make Zack pinkie-swear he won't tell anyone where we're going. Even if he blabs, I don't care. I'm going to have to tell Mom sooner or later, and I'm beginning to believe sooner might be better.

Zack and I reach the lobby. He enters, shoulders back, neck stretched high, proudly displaying his clothing. People giggle when they see him, and I get it. Nearly thirteen, he's too old to be wearing regalia and, on top of that, owning it, but still, I wish they wouldn't stare. I swear I catch a glimpse of Cameron just beyond the doors peeking through the glass, but by the time we step outside, there's no sign of him. I let out a deep breath. My nerves are so bad I'm seeing things.

John is parked on the back of the lot, in our regular meeting place. He's leaning on the front bumper, staring at his phone. When he sees how Zack is dressed, I'll be lucky if he doesn't hop in the truck and drive off.

Zack's head snaps up. "There's John!"

He dashes across the parking lot with me trailing behind him shouting warnings to watch out for cars. I finally catch up and nab him by the shoulder.

"Hey," he says, as he wiggles out of my grasp.

At least I've got his attention. "You have to be careful in parking lots. You're going to get hit by a car."

"Oh, yeah. I forgot." He walks beside me but hops out of my reach every time I try to take hold of his hand.

When we get closer, Zack races to John, screaming, "Hey, look at me."

John's eyes go wide, and I brace for the impact. Instead of getting angry, he covers his mouth to hide a smile.

I shake my head. "I told you I shouldn't bring him. What is your family going to think?"

John tugs the collar of Zack's shirt. "Don't worry about it, you look great."

Zack doesn't shy from John's touch as he would with someone else. Like me, for instance. Instead, he smiles at me, showing all his teeth, and says, "See?"

"It's a good thing John likes you," I say, then mouth "Thank you" to John when Zack turns his head.

Zack pulls the fringe on his pants. "Why aren't you wearing your pants like this? Are you going to put them on when we get to your house?"

John glances at me, his eyes twinkling, then back to Zack. "No, not today. It's my day off from being a Cherokee, so I'm wearing jeans."

Zack's brows come together. "Okay, I suppose everyone needs a day off. You'll wear your Cherokee clothes next time I come to your house?"

"For sure, kid." John rubs his nose to hide his amusement and swings the passenger door open.

Zack races past and wiggles into the middle seat.

John catches my arm before I climb in and plants a kiss on my cheek. "You look great, too. In fact, you're more beautiful than I remember."

"Thanks." I breathe deeply to slow my runaway

heart. “So are you.”

The horn honks. John and I startle.

“It’s time to go,” Zack insists.

I open my mouth to scold him, but before I get a chance, John says, “Okay, boss, here we come.”

*Brat attack, thwarted once again by my superhero boyfriend.*

When we have our seatbelts on, John cranks the truck and we’re on our way.

It’s not particularly hot outside, but my underarms are wet. I don’t think I’ve been this nervous since I had to do an oral report as part of my final grade in history.

Zack keeps John busy asking millions of questions about Cherokees and comparing John’s answers to information he’s memorized from his encyclopedia. He takes in everything John says, repeating the inaccurate facts to himself as if he’s committing them to memory. Perhaps he plans to rewrite the encyclopedia one day.

Before I know it, we’re at John’s house. Multiple cars clutter the front yard. A few kids run past, chasing each other in a game of tag. Laugher floats from the backyard along with the smell of meat cooking on the grill. My stomach feels as if it’s harboring a lead weight, making the thought of eating almost unbearable.

John takes my hand and we go inside, with Zack skip-jumping along beside us. As soon as John shuts the door, Rae comes tearing out of nowhere and gives me a big hug. She’s wearing a black tee with silver studs across the front. Her makeup consists of bronze lipstick and cat’s-eye liner, making me wish I’d dolled myself up a bit more.

“Ace,” she says. “I’m so glad you made it. Are you

ready to meet the family?"

"Yes." I swallow and try to smile. Meeting everyone makes me nervous, but the thought of being in the same vicinity as Elisi terrifies me. John cares so much for her though, that as hard as it may be, I have to try to make peace. But how?

Zack is hiding behind John. He peeks around him and studies Rae.

Thankfully, she appears more amused by his appearance than angry.

"Hey, Chief," she says to him. "What's up?"

Zack doesn't answer.

"This is John's sister, Rae," I say. "Tell her hello."

He looks at the ground. "Hello," he says, mimicking my cheery inflection.

"Rae," John says, "quit scaring the kid."

Rae shoves John. "Don't tell me what to do. There's only one scary person around here." Her eyes dart into the kitchen where Elisi sits at the table, scowling. "And you need to talk to her. Now."

John nudges me and we walk into the kitchen with Chief Zack following close behind.

"Elisi, Ace is here and we've brought her brother, Zack," he says.

Elisi looks Zack up and down.

"I'm sorry." I wince, praying she doesn't chew me out too badly.

"What are you sorry about?" She huffs. "He's the only one around here who knows how to dress for a party."

Omigod, she's not mad? The tension in my shoulders releases for the first time today.

"But you." She points at me, and I stiffen up again.

"Where did you get that shirt? From one of our rival retailers, no doubt. Didn't John tell you we have a store with beadwork clothing? We stitch *our own* designs."

I clasp the collar of my jean shirt where I'd stitched two detailed roses. "This didn't come from a store. Well, not totally. I bought the shirt, but I did the beadwork myself. It's sort of a hobby."

She's speechless for a few seconds. "Hobby, humph," she finally grunts. "Some of us have to work for a living."

It's clear she hates me, but if I don't make things right between us, I'll never find the courage to face her again. "John," I say. "I'd like to speak with your grandmother for a moment. Could you take Zack out to play?"

He shakes his head. "Ace, I don't think…"

I touch his arm and squeeze, but when Elisi frowns, I stuff my hands in my back pockets. "I'll be okay. Really."

"Come on, Zack," John says. "I'll be waiting right outside the back door if you need me."

"Thanks," I say. Bile churns in my stomach as I watch them disappear.

The room goes silent. So does the house. It's as if everyone has evacuated along with John, expecting some huge natural disaster to roll in, like a hurricane or maybe a tsunami. What I have to do isn't pleasant, but facing Elisi is the only way to undo the damage from the other day.

A lump that feels like a giant hairball clogs my throat. My cheeks burn, and I dig my toes into the floor to keep from running out the door.

"So, where are you from?" Elisi asks me.

"New Jersey," I croak.

"What are you doing here?"

"My dad works at the casino. He brought my family here for the summer."

"A gambler, huh?"

I nod. Some consider gambling an occupation. I hope Elisi's one of them, because it's the only thing my dad does besides invade his trust fund.

Elisi raises a brow. "So, you came from six or seven hundred miles away and manage to meet John?"

I shrug, still super glad I did despite my current predicament.

She sighs. "I suppose two lame donkeys can find each other anywhere in the world."

I suppress a smile because I'm not sure if she's trying to be funny. "Look, Mrs. Spears—"

"Spears is John's last name, mine is Youngdeer."

"Mrs. Youngdeer, I am really sorry if I disrespected you in any way, but it wasn't my intention. I didn't expect to get wet and muddy while we were riding. Nonetheless, I should have made sure you were home and gotten your permission before I used your shower. I wish I could change what happened, but I can't, so I hope you'll accept my apology."

She stays silent while the air grows thick and sticky and breathing becomes difficult.

"John is my grandson," she finally says, "but I've raised him since he was four years old, and he's like my own child. I don't want to see him hurt or his future ruined. I won't stand for it, do you understand?" She cups her fist in her hand.

"Yes, ma'am."

"I have a question to ask you."

"Anything," I say.

"Where do you think this little infatuation between you two is going?"

I pause to collect my thoughts and then choose my words carefully. "We're still figuring it out for ourselves. Look, I can't promise you that he won't get hurt or I won't get hurt or where we'll end up in the future if that's what you're asking. All I can promise you is that I really, really care for him."

Elisi rises. She stops in front of me and looks me straight in the eyes. "We'll see how far that gets you."

Then she steps around me, leaves the kitchen and disappears into her bedroom.

She still doesn't like me. Hell, she may never like me, but it sure feels better to have cleared the air.

I head for the backdoor. John's peeking through the paned-glass. He meets me in the living room. "Are you okay?"

"I needed to apologize for the other day. I don't know how much she forgives me but things are a little better. I think."

John's mouth twists into a lopsided grin. "You are special, aren't you?"

"Not really. Just determined."

"Determined about what?"

"To make this work between us."

The warmth in his eyes lets me know he wants the same. We hug for just the right amount of time to stay respectful to his grandmother and then join the family and friends in the backyard.

Jack, Chloe, and Simon rush to greet us and make a point to make me feel welcome. Victor has Zack involved in a game of croquet with the other kids.

Zack's not talking, but he's smiling and seems to be enjoying himself. John introduces me to so many people I don't know how I'll ever remember everyone's name.

One thing stands out to me. John's family and friends are laughing, talking, and having fun and not one of them has an alcoholic drink in their hand. When my parents entertain, a party isn't a party without a fully stocked bar.

Rae comes up beside me and weaves her arm through mine. She's holding a set of tongs and a bead of sweat rolls down her temple "I'm stealing Ace."

John grabs my other arm. "What for?"

She pulls me closer. "You've got to learn to share. Besides, it's your turn to watch the grill." She shoves the tongs into his hand. "Don't worry, we're only going to talk about what a fantastic boyfriend you are."

John rolls his eyes.

Rae continues, "Remember to be gentle with him, Ace. He thinks the world revolves around him, so we have to feed his ego."

"Of all the sisters I could have had, why'd I get stuck with you?"

"He knows not what he says." Rae tugs me. "Come on, Ace."

I wiggle my fingers at John and let Rae drag me to a spot underneath a large elm. Rae stares at the picnic table where Jack and Simon sit stuffing hamburgers into their mouths.

"So tell me," Rae says. "What do you think of Simon?"

"I hardly know him, but he seems nice."

"Is that all?"

"I guess he's kind of cute. But nowhere near as good looking as your brother."

"That's a matter of opinion."

"I suppose, but you probably don't see your brother the same way other girls do."

She shifts and leans closer to me. "Can you keep a secret?"

"Trust me. I'm an excellent secret keeper." I should be, I've had to practice my whole life.

"Simon and I started dating a few weeks ago."

"Why don't you want anyone to know?"

"It was an accident. We were watching a movie and the next thing I knew we were kissing, and he kisses sweeter than any guy I've ever known. But he and John have been best friends since they were toddlers, and John thinks of him as family. I'm afraid he'll think it's weird."

"I'm sure John will be happy for you both."

"I don't know. Simon and me hooking up sort of throws off the dynamics of all of our relationships. Simon's scared to tell him, too."

"If you're asking me for advice, I'd tell you to let John know as soon as possible. Keeping secrets isn't good for the psyche. I should know."

"You're right, but I think I'll wait, at least until after the party. Please don't say anything."

"My lips are sealed." I tick a lock on my mouth.

When the sun goes down over the horizon, the sky becomes a decoupage of midnight blue, charcoal gray, and black, sprinkled with thousands of winking stars. In the distance an owl hoots. A cool breeze rustles through the pines and swoops across the yard.

John and his uncles start a large bonfire. Zack stays

by John's side, tossing tiny sticks into the flames. Once the fire is ablaze, I call Zack over and have him take a seat on a log near me. He slips to the ground and rests his head on my knee. My heart swells. Zack so rarely trusts me enough to share his precious contact. I stroke his hair while the embers crackle and pop, and float to the ground like fallen fireflies.

But after only a stolen moment of closeness, he moves my hand. Poor baby can only tolerate so much. It must be horrible to be over-stimulated from something so important as human touch.

John and Simon disappear into the house. When they come back out, John's carrying a long, hand-carved wooden flute with leather straps tied around the sound chamber. Simon holds a small vase-shaped drum with suede cord binding a leather hide to the base. One of John's uncles takes a mandolin from its case, and another man joins the circle with a drum of his own.

John settles in next to me. Elisi crosses her arms on her chest and turns her head away as if seeing us together is too painful to bear. A dull ache pulses in my chest. I'm afraid no matter how hard I try, she'll never like me.

John seems to notice his grandmother's slight bothers me. He rests his hand on my knee and whispers, "Once she gets to know you, she'll love you, too."

A bet she won't carries better than stellar odds, but I keep my feelings to myself nonetheless.

Simon and the other drummer thump out a one-two beat. The guy with the mandolin joins them strumming an upbeat tune that sounds similar to bluegrass music. John comes in playing the melody on the flute. His notes are crisp and clear. Flesh bumps shimmy down my limbs as I listen to the whispering, high-pitched sound.

Everyone is smiling—even Elisi. While John doesn't have a traditional family per se, I sense a feeling of spirit and belonging amongst the group. Something that's missing in my life even though my family is intact. He's so lucky.

Rae makes her way to my side of the circle and sits beside me. She takes my hand and squeezes. John raises his eyebrows and smiles behind the mouthpiece of his flute.

The musicians start jamming. The mandolin player sets his instrument to the side and picks up a pair of maracas. John stops with the melody and plays a single shrill note every now and then. The drumbeat is heavy. Everyone claps, stomps their feet, and shouts random cheers of encouragement, some in Tsalagi. Zack, who always hides his enjoyment of music, taps his pinkie finger into the sandy ground in time with the beat.

When the jam ends, the trio shifts into a musical version of the song I learned in chorus named "El Condor Pasa". Rae starts singing, so I join her with the harmony. Everyone is looking at us and smiling.

Everyone but Elisi, who has taken to drawing a line in the dirt with a stick, glancing over every so often to give me a disapproving look.

A few songs later the concert is over. The crowd quiets and an older gentleman gets up. He tells a story filled with humor about things that have happened to him throughout his life. He keeps the crowd in stitches.

When he's through, he turns to Elisi and thanks her for hosting a wonderful evening. Everyone rises and happy voices fill the night as people go about saying their goodbyes.

Zack has fallen asleep. I gently shake him. He groans but doesn't wake.

"I think I better get him home," I say to John.

John lifts Zack to his feet.

"Give me a minute, I want to say goodbye to your grandmother." I circle around the fire, but when Elisi notices me coming, she rises and hurries into the house. Instinct tells me not to follow. I return to John and shake my head.

He pats my shoulder. "Let's get Zack home, and I'll have a talk with her when I get back. Everything will be fine. I promise."

Darn it. No matter how bad I feel, I won't let Elisi's slight ruin my night. It was only the first time we were properly introduced, and I'm a tolerant person even if she isn't. If I have to come over and visit every day for the rest of the summer to get her to accept me, I will.

## Chapter 18
## John Spears and Ace McAllister

By the time we reach the casino, Zack is sound asleep with his head resting on my shoulder. Ace asks me to drive them to the front door. Ah…progress.

When I park, Ace leans across Zack, and parts her lips. They glisten, making them even more impossible to resist. I gently position Zack against the seatback and we kiss. I'm transformed into another dimension, one that's sizzling and sparking with electricity.

Zack stirs and we break away. Both of us are breathing heavily.

She dips her head and runs her fingertips over her lips. "That was nice." She looks up from under her long lashes. "If I didn't have to get Zack to bed, I don't think I'd ever leave."

"There's always tomorrow," I say.

The corners of her mouth tip up and she sighs, cementing my belief there will be a tomorrow even if it isn't exactly tomorrow. Reluctantly, I climb from the truck and open her door.

She pulls Zack's arm and he flops over on the seat. "Wake up."

The doorman comes up behind us. He scopes me out. "Is everything okay, Miss McAllister?"

"Oh…yes." She glances at Zack. "He's fine. Just sleeping."

“Would you like me to call your father?” he asks her, staring directly at me.

Ace sucks in air and nearly chokes.

She’s frazzled. I’ll have to help her out. “Listen,” I say to the doorman. “I was just about to carry him upstairs. Can I leave my truck here for a moment?”

The doorman turns to Ace. “Is this okay with you, miss?”

“I asked him to help,” she says with a hint of defensiveness in her tone.

“Park over there.” The doorman points to a spot just beyond the overhang. “A few minutes won’t be a problem.”

I close the truck door and leave Ace standing with the doorman while I park. Then I carefully lift Zack out of the seat. He hangs dead weight in my arms, his soft hair tickling my cheek.

“I don’t want to leave the party,” he mumbles before laying his head on my shoulder and drifting back to sleep.

Ace says goodbye to the doorman, and we head to their room.

The kid’s not heavy, but I’m a sweaty mess thinking about meeting her family. “Your parents won’t mind, will they?”

“I hardly think so. My mother isn’t home. Remember? And my Dad is hardly ever home.” Ace opens the door.

The place is pitch black. When she flips on the light, my jaw drops. I’ve been in the casino before, but never in the suites. This one’s the size of a small apartment and it’s stuffed with swanky furniture. Her dad must have dropped a load to rent this place for the summer.

I follow her into a room off the hallway. Ace bends and whisks a pair of lacy pink underwear off the floor and shoves them into her pocket. Her cheeks color as she tries to act like nothing happened. Seeing her underwear on the floor is no big deal, but imagining her in them…man-o-man. I've got to remain cool. I draw an imaginary cross over the image of Ace in her underwear and change my thoughts to cleaning horse dung out of Billy's stall.

Ace pulls the covers down on one of the beds and gestures for me to lay Zack there. After he's tucked in, she approaches me. The light from the hallway casts angles on her face, high-lighting her deep-set eyes and full lips. Billy's poop dematerializes.

She runs a slow finger down my chest. "Thanks for helping me, and for the fun day," she says.

"No, thank you for coming. Everyone thinks you're great. You even found a way to tame Elisi, and that's not easy." I wrap my arms around her. She feels so good, so natural pressed up against me. It's as if we've always been together. I kiss the top of her head, then lift her chin till her mouth meets mine. She clings to me and pulls me closer. Unable to resist any longer, I melt into her.

The door to the suite opens and closes.

"Ace, I'm home," a female voice calls.

Ace draws in a sharp breath. "Oh, damn." She looks like a canary about to be confronted by a cat.

I swing around to face a woman small in stature but bearing a look that could frighten an ogre.

"What the hell is going on?" the woman asks.

"Mom, I thought you were at the Biltmore."

"I was, but Susan wanted to come home because Cameron's upset. He wants to go back to New Jersey because he's bored. You were gone all day again. He says you won't hang out with him anymore. I suppose this is the reason." She points at me like I'm an object and not a person.

Ace steps between us. "Stop it, Mom, you're embarrassing me." She slips her hand into mine. "Mom, I'd like you to meet John."

The look of disgust on her mother's face makes it clear I'm not a welcome commodity. "Look, it's late. Maybe we can save the introductions for another time."

Her mom braces her hands on her hips. "That's the first smart thing I've heard tonight. Why don't you leave?"

"Don't talk to him that way, He's my boyfriend, so you're going to have to accept him whether you like it or not."

Zack lifts his head. "What's all the yelling about?"

Ace drops my hand and rushes to the bed. "Lie down, Zack. I'm talking with Mommy."

I step outside the room. "I think I'd better go. It seems you two need to talk privately."

Her mother frowns. "You bet we do, buster."

I open the door and look at Ace. "I'm a phone call away if you need me."

She nods, and I leave the suite. I hear the two fighting through the door. I place my hand on the knob, debating whether I should go back in.

"How dare you bring someone like him into our suite?" The iciness in her mother's voice cuts right through me.

"Someone like what, Mother? Go ahead, don't hold

back," Ace counters.

I think I know where her mother's going with this and if I listen to any more, my head is going to explode. Pulling Ace away from that woman is definitely on the forefront of my mind, but I'd better leave before my anger gets the best of me and I say or do something I can't take back.

****

"Quit yelling," I whisper. "You'll wake Zack."

"You lied to me," she snarls.

"Yes, I did, and I'm sorry. I wish I hadn't but I can't change it now. From this moment forward, I assure you, I'll be completely honest."

Mom paces. "I forbid you to see that boy again."

"You don't even know him. Your prejudice is unfair and really ugly."

"So is your insolence." She grabs a chair and rummages in a cabinet above the refrigerator. With a bottle of wine under her arm, she practically leaps for the drawer that contains the corkscrew.

*Not on my watch.* I wedge myself between her and the drawer. She bumps me out of the way.

"Wine won't fix your problems, Mom," I say as I grab for the bottle.

She clasps it to her chest as if she's guarding a child from harm.

Nine years ago, Zack was diagnosed with autism. Nine years ago, her drinking soared out of control. Even a DWI last year didn't stop her. I've had enough.

She grabs a corkscrew from the utility drawer and jabs at the cork with the pointy end.

"Mother, don't."

She ignores me.

Alcohol has come before Zack and me for long enough. Anger bubbles in my craw and my neck grows hot. I snatch the bottle from her hand and slam it against the side of the sink. Wine and glass spray everywhere. Some splashes me. Some hits mom and spatters onto the floor. Most seeps into the drain, leaving a slow, winding burgundy trail, diverted by shards of glass. A pungent scent consumes the room—a scent that for too long has reminded me of home.

"What is wrong with you?" she screams.

"Your drinking is out of control. You need help."

She turns fiery red. "How dare you speak to me like that? My drinking isn't the problem here. You are."

"I suppose having to peel you off the floor at night is normal?" She doesn't respond. "If I see any more alcohol in the house, I'm going to pour it down the drain." I grab some paper towels and soak up the wine on the floor, then get a broom from the closet.

I feel Mom's glare on my back and she growls, "If you think your little tantrum is going to divert the attention from the real issue, you're wrong. You are not hanging out with that boy any longer. You're grounded."

"You can't ground me. I won't let you. Not this time, Mom. I'm through being your minion."

She presses her lips together and makes a sound similar to a snarl, then marches into her room. "No wonder I drink. I've got a kid with autism and another kid who shows me no respect. Defy me. Go ahead. You'll see what happens," she says before slamming the door.

I'm sick and tired of her threats. I'm sick and tired of her drinking. Most of all, I'm sick and tired of her.

After I've cleaned up the spilled wine and broken glass, I search the kitchen for hidden bottles of booze. When I don't find any, I head to my room. Despite all the noise Zack's still sleeping. He's kicked his covers off, so I tuck him in again. Then I grab my cell phone, throw myself onto my bed, and text John.

Me: *Sorry about my mom.*

I wait but he doesn't respond. He must still be on the road.

I rest my phone on my chest and close my eyes.

****

The drive across town gives me time to sort through what happened. By the time I reach my house, I'm calm. In Ace's mother's defense, we surprised her—the same way we did Elisi. Maybe she'll chill once the whole thing sinks in. She'd better. And Elisi better, too, because I'm not giving up on Ace as long as she still wants me.

As soon as I get inside, Rae greets me, her brow creased with worry. "Thank God you're home. Something is wrong with Elisi."

"What? She was fine when I left."

"I know, but she's in her room curled in a ball. She looks like she's in pain."

I roll my eyes. "She's faking. Look, Elisi's been playing sick since I told her Ace was coming tonight. It's a trick to make me dump Ace. Now she's working on you, too."

"No, I don't think so. Not this time," Rae says.

I've had it with this nonsense. Between Ace's mother, my mother, and Elisi, I'm beginning to think all parents are messed up. I stomp into Elisi's bedroom. She's on the bed, her color's ashen and her teeth clenched.

I'm the biggest jerk on the planet.

I rush to her side and kneel beside the bed. "Elisi, what's wrong."

"I'm fine," she says, but she's not. She's out of breath and her lips are blue.

"Don't lie to me, old woman."

Her face twists and she strains to speak. "My shoulder hurts."

Her body contorts in an inhuman way and she closes her eyes.

I blink to process what happened.

"Oh, god," Rae screams. "Is she still breathing?"

I jostle her. "Elisi?" She doesn't answer. "Elisi, don't you dare check out on me. Not now."

Rae lets out a sob so loud everyone in the house comes rushing into the room. There's a big commotion around the bed with my family screaming stuff like.

"What happened?"

"Someone give her CPR."

"Move out of the way and let me see her."

"Is she dead?"

Elisi's eyes shoot open. "Stop it," she spits. "I'm not dead. I need to go to the hospital."

"I'll take you." I bend to pick her up, but she moans when I try to lift her.

She looks bad, real bad. I grab my phone and call 911.

****

My phone buzzes, and I jerk awake. I have a text from John.

JOHN: *Sorry so late. Something bad happened. Elisi's in the hospital.*

ME: *OMG*! *What's wrong?*

JOHN: *Don't know. They think she had a heart attack.*

ME: *Where are you?*

JOHN: *The hospital on the Rez. Being called, have to go.*

ME: *K. Let me know if there's anything I can do.*

He doesn't respond. John's family is everything to him. He must be so upset. I have to go. I have to go now. Elisi won't want me there, but I can stay out of sight in the waiting room. I kiss Zack on the forehead and rush to find my purse. Mom's door is locked. I pound on it. "Mom, I need the keys to your car."

"Go away."

I pound harder. "Open up, please?"

Mom swings the door wide. "If you're here to apologize, it won't work."

"John's grandmother has been taken to the hospital. Where are your keys?" I hold my hand out, half begging, half demanding.

She crosses her arms. "You're not going anywhere in the middle of the night."

I spot her keys lying on the dresser, then dart around her and snatch them. "I'll be back as soon as I know she's fine."

She blocks the door. "You think you're so smart, don't you?"

I glare at her, and we get into a stare down. She's small and it would be easy to overpower her. I stand tall. "Move, please?"

She shrinks and, she steps to the side. "If you leave this suite you'll be sorry. I'll kick you out. Then what will you do?"

More like what would she do without me to care for Zack. I feel like laughing but decide to take the high road. No one deserves to be laughed at, no matter how messed-up they are. "I'll be home later, and we can talk about it."

Soon I'm in the hospital waiting room. It's empty except for a woman holding a child, and a man sleeping across three chairs. The lights are bright and the smell of antiseptic and illness linger in the air.

"Can I help you?" the triage nurse asks.

I approach her and lean over so I don't speak too loudly. "I heard Mrs. Youngdeer was brought here earlier."

"Are you family?"

"No, ma'am. She's my boyfriend's grandmother."

"I'm sorry. I can't give you any information."

"I understand. I'll wait anyway." I gesture to a chair in the waiting room. "If it's okay."

The nurse nods, and I take a seat near the door and search for my phone to text John. My phone isn't in my purse, so I go outside and search the car. It's not there either. I must have left it on the bed table. All I can do is return to the waiting room and hope John comes out with good news.

The black and white analog clock on the wall seems to move backward. Every time I look, only minutes have passed, though it seems more like hours. The woman with the baby comes and goes, as does the sleeping man. The cops drag in a scruffy-looking guy. His head is droopy and he reeks of alcohol. A large man in blue scrubs comes out and hauls him off in a wheel chair.

Once the room is still, the nurse glances at me. Her

expression softens. “It’s late. I can let the family know you’re here.”

“No, please don’t bother them. I can wait.”

She smiles at me and shakes her head, then continues typing at the computer.

I grab a magazine from a nearby table and settle in my seat. None of what I’m reading is getting in. My mind is too full of worry for John and Rae and most of all Elisi. What if she dies? Even though my parents and I have our problems, I’d be devastated if anything happened to one of them.

I toss the magazine on the table, prop my elbows on my knees, and rest my head in my hands. I’ve never known anyone who died. I’m really scared.

“Ace,” John says. “What are you doing here?”

I rise. John and Rae are coming toward me. Rae’s cheeks are blotchy and John has purple craters under his eyes. The three of us fall into a hug.

“How is she?” I ask.

Rae lets go, but John hugs me tighter. I can’t tell if he is trying to comfort me or if he’s holding on for support.

He kisses the top of my head. “It’s been a long night, but the doc says she has a really good chance of pulling through.”

“Oh, I’m so glad.”

“Luckily a cardiologist was on call, and he was able to insert a stent in her artery.”

“What’s that?” I ask.

“I’m not sure. I couldn’t concentrate on what the doctor was saying.”

Rae traces her breastbone with three fingers. “It’s a little tube that keeps the artery open and the blood flowing to the heart."

"I'm so sorry this happened," I say. "Is there anything I can do to help?"

John shakes his head. "She's sleeping now. The doctor said we should go home and get some rest. I'm walking Rae to the truck. She's going home, but I'm staying."

Rae rubs her eyes. "John's got the first shift. Aunt June will relieve him in a few hours."

John takes my hand, and the three of us head for the parking lot.

When we reach Old Blue, John turns to me. "Your mother was pretty mad when I left. Are you okay?"

"She's calmed down. Everything will be fine," I say, not wanting to put him under any more stress.

Rae climbs in the truck and settles behind the driver's seat.

John lovingly strokes the fender. "Take care of Old Blue. And be careful."

"Always." Rae smiles, then cranks the truck and drives off.

John rests his forearms over my shoulders and clasps his hands behind my neck. "Thanks for coming."

"Don't thank me. I'm just glad your grandmother is okay."

He glances around the lot. "Where is your car?"

Forgetting where I parked, I scan the lot. "There it is." I point to a row near the back. "I lost it for a moment. The gray paint seems lighter under the fluorescent glow of the streetlight."

"You drive a Mercedes?"

"It's my mother's car."

"Wow."

I suppose I should have told him my family has money, but I don't like to talk about it. People think because we're wealthy we don't deserve to have problems. "The car is pretentious. I know."

"No, it's nice." He tries to sound nonchalant.

"It's okay." My stomach clenches. I hope this doesn't change things between us.

"Don't look so worried. I've seen better." He winks, then bends and kisses me on the lips.

His kiss is sweet, but it's weak, missing the sort of passion he usually offers. Under the circumstances, it wouldn't be fair to expect more.

"You've come all this way," he says. "Do you want to get something to eat? There's an all-night diner nearby. We could go for an hour or so." He looks over his shoulder at the hospital, and I can tell he's concerned about leaving.

"No. Your grandmother needs you. Besides, I have to get home. Do you want me to bring you something?"

He rubs his stomach. "I don't think I can eat right now."

"Okay then."

He wraps his arm around my shoulder and walks me to Mom's car.

I press the lock button on the fob and the lock snaps open.

John opens the door, then bends and looks inside. "You'll have to take me for a spin sometime."

"I don't think so. I like your truck better."

"Sure, sure," he says, shaking his head.

"I mean it."

He shoots me a look, then kisses me on the cheek. "I have to go."

“Call me when you get a chance.”

“You got it,” he says, before he walks away.

I lean against the fender and watch him until he disappears inside. Then I kick the tire of Mom’s high-dollar bucket of bolts. Why can’t she drive a mini SUV like most moms?

## Chapter 19
## John Spears and Ace McAllister

Aunt June arrives and I leave somewhat reluctantly.

Outside the hospital the sun casts a golden haze across the horizon and the air is cool and scented with a hint of pine. Though fragrant, it's not pleasant enough to flush the antiseptic smell from my nose. It's beautiful, but it doesn't bring me complacency. I wish I could rewind time to when Elisi was well and things were normal. She's taken care of me for as long as I can remember, and up until this time, I never thought about her not being here. For the first time in my life, I feel completely powerless.

I promised Aunt June I'd go home and sleep, but I'm going to work. The river is my steady. My constant. It swells and ebbs, never ages or runs dry, and rarely disappoints.

Though I barely remember the ride, I reach the Adventure Center in one piece. Before I have a chance to get out, a familiar black BMW pulls in a few spaces over. The idiot driving is none other than Cameron. His timing makes me suspect he's been tailing me. What the hell does he want?

He struts over to my truck, elbows out, chest forward, like he thinks he's bad. I'm not in the mood for any bull. If he says the wrong thing, I'm likely to flatten him.

I get out and slam the door behind me. "What do you want?"

"Not a river ride if you're driving." He smirks.

I straighten until I'm my tallest and stare down at him. "Just get to the point."

He runs his hand through his spiky, beauty-parlor hair. "You need to leave Ace alone."

"What I do is none of your business. Besides, the way I hear it, you're the one she wants nothing to do with."

His grin twitches down a notch. "This thing you have going with her won't last. You'll be on the chopping block soon. I'll see to that."

Last time I got into it with him, I was nearly fired. I turn to leave. "I don't have time for this."

"Once she satisfies her curiosity, she'll leave you flat. Ace isn't used to your kind of lifestyle."

I spin around and nearly run into the phone he's holding in my face. On the screen is a picture of a house. No, more like a mansion. It's five times the size of my house.

"What the hell are you doing?" I ask.

"This is Ace's house." He flips through the pictures, showing acres of backyard, and a pool meticulously landscaped complete with a cabana bearing a showy, red-tiled roof.

Ace's family must be rich. Really rich. Why didn't she tell me? "Look, I have no interest in looking at real estate. I've got to get to work."

"Ace stole her mother's car last night because of you. She's in deep trouble. She and her family were tight. They had no problems until you came along. Now she's on the verge of cracking up."

"I don't believe you. So, if you think coming here changes anything, you're wrong."

He clenches his jaw and the veins pulse in his neck. He's a Jekyll-Hyde if there ever was one. "Dammit," he spits. "She was supposed to be my girlfriend. You won't win. I promise you that."

That's it. It's time to end this thing one way or another. I crack my knuckles. "Are you through?"

His cheek twitches as he stares at my balled fists. A hint of apprehension flashes across his face. With his eyes locked on mine, he walks backward to his car.

Good choice.

"This isn't over by a long shot," he says. "If you know what's good for you, and Ace, you'll stay away from her."

My instinct is to pounce, but I count back from ten in my head instead. Elisi needs to get well and if I get into trouble, it will kill her. Especially if the trouble is connected to Ace.

He revs the engine and peels out of the parking lot. Dust and rocks go flying. The tires leave twenty feet of burned rubber on the pavement.

What a psycho. I text Ace to warn her he might be coming her way.

****

I jerk awake consumed with the overwhelming feeling I'm being watched. I scan the room. Zack isn't in his bed and the suite is quiet except for the slight hum of the TV in the other room. I grope around the bed table for my phone. It's gone?

Mom was sleeping last night when I returned. I'm surprised she hasn't yanked me out of bed to chew me out. I almost wish she would. We've got to come to an understanding. More importantly, she needs to know I love John, and there's nothing she can do to keep us apart.

I peek out my bedroom door. "Mom?"

She doesn't answer, so I tiptoe into the living room and stumble back a few steps. Cameron is lying on the sofa, his hands behind his head and his feet propped on the arm like he owns the place.

He smiles. "Hey, beautiful."

"Why are you here?" I place my hand over my thumping heart but it doesn't still.

He sits upright. "Your mom asked me to hang out here while she runs some errands. She told me not to let you go anywhere."

"Where's Zack?"

"She took him." His eyes fall on my chest.

Suddenly, I'm hyper aware that I'm alone with Cameron, dressed in a long T-shirt with no bra. I cross my arms. "I don't need a sitter, so leave."

"Calm down. I come in peace." He holds his hands like he's praying and dips his head.

"Fine. Then you won't have a problem leaving in peace either."

"Ace, what I did to you was totally wrong. Please believe me when I say I'm sorry. Really sorry."

He sounds sincere; however, what he did is unforgivable. "Get this in your head. I don't want to be around you and nothing you say will change it."

"Believe me, I get it, Ace. Your mom told me about John. I sort of wish we could have gotten together, but I'm not mad. If it can't be me, I'm glad you found someone else to make you happy. John seems like a decent guy."

I lean against the wall and stare at the ceiling. "I thought you hated him."

"I barely know the guy. Sure, I was angry when he dumped me in the river, but looking back, it was sort of funny."

"Your emotions swing like a pendulum. Why the change of attitude?"

"Let's just say I've done a lot of soul searching over the last few days, and I saw the light. I don't know how to act around girls. There are only guys at my boarding school, and my father wasn't the best example. Perhaps I took it all the man talk too seriously. Let me prove to you I've changed. I'll take you to see John, and I won't tell your mom either."

"I don't know. How about lend me your car instead?"

"You know I can't do that. If my mom finds out I disobeyed your mother, I'll lose my driving privileges and maybe my allowance."

He's not remorseful enough to quit worrying about himself, but if he takes me to John… "Okay. You can drop me off, but you can't come with me. You can tell my mother I snuck off while you were napping or something so you won't get in trouble. I will back you up."

"If that's how you want to play it. I'm game."

I need to text John. I glance around. My phone is nowhere in sight, so I run back to the bedroom and rummage around. It's not there either. I go back to the living room to have another look. "Have you seen my phone?"

"Your mother took it. You can use mine."

The last thing I need is for Cameron to have John's number. "That's okay. I can go without calling. Look, I'll ride with you, but you better not try anything funny."

"Ace, I swear"—he places his hand over his heart—"I want to make amends."

If I didn't want to get back to the hospital, I'd never accept this deal. Right now, it's my best option.

Cameron is waiting for me outside the hotel. I get into the BMW and place my backpack between my feet, so I'm prepared to exit quickly should things go sour.

He hands me a cup of coffee and a doughnut. "I picked this up at the cafe downstairs. I thought you might be hungry."

I set the doughnut on my thigh and place the coffee in the cup holder.

"So, where are we going?" he asks.

"Take the main road into town."

He puts the car in drive and we're on our way.

The coffee is just the right temperature and the flavor is out of this world. "Thanks. Hazelnut is my favorite."

"I know you better than you think." He rests his hand on my knee.

I remove it. "Please don't."

"Sorry." he says. "But you know it's not too late to choose me."

The inside of the car grows smaller and more uncomfortable. "Cameron, I appreciate your help, but John or no John, it's not going to happen between us. Ever."

"No problem. You mean so much to me, I'd do anything just to make your life better."

I take a bite of my donut, and sip on my coffee. If I keep my mouth full, I won't have to talk to him.

"You know, Ace," he says, "when I went on this vacation I thought our moms were fixing us up. That's why I agreed to go."

The hint of anger in his voice makes me uneasy, as does his comment. Still, I think it's best not to say anything. I tug at my collar. The weather is cool, yet I'm sweating. "Mind if I put on the air conditioning?"

"Sure, go ahead." He hits the button and our windows go up.

I reach for the controls but can't figure out which button to push because the writing is blurry. The car hits a slight dip in the road and my stomach roils. I fall back into my seat and rest my head on the window glass. "Can you pull over? Everything is spinning. I think I'm going to be sick."

He ignores me and keeps driving.

Beads of sweat roll down my temples, and my chin drops to my chest. No matter how hard I struggle, I can't lift my head. I roll in his direction. "Something is wrong with me."

He turns and smiles. His perfectly straight white teeth and curved up lips don't match the evil in his eyes. He's the devil, and I've let him trick me again.

I've got to get out of the car.

Through the haze that's become my vision, I zero in on the door handle. Just as I latch onto the metal handle, the door locks click.

"Let me out," I scream.

Cameron laughs.

My heart hammers against my ribs while the world tailspins in a looping circle. I'm in a nightmare. I'm falling and straining to grab onto something to stop myself, but everything I touch slips through my grasp. It's then I understand he's drugged me.

"Ace," Cameron says, "you're going to be with me. You're going to be *my* girl."

"I hate you," I say, right before everything goes black.

## Chapter 20
## John Spears

After I return from my first river run, I tell my boss about what happened to Elisi. He insists I go home even though I've only worked half a day. I don't fight him. I need to shower so I can get back to the hospital.

I lay a towel across the seat, climb in, and take my phone from my glove box. As soon as I swipe the screen, it buzzes in my palm. There is a text waiting:

ACE: *I appreciate your concern, but warning me about Cameron isn't necessary. Jealousy doesn't become you.*

Whoa…where did that come from? I thought she'd want to know that dude came at me like a lunatic.

ME: *Are you serious*?

ACE: *Can you read?*

Ouch. This doesn't sound like Ace.

ME: *Did I do something to tick you off?*

ACE: *Yes. Cameron hasn't done anything to hurt me, so stop with the drama.*

ME: *Sorry. I was afraid you might be in danger.*

ACE: *I'm a big girl. I don't need you to look out for me. The sooner you understand that, the better we'll get along.*

Something's wrong. Really wrong. I switch to phone and call her. My call feeds right into voice mail. I hang up.

ACE: *Can't talk. Mom's watching me. Got to go. Bye.*

ME: *Bye.*

I stare at my phone screen, re-reading Ace's texts. First, I almost lose Elisi and now Ace is on my case because I wanted to protect her.

A sharp pain hits me in the gut, and my mouth waters. I bend over some nearby bushes and ralf up what little I've eaten. Can my life get any worse?

After a long, hot shower, the sick feeling leaves me, so I go to the kitchen to fix a bowl of wholegrain cereal. I eat it at the counter, not bothering to sit.

I can't stop thinking about how angry Ace was and how I could have handled the situation differently. No matter how many times I play the whole thing over in my head, I come to the same conclusion. I didn't do anything wrong. Cameron was the one acting like a fool. Not me. I pick up my phone and dial Ace's number. I let it ring. She's avoiding me. But why? She can't be mad at me for staying with Elisi last night, could she? I decide not, she's never shown any signs of being selfish. The call feeds into voicemail again.

"Ace, I need to talk to you," is all I can manage to say before pressing END.

Maybe Cameron got to her. Maybe he convinced her she'd be better off without me. She knows I'm not into making tons of money. If I do prosper, there are lots of charities that need help. A huge house and matching bank account aren't a priority of mine. Just because I'm going to college doesn't mean I'm going to forget my roots.

College. Me and my stupid aspirations. So far, they've only led to heartache. Elisi was perfectly fine until I got accepted to Duke and then introduced her to Ace. Maybe my selfish choices are the reason Elisi's lying in that hospital bed now.

My phone buzzes. It's a text from Ace: *John, I've been thinking. Summer's over soon. I'm leaving. Maybe it's best we break up now.*

What the hell?

JOHN: *Where is this coming from? Last night all was fine. At least I thought it was.*

ACE: *I can't handle the pressure from my family.*

My blood turns to razor blades. It pumps through my veins at record speed. No part of me is left uncut. I never thought anyone, especially Ace, would break up with me by text. The phone slips from my hand and plops onto the floor.

I hurl my bowl into the sink. It shatters and pieces go flying all over the kitchen. I stomp from one end of the room to the next, trying to process what just happened. A shard of glass bites into my bare foot.

"Damn it."

I pick it out and hold a wadded paper towel to the wound to stop the bleeding. My foot will heel, but the hole she just shot through my heart is not repairable.

What we had felt so real. Hell, it was real. At least for me.

She loves me. I felt it. She must be having a moment of doubt. That's it. A moment of doubt. I had a few of my own. I grab my phone and text her.

JOHN: *I'm going to the hospital to see Elisi. I've got some free time later. I'm coming to the casino to talk to you.*

ACE: *No, you can't come here.*

JOHN: *Ace, you're killing me. I've got to see you.*

*You owe me as much. Meet me on the bridge by the river at nightfall.*

I wait and wait some more. Just when I'm about to toss my phone out the window an answer comes.

ACE*: Okay, I'll be there.*

## Chapter 21
Ace McAllister

My eyes open. The sun burns heavily through a large paned window on the far wall. The colors. The layout. The rustic furniture. They're all foreign to me.

I squeeze my eyes shut and concentrate until the white space in my head clears and my memory kicks in. I was in the car with Cameron. He was taking me to see John. I drank the coffee he gave me…oh, no. What has he done?

I'm in a strange bed, somewhere. At least I'm still wearing clothes.

I try to sit but the pain in my head knocks me flat. "Cameron. Where the hell am I?"

He doesn't respond.

I scream until my throat burns and my ears ring. Tears stream down my cheeks and into my mouth.

The door cracks open and Cameron walks in. He's dressed in the clothes from yesterday. Sweat stains soak the material under his underarms. Gone are his cocky gait and the smirk he flashed right before I slipped into oblivion, replaced by a blank stare, disheveled hair, and dark craters under his eyes. He looks like an apparition who's just risen from the dead.

A volcano of fear erupts inside me.

"No point in yelling," he says in a voice as worn and flat as he looks. "No one can hear you." He sits on the bed beside me and brushes a stray tendril of hair off my face.

He sickens me like no other. I'm dying to recoil but lie perfectly still. Something tells me now is not the time to exercise my First Amendment rights. If he's desperate enough to drug me, who knows what he'll do. If I stay calm, maybe, just maybe, I can talk him into taking me home.

I wipe away my tears and swallow to moisten my throat. "Let's go back to the casino now. I won't tell. We can pretend nothing happened."

"As if I'd believe you." He rubs his temples while his lips move as if he's having a conversation with himself.

I resist the urge to claw out his eyes. *Not yet. There will be a better time.*

"I could tell from the day on the river that guy was trouble. The way he looked at you. If it weren't for him, none of this would have happened." He stares at me unwaveringly. "How could you let that Indian touch you?"

"He never touched me. We're just friends. I swear," I blurt out.

He slams his fist on the bed. "Do you think I'm an idiot? I hate it when people lie to me."

He hates to be lied to? Indignity replaces the fear inside me. "The same way you did to me when you tricked me into getting in your car and drugged me?"

He looks down, and then back at me, his expression smug.

"Cameron," I say, "we have to go back. Our parents will be looking for us. Zack needs me. Please?"

"I don't have to do anything. Besides…I need you

more than Zack."

"We can't stay here forever."

He jumps to his feet. "We can if I say we do."

Clearly, he is not well. I've got to find a way out of this. "Fine, we'll stay, but I need to use the bathroom."

His eyes shift to the door. "All right."

I grit my teeth and rise to my feet, fighting a blinding migraine as the blood leaves my head. He motions for me to follow him. The bathroom has a small window high on the wall, making it hard to reach. Still, I can lock myself in until I figure out what to do.

He leans against the door jam. "Go ahead."

"I can't. Not with you watching."

He glances up at the window. A bead of sweat trickles down his cheek. "I'll be right outside. Don't lock the door."

As soon as he shuts the door, I cover my mouth to stifle a wail and lean against the sink to keep my knees from buckling. If I don't pull it together, I'm sure to have a full-blown panic attack.

"Hurry up," he shouts.

My personal needs are urgent so I take care of them as quickly as I can. Then I dig through the medicine cabinet. There is a bottle of aspirin. I take two and gulp them down with a swallow of water. My reflection in the age-worn mirror matches the horror show that has become my life. My eyes are puffy and black streaks of mascara line my cheeks. Whatever he drugged me with has aged me ten years.

"If you don't come out right now, I'm coming in," he says.

In this exact moment, I learn about fear. Real gut-wrenching fear. It's like the feeling you get when the heroine in a horror flick has her hand on the door knob, and the entire audience is screaming for her to stop, but she opens the door anyway and subjects the audience to a second of terror so intense that knees hit chins and heartbeats thunder. That's my fear, only it isn't make-believe, and I can't close my eyes and will it away. I have no choice but to face it.

Or not.

Light from the small window glints off the mirror and holds my attention. To me the flicker of light is more than merely a cloud shifting. It's a sign to seek other options.

I stand on the toilet and undo the latch. With a few more inches, I'd be high enough to climb out. I hop down and eyeball the room. A small metal trashcan sits beside the sink. If I put that on the toilet lid…

The door flies open.

In a single gasp, I suck all the air out of the room.

Cameron glances around. He stalks toward me, not stopping until our toes touch. "You've been in here long enough." He glances up at the window.

What will I do if he sees the latch? I'll have no choice but to fight. He's a lot bigger than me, and a lot crazier, but perhaps not as desperate.

He grabs my upper arm.

My breath hitches. I can't breathe. I can't move. I'm paralyzed.

"Come with me," he says. "It's time to eat."

He didn't see? No. He didn't see.

I fight dizziness from lack of oxygen, and I allow him to drag me to the kitchen.

## Chapter 22
John Spears

Aunt June arrives at the hospital twenty-five minutes late, dressed in yoga clothes. She's too large to be wearing spandex in public, but she's doing double-time at the gym, trying to get healthy. Elisi's ordeal scared the hell out of her, too.

"Sorry I'm late, John," she says, hurrying into the room.

"It's okay," I say on my way out. I totally don't mean it, but it would be uncool to take my aggravation out on her, especially when she's here to help.

I pass the nurse's station without saying goodbye. There's no time for small talk. Ace is waiting for me at the river. I have to find out what caused her sudden change of mind. Sure, we both have a lot to deal with family-wise, but I never pegged her as a quitter. Well, I'm not one to roll over and play dead. I'd trade every single time I hooked up with a girl to sit by the river with Ace one more time, watching the sunrise.

By the time I get to the park, it's dusk. I head straight for the wooden walking bridge that spans the river. A few people pass over, but none of them are Ace. Even from a distance I'd recognize her slender frame with the soft curves in all the right places.

I stop on the top and lean against the railing. The orange glow of the sun fades into the tops of the mountains, succumbing to the purple haze of darkness. Nightfall is seconds away. She's not late. Not yet.

More time passes and she doesn't show. Standing still makes my legs twitch, so I go down to the riverbank below, and perch on a rock.

Elisi says rivers are sacred. If you listen to the water curling and whooshing around the rocks, you'll hear the songs of our people written before road noise, tourist shops, and the English language were ever forethought. I wonder if there would have been a place for a couple like Ace and me in that world?

Night crashes down black and cold. I pick up a handful of pebbles and skip them one by one across the water. Maybe she forgot where we were supposed to meet and went to our special place instead.

I toss the remaining pebbles into the water and jog along the river's edge until I reach the spot, our spot, hidden behind the trees. It's empty, the ground washed clean by an afternoon shower. There's not even a footprint to prove we were ever there. I pull out my phone and call her.

When the call feeds into voice mail, I don't bother to leave a message. Her absence says it all. She really doesn't want to see me anymore.

The star-bear looms in the same spot it was the night I confessed my childhood fear to Ace.

It's time to face the facts. I totally got it wrong again. Elisi warned me. Ace could never really care about me. Well, I've wasted enough time on her. The one thing I've learned in my eighteen years is that people you love screw you over. First my mother. Now Ace. Why do I always cling to false hope? Why can't I make my heart let go when holding on only brings me pain?

When I return, Elisi's propped up in her hospital bed, reading a gardening magazine. Her cats-eye glasses rest midway on the bridge of her nose. I sit in the wooden chair and perch my feet on the rail of the bed. She looks over and smiles.

"Where's Aunt June?" I ask.

"She went to the cafeteria to get something to eat. All that yoga made her hungry." Elisi chuckles.

"Never mind that. What are you doing up? It's late. You should be sleeping."

"Stop fussing over me. I'm tired of laying around doing nothing."

"Elisi, the doctors say you need to get your rest."

"If I listened to what the doctors said I'd have been in the ground five years ago." She loosens her blood pressure cuff and the machine starts to beep.

"Don't do that." I jump up and attempt to wrap the Velcro around her arm.

"That thing is bothering me," she moans.

A nurse hurries into the room. "Mrs. Youngdeer, how many times have I told you, you have to wear the cuff?"

Elisi drops her magazine across her lap and holds out her arm in the air while the nurse straps her back up. "Darn thing itches. How much longer do I have to wear it?"

The nurse closes the Velcro band and readjusts the monitor. "You'll wear it until the doctor says you don't have to." She looks at me. "Holler if she tries to remove it again."

When she leaves, I rise and stand guard at the foot of Elisi's bed. She rolls her eyes and makes a *pffff* noise.

"If you want any peace, you better do what she says," I warn.

She grunts, then holds her magazine up in front of her face.

"Go ahead and ignore me, but I'm staying right here to make sure you follow the doctor's orders."

She continues to pretend I don't exist. She'll never listen to the doctors, and she won't slow down either, especially if no one is here to make her. How can I go away when she's ill?

"I've been thinking," I say. "How about I put off school for a year or maybe go to a community college nearby? That way I can still help out around the house."

Elisi peeks over the top of her pages. "I thought you were dying to go to that fancy-pants university. How will you pay for school without a scholarship?"

If staying will keep her alive, I'll find another way. "I don't know, maybe student loans until I can apply for tuition assistance. Or even better, I could take a year off and work for Jasmine's father. There's no shame in doing construction work. In fact, I think it would be great. I've been having second thoughts about leaving the reservation for a while now."

Elisi closes her magazine. "Let me see your eyes."

I hadn't realized I was staring at the floor. It takes all my concentration to look at her.

"I've raised you since you were a tot and not once have you tried to get away with such a lie. What makes you think you can now?"

"School means nothing if you aren't here to watch me graduate."

She settles into her pillow. "If you stay, it is only

because of me. Right?"

The blood pressure monitor blips a little higher.

"Answer me." She rolls her hand, gesturing for me to speak.

"Yes," I practically whisper.

She slaps the mattress. "I won't have it. I won't bear the burden of your disappointment. I will not allow you to resent me. Besides, the *yonega* won't want you if you don't become a lawyer, will she?"

"Why do you care what Ace wants? You hate her, remember."

"I don't hate her. I hate her kind."

"It's the same thing, Elisi."

"No, it's not."

I press my lips together tight. She's not going to bait me into an argument. It's not good for her health.

"Getting sick has given me time to think," she continues. "There's something you need to know before I'm in the ground."

Here she goes again. I should tell her Ace dumped me and spare myself the lecture, but if I say the words, I'll be admitting we're over, and I can't handle that. Not yet.

"I'm listening," I say.

"When I was your age, there was a boy who worked in the same forest station as your Uncle George. He had red hair and freckles and crystal blue eyes. He was of Irish ancestry, I believe, and he sure was a looker." She presses her lips together and pauses a moment. After a deep breath she continues, "I saw him nearly every weekend for close to a year. We were serious, and I was sure we'd be married one day."

"What happened to him?"

"He moved to Baltimore to be with his family."

"Why didn't you go with him?" I ask, even though I'm sure I know the answer. Elisi would never leave the reservation.

Elisi's face melts, the wrinkles forming a road map of pain. "We did what young people who are in love do, and I got pregnant. He said his family would never accept me, especially in my condition. So, rather than marry me, he fled, leaving me to carry our child. What a fool I was."

Sticking a fork in an electrical outlet couldn't have shocked me more. "The baby? Where is it?"

Elisi places her glasses on the bedside table and rubs her eyes. In my whole life, I've never seen her cry. I don't know what to do. She answers, "In those days there weren't TV shows glorifying teen moms. Unwed mothers were looked down upon—at least by white people. His family thought there was something morally wrong with me and got social services involved. I didn't have a way to support myself, and I let the social worker talk me into giving up my baby for adoption. Somewhere in this world, there's a red-haired boy with dark piercing eyes that I will never know. So, John, when I tell you the path you're on with that girl can only lead to your unhappiness, I speak from experience. I don't want you to bear the same pain I do to this day."

"We can find your son. I'll help you."

Elisi shoots up in bed. She's beet red and looks as if any second she'll detonate. "Stop. It's over and done. He's gone. I never want you to mention this again. To anyone. Do you understand?"

"Please, calm down. I swear I won't say another

word." I ease her back down.

She nods and pulls her covers up around her neck. "I want to sleep now."

I take a few unconscious steps backward before settling in the easy chair in the corner. Until tonight, I thought Elisi lived almost a saint-like life. But she's human, with flaws like me and Rae and my mother. Her perfection is no more than a childhood fantasy of mine.

The nurse walks into the room. "John, there's someone here to see you."

Still reeling from Elisi's revelation, I consider her words for a moment. Maybe it's Ace. At least some good might still come from this day. I leap to my feet and follow the nurse into the lobby.

Two cops are standing at the nurse's station. I know them. Officer Stomper has patrolled this area for years; the other graduated from high school a few years ago. I wave, then scan the waiting area.

Ace is nowhere in sight.

I turn to the nurse. "You said someone wanted to see me?"

The nurse gestures to the policemen. Officer Stomper is a friend of Elisi's. He must have come to see how she's doing. "You're a little late. She's sleeping," I say.

"How is Pearl?" he asks.

"Getting stronger every day."

"That's good to hear, John. But my visit today doesn't concern your grandmother." His eyes sweep the waiting room.

"What's up?" I ask.

"I hate to burden you at this time, but I need to talk with you outside in my patrol car for a minute."

“Sure,” I say, wondering what the heck is so important that we can’t talk inside.

By the time we reach the parking lot, I’m buzzing with adrenaline. Officer Stomper opens the front door of his car and asks me to get in.

We sit in silence for a moment, and an uneasy feeling settles in my gut. “What’s this about?”

Officer Stomper glances at the floorboard. “John, I’ve known your family for a long time. You’ve never given me an ounce of trouble. But something’s happened, and I have a few questions for you.”

All the possibilities of what could be wrong rattle my brain. If it’s not Elisi—

“Is my mother in trouble?”

“It’s not about her.”

“Then what?”

“There’s a couple of teenagers staying with their families at the casino, Ace McAllister and Cameron Mitchell.” He stares at me. “They’ve gone missing. Do you know them?”

Ace? Missing? The world starts to spin, and I thump my skull against the headrest. “Ace is sort of my girlfriend—at least until a day ago. And I’ve met Cameron, but don’t know him well.”

“Do you know where they might’ve gone?”

“No. But if Ace is missing, I want to help find her.”

“Her family says she’s been hanging around with a Cherokee teen named John against her mother’s wishes, and you’ve just admitted as much. So let me spell it out in plain English. The mother believes you might have something to do with Ace’s and Cameron’s disappearance.”

"Cameron is crazy. He's the one they ought to be worried about. He came to my work and threatened me. I tried to warn Ace about him, but she wouldn't listen. If he's done something to her, I'll—" I stop short. Somehow spouting how I'll kill someone to a police officer doesn't seem like a smart move.

Officer Stomper stares at me, his dark eyes probing. "Her phone was found by the river. There are texts from you asking her to meet you there. The kids' parents think Ace went to tell you she didn't want to see you anymore and Cameron went along to protect her. Neither has been seen since."

Common sense tells me to ask for a lawyer, but it might delay helping Ace. If that creep hurt her, I'll make sure he's more than missing. "So what are you trying to tell me?"

"We don't have enough evidence to charge you. However, if more information comes in, I might have to bring you in."

I throw my hand up. "I can't believe this."

"Calm down. My experience tells me those two took off for a day or two of alone time and they'll show up soon. But until this situation is resolved, I'd advise you lay low and not make any moves that might arouse suspicion."

"How can I sit back and do nothing? Ace might be in danger."

Officer Stomper lays a heavy hand on my shoulder. "John, when you're not with your grandmother or at work, I want you to stay home. It's for your own good. The further you stay from that girl, the better—at least until we can clear your name. And don't go off alone. Make sure you have a witness at all times."

Don't go off alone? Clear my name? I've done nothing wrong. There's no way I can sit around doing nothing if Ace is possibly in danger. "Can I go now?"

He nods. I get out of the patrol car.

"Do what I say, John," he calls after me.

This makes no sense. Even if Ace wanted to be with Cameron, she'd never run off and leave Zack.

I head to Old Blue and call Rae. She doesn't answer so I leave a message. "Get to the hospital as soon as possible. Ace is missing and I've got to find her."

## Chapter 23
## Ace McAllister and John Spears

I wake abruptly. Sunrays burn through the large paned window at odd angles, warming one of my bare feet. Cold sweat drips from my forehead to the back of my neck. The last thing I remember is eating a hamburger and baked potato, and now I'm back in bed dressed only in a T-shirt and panties. He's drugged me again, and from the way my stomach's growling, I doubt I ate much.

A door opens and closes in another room. Keys jingle and drop onto something hard—maybe a counter or table. Sprawled on my back, I'm more vulnerable than I've ever been. Panic fires through me and nearly lifts my body off the bed. I thrash and wail in a voice not my own, but one that sounds more like a wolf in mourning.

The door to the room opens. Cameron's face is covered with stubble and his usually perfect hair is greasy and sticking every which way. My heart beats between my ears like a demented drummer in a heavy metal band.

"I see you're awake," he says.

My chest rises and falls as I labor to catch my breath. "What did you do to me?"

He comes to the foot of the bed and wiggles my toe. "Did you miss me?"

Any closer and I'll spit in his face. I collect saliva in the side of my cheek, but then something one of Mom's rehab therapists told me crosses my mind: *Calm down. Don't get caught up in the toxic swirl. Wise decisions are made with a clear head.*

Instinct tells me I need to gain his trust. If I'm going to survive this, I'd better start trusting my gut. "Of course, I missed you."

He presses his lips together and impales me with the intensity of his stare. The tiny hairs prick on the back of my neck. If he remains silent much longer, I'll lose it.

He sits down beside me and runs a finger along the inside of my thigh.

Protected only by the thin layer of silk of my panties, I squeeze my knees together.

He stops moving and rests his hand on my thigh. "You don't want me to touch you, do you?"

Oh boy, he's more out of it than I thought. I steady my voice. "Really, Cameron? Drugging and kidnapping me isn't a good way to get me to be your girlfriend."

"This"—he swings his arm in a wide circle around his head—"is your fault. You chose a lowlife over me. If you only knew how bad you hurt me."

Remain calm and appease him, I remind myself. "You're right. I never gave you a fair shot. But that doesn't give you the right to strip me and do whatever you want while I'm out cold."

"Don't worry. I haven't stolen your precious virginity. I'd prefer you gift it to me."

"Then why drug me?"

He leans over until his nose almost touches mine. His breath reeks of alcohol and sour milk. "I had to go out. I can't trust you to stay put, so…"

"How do you think you'll get out of this one, Cameron? What have you told our parents?"

He smooths his hair, stopping midway back to squeeze his head between his hands as if trying to force out his thoughts. "Nothing. They don't know anything."

"Are you crazy? They're probably freaking out." I stop myself short of blurting my next thought—that I'm sure they've got the police looking for us. I don't know what he'll do if I send him into a panic.

He clears his throat. "How about this? We can run away together and start a new life. We can change our names and forget the past, our parents, Zack, and that Indian. I can forgive you."

"We need to make a decision like that as equals and right now I'm your captive."

Cameron shifts on the bed and cups his chin in his hand, pondering my suggestion for way too long. "You told me to get lost. You told me you didn't want to see me again."

"I did, but I'm here now and I'm listening." I roll away from him and rise to my feet.

He dives and snatches me by the wrist. "Where do you think you're going?"

Realizing I've made another big mistake, I suck in a sharp breath and blow it out slowly, allowing the tension to leave my body. "I'm stiff from lying for so long. I need to stretch."

"You said we were going to talk?"

I stare at his hand, the one with the white-knuckled grip holding me in place. "You're hurting me. Real men don't hurt their girlfriends. Everyone knows that."

He reddens as if he's embarrassed, before finally

letting go.

Relying on the slim chance he has some sort of a conscience, I take a cautious step toward the large picture window. When he doesn't stop me, I take another, and another, and soon I'm standing at the sill. Outside, the mountains span forever. There's not another cabin in sight. How will I ever find my way back? "The view is beautiful. Is this a rental?"

"I found this place while I was scoping out the area. The owners drove off in a camper. Stupid people left the key in a planter near the porch."

No one knows we're here. A sob threatens to burst from within. I swallow, thankful my back is to him.

"Can we go outside and get some fresh air?" I manage to squeak.

He opens a small closet, retrieves my jeans, and tosses them to me along with a pair of flip-flops that must belong to the owner. I slip them on.

Then he takes my hand and leads me from the bedroom to a large open room with a kitchen and living area. The walls are made from logs and the floor is raw timber. The furniture is mismatched and most appears to be handmade.

He opens the latch on the front door. The yard is a mass of overgrown foliage. The only way to and from the house is a dirt drive that disappears into the forest.

"Where's the car?" I ask.

"It's gone."

"How will we get out of here?" I ask, though I'm almost positive he won't tell me.

His grip tightens to the point the small bones in my hand grind together. "You ask too many questions."

This is bad. Much worse than I thought. I'm in the

middle of nowhere. No car. No map. No phone. "I'm sorry. I didn't mean to make you angry. It's really sweet of you to bring me to such a nice place. I should be grateful."

His face softens. He seems all too happy to buy my lies.

We continue walking through the overgrown grass to the edge of the back yard where it drops to a steep decline. Trees cover the mountainous terrain on both sides of the valley, breaking only for a narrow river running between the two.

Cameron comes from behind and wraps his arms around my waist. He presses his chin to the side of my face. "This is how it's meant to be. Just you and me."

The smell of his body odor is overwhelming. I'm suffocating. If only I'd called Grandma back and told her how bad things really were in our house. If I hadn't hidden Mom's drinking problem, I wouldn't be in this mess.

My knees go rubbery, and as much as I don't want to, I slump against him. Above me the clouds waft by. I close my eyes and I pray to whoever lies behind their milky veil of fog that I'll survive when I decide to bolt from his arms and throw myself down the hill. I picture my body mangled and lifeless at the bottom

No. I don't want to die. I want to survive. I will survive. Zack needs me and the thought of never seeing John again is more than I can bear. John Spears. I open my eyes, and the clouds part, revealing a miracle in the distance. A tree. John's tree—the one that juts out at an angle. The one where the hawk landed the day we rode Billy to the place with the magical sun showers. A spark flickers inside me. It's small but fueled by hope. I can do this. I can make it to the other side. But I'll have to wait for the perfect time—one where I can get a head start.

I remove Cameron's hands from my waist. "Let's go inside and talk."

"First you want to go out and now you want to go in?"

I take a step toward the cabin, coaxing him along. "I need a drink of water. My throat hurts."

He nods and allows me to keep moving.

Inside, he takes a plastic bottle of water from the fridge and thumps it down on the kitchen table.

The seal isn't broken, so it's probably safe. "You've been working hard taking care of me. Why don't you let me make you something to eat?"

He drops into a chair at the table and rests his chin on his fists. His eyes hang half-mast.

"I need to use the rest room first," I say.

He yawns. "Go ahead."

I expect him to follow, but he doesn't, so I force myself to walk slowly as to not insight alarm.

Now I'm in the bathroom. Alone. I eye the small window and look for the trashcan to use as a stool. It's missing. Cameron must have taken it. I'll never be able to climb out without it. The window in the bedroom is close to the ground. My heart thumps as I tiptoe through the hallway.

"Ace," Cameron yells. "What are you doing?"

I startle and bang my head on the doorframe. Cameron barrels through the door, leaving me barely enough time to jump out of his way. He examines the room from corner to corner, stopping to stare in the direction of the windows. Finally, he turns toward me.

"Why are you in here?"

"Just looking for something to tie my hair back. You're going to have to trust me if you want me to be your girlfriend."

He points at the bed. "Sit." When I don't move, he screams, "Now!"

I sit on the edge of the bed. "Please don't yell. It scares me."

"You need to go only where I say you can and nowhere else. Don't move," he says as he backs out of the room.

He returns promptly with two paper cups and an open bottle of wine tucked under his arm. He sits down next to me, and hands me a cup, no doubt laced with something.

My hand shakes so badly, burgundy liquid splashes over the side.

He holds his cup of wine up. "Cheers."

I raise mine. The plastic bends as we meet somewhere in the middle.

"Now, drink," he insists.

****

Rae rushes into the hospital lobby. I fill her in on everything except the part about Officer Stomper ordering me to stay home. As soon as she understands Ace might be in danger, she shoves me out the door.

Mid-afternoon comes and soon passes. And after driving half the roads in and around the area, searching multiple campsites and motels, I'm still no closer to finding Ace or Cameron. I've always kind of liked that the Cherokee Rez was a little backward technology-wise—kept me from being too caught up in Computer Land—but what I wouldn't do for my GPS to work right now.

My fruitless search has made me come to the realization that I need help, so I phone Simon. He answers on the first ring, despite the fact I've been ignoring his texts. The word that I'm in some kind of trouble has already reached his ears and most of the people on the reservation, or so he says. Like a true brother-from-another-mother, once he knows the deal, he hops-to and assembles a posse of our closest friends.

I'm just about to hang a U-turn and drive in the direction of his house, when my phone rings, again. The screen flashes Jasmine in big white letters. Damn, I thought I deleted her contact information. I'm not in the mood to deal with her, but as I've learned from past experiences, she'll keep calling until I answer. "What do you want?"

"I hear you are in trouble." Her voice is laced with concern.

"Good news travels fast." My voice, unlike hers, is laced with sarcasm.

She sighs, and silence fills the radio waves between us.

I don't have time for her games. "Look, I'm busy. I've got to go."

"No, don't. Please? I have some information about the *yonega* and her boyfriend, but I can't go to the police."

Now she has my attention. I pull over to the side of the road. "Do you know where they are?"

"No. Listen, I've said more than I should have over the phone. Meet me at the place where we used to go when we wanted to be alone. I'll tell you all I know."

"This better not be a trick, Jasmine, or I swear…"

"We've had our differences, but I'd never want to see you in trouble. Hurry please. And don't park near my house or I won't show. I don't want to be seen with you."

A sickly feeling hits me right in the gut, similar to one I had when I feared Elisi might die. I text Simon and tell him to start without me, then drive to the trail that leads to the pasture behind Jasmine's house. I park my truck a quarter mile down the road and jog the rest of the way.

I'm winded when I reach the dilapidated cabin hidden in the woods behind her family property. The door is ajar so I step inside. The place is covered with cobwebs and dust and makes my nose itch. I don't remember it being so dirty. Has it really been that long since the two of us were here alone together or does the place look worse without an ulterior motive in mind?

The door behind me creaks and I spin around.

Jasmine and Yarrow enter.

Faced with an ambush, I curl my hands into fists.

Yarrow smirks. "Aren't you going to say hello?"

"Quit with the small talk. What do you know about Ace?"

Jasmine glances at Yarrow as if asking permission to speak and then back at me. "The *yonega's* friend has been hanging out at the river. He loves to smoke weed and has plenty of cash to do it."

"How do you know it's him?" I ask.

"He's on missing persons posters all over the reservation."

"So, what are you trying to tell me?"

She glances down at the floor. "The day before they disappeared, he came looking for something a little stronger."

I glare at Yarrow. "What did you sell him?"

Yarrow holds up his hands in a "don't shoot" position. "He said he had a date with a chick and wanted to have a good time."

The blood pounds between my ears. "What did you sell him?"

Yarrow glances at the floor and back up. "Just a little Easy Lay."

"A date rape drug?"

"Yeah, but I didn't know he was going to use it on *your* girl."

My mind stops working, and before I know what's happening, my fist slams into his jaw. He crashes to the floor and bangs his head on the wall. Jasmine screams and falls to her knees beside him

Yarrow rolls to kneeling and fondles the knife sheath on his side.

I take a step toward him. "Go ahead and try."

Jasmine spreads her arms wide. "Stop it."

"Yeah, back off," Yarrow says. "This ain't the way to treat a brother who's here to help."

He's lucky we were buds at one time or I'd finish what I started. "You're no brother of mine. If you really want to help, leave me the hell alone and get onto the road and find Ace before something happens to her. Unless you want to have her blood on your hands."

He wipes a trickle of blood from the side of his mouth. "Okay. I'll do it."

I offer him a hand up. After he's on his feet, I grind his palm until I feel the bones crack together. "Once we find her, if you see me or her on the street, cross to the other side."

I let go and he flexes his fingers. “Remember, this will even the score—no bad karma between us. Right, man?”

He can believe whatever he wants, but I have no control over cosmic laws. “Don’t tell anyone you’ve seen me.”

Yarrow cranks up a crooked smile. “You know me better than that, man.”

“Yeah, unfortunately I do,” I say as I head for Old Blue.

****

Cameron sits on the opposite side of the bed, using the headboard as a backrest. He stretches out, putting his shoes on the comforter. Then he pats the mattress, indicating he wants me to sit next to him. Reluctantly, I do.

He lifts my hand, the one holding the cup of wine, and urges me to drink. I keep my lips tight, limiting my intake to practically nil, and fake a swallow. He guzzles straight from the bottle and closes his eyes. The silence between us is a gift that keeps giving. Soon his breathing grows heavy and his chin sags to his chest. He’s sleeping. I shift ever so slightly and dump the cup of wine onto the floor behind the bed.

He snorts and his hand clamps down on my thigh. “What are you doing?”

“Nothing. My leg’s cramping and I need to move.” My face burns liar’s hot.

He brushes my cheek with the knuckle of his forefinger. “You’re blushing.”

“Am I?”

“Uh-huh. Why?”

“How should I know? Maybe it’s the wine.” I say,

showing him my empty cup.

He leans over until I feel his lips on my ear. "Oh, yeah. Well, I can think of a few positions that will make you blush a lot harder."

When I think things can't get worse, he grabs my breast and squeezes it like a melon he's checking for ripeness.

"Cameron, stop." I remove his paw and place it on his lap. "I need to shower first."

His face screws up. "You don't want to be with me."

"Of course I do. I just want everything to be perfect." I cross my arms and shove my hands into my armpits to stop the trembling, all the while praying he's vain enough or maybe crazy enough to believe me.

He hits off the bottle again and wipes his mouth with the back of his hand. "I'll join you."

I shoot to standing. "No!"

*Don't blow this. Breathe in, breathe out.*

I force myself to touch his shoulder. "I can't relax if I'm worrying about not being clean."

"Fine, but hurry. Today is the first day of our eternity." He winks.

Hearing those words from him makes me feel as if I'm ensnared in a steel cobweb ready to be gobbled by a spider. "It won't take long. I promise."

He slaps my butt. "Better not."

I hurry to the bathroom. As my bare feet meet the hard, cool ceramic tile, I'm reminded my shoes and backpack are still in the bedroom. Making it all the way to John's mountain shoeless would be next to impossible.

I turn on the shower and leave the water running

while I prop open the small window above the toilet. Then I creep back to the bedroom. Cameron is hugging the bottle of wine like a teddy bear and snoring lightly. I toe-heel back to the closet, get my backpack and stuff my feet into my shoes, walking on the backs of my heels until I'm back in bathroom with the door closed. I turn the lock on the door, but it doesn't catch, so I wet a towel and wedge it in the crack at the bottom.

Standing on the toilet lid, I toss my backpack outside, then slip on my shoes, leaving the laces untied. I grab the sill with my forearms and try to climb the wall. My feet slip, leaving me hanging. I have another go at it, and another, until I'm nearly out of breath and my hands and elbows are bruised.

I'm botching my escape the way I've been botching things my whole life. If I don't get out of here, I might not be around to help my brother, or my mother. I won't go to college or have children of my own. Cameron will probably kill me when I reject him, but I will reject him with pleasure, because my body belongs to me, not him, and I'll spend my last breath defending it.

I hop down and open the cabinets below the sink, seeking something, anything, that will give me height. Inside, I find the trashcan. Evidently, Cameron is really bad at hide and seek.

Climbing up to the window is the easy part. Balancing on a small metal can is another. It raises me just high enough to finagle my body into the rectangular space beneath the glass. The frame digs into my ribs, but I don't care. The cool air outside invigorates me, and I push off with my toe. The metal can slips from beneath my foot, and I'm left dangling half in and half out as the can rolls across the floor, tattling on me with each clink of its tinny trail.

My adrenaline spikes and I shimmy like mad. In the next instant, I'm suspended in air. *Tuck and roll. Tuck and roll.*

*Ouch.* I think I flipped and flopped instead.

Flat on my back, unable to catch my breath, I wiggle like a goldfish out of water, gulping for air. Above me the three-quarter moon peeks through the dimming scarlet sky.

Bang, bang, bang. The bathroom door rattles.

"Open up, Ace." Cameron shouts from inside. "Open up now, before I kick down the door."

I need to get up and run, but all I can manage is to roll onto my side. My backpack is beside me in arm's reach. I catch hold of a strap and pull it to my chest, hugging it like a long-lost friend.

There's a loud crash. I imagine an unhinged door flying across the room. I gasp and air fills my lungs.

"Goddamnit, where are you?"

My brain doesn't register my actions, but somehow I'm on my feet and running toward the edge of the yard where the mountain drops off to a steep incline.

"Ace, wherever you are, I'm coming for you." Cameron's head pops into the bathroom window. I drop down onto my butt on the grassy overhang and push myself over the edge into the unknown.

## Chapter 24
## John Spears and Ace McAllister

I've ridden around for hours, checking every campsite in the area, some remote and some not so, but still no sign of Ace or Cameron. My hope dims along with the sun as it disappears into the horizon. They could be in New Jersey by now, and somehow the bastard has managed to make it look like I'm responsible for their disappearance. I should have gone to the police the moment he threatened me. I thought he was a jerk. I didn't think he was a real psychopath. What the hell do I do now?

My phone rings. I retrieve it from the seat next to me, hoping it's Ace calling to tell me everything is a mistake that she's not missing, and she didn't ditch me at the river on purpose. Hell, I'll even accept it if she never wants to see me again if it means she's safe.

Instead of Ace, Simon's name flashes on the screen. My chest tightens.

"What's up?" I ask, trying not to sound totally bummed.

"John, you need to get to the Crows' cabin, fast. Their camper is gone and no one answers the door. At first we thought they may have gone to visit their daughter, but the back door's wide open. I'm going to call the cops."

"What if it's nothing? I promised Officer Stomper

I'd lay low. I'm only a few minutes away. Don't do anything until I get there." I step on the gas.

"Wait," he says. "I don't think…"

The phone cuts off. Another dead air spot. Doesn't matter. We can talk when I get there. Besides, if Cameron has Ace holed up in the cabin against her will, I want the first crack at him.

When I pull onto the drive, Simon, Jack, and Chloe jump out of the Cavalier, waving like flagmen. I cut the engine and bolt to the backyard, motioning for them to follow.

I shout through the open door. "Anyone there?"

No one answers, so we step through the entryway one at a time, and tiptoe into the living area. Dirty dishes fill the kitchen sink and a chair is tipped over on the floor. Agnes Crow would never leave with her house in this condition.

I point at a closet in the entry way and nod at Simon to check it out. Then I move into the bedroom.

As soon as I enter, my heart sinks into my stomach.

The bed sheets are a tangled mess. Male clothing is tossed around on the floor. A pink polo shirt lies conspicuously in the corner. I stick my head into the living room. "Come in and check this out."

My friends hurry into the bedroom and skid to a halt in front of the bed.

Simon's eyes go wide. "What the…."

Jack shakes his head. "Aren't Mr. and Mrs. Crow too old to be doing kinky stuff like that?"

"No, stupid, Cameron has been here." I point to the pink polo in the corner. "No self-respecting Cherokee man would wear that."

Chloe swipes her phone and starts pecking. "That's

it. I'm calling the police."

"Don't," I insist. "They already think I'm responsible. If they find me here, they'll arrest me."

Jack throws his hands in the air. "But if we don't tell, we're all involved. Some of our records aren't squeaky clean like yours. Mine for example."

He's right. The last thing I want to do is get my friends tossed in jail. "Ya'll go. I'm going to stay here and wait until they come back."

Simon nudges me. "I'll wait with you, man."

"I can't let you do that. It's too risky. If anyone asks, you haven't seen me. Okay?"

"All right," he says. "But I'm a phone call away if you need any help."

"Thanks, brother."

The three of them scuff to the door. Chloe and Jack leave. Simon stops at the threshold and glances over his shoulder. "I don't feel right bailing on you."

"Go," I insist. "Call me if you see anything."

He nods, then disappears outside.

After my friends drive off, I hop in my truck and move it a mile up the road. By the time I jog back it's full dark.

I enter the cabin cautiously. It's still empty, so I clear out a space in the bedroom closet, shoving everything under the bed. Then I take a sleeping bag off the top shelf, and crawl inside and close the door behind me, leaving it open just enough to have a view of the doorway. Boy, will Cameron be surprised when he gets back. I only hope I can hold my temper, because if I can't, he's a dead man.

****

In purple darkness as I slide down the side of the

mountain. Foliage and briars tear my flesh, and rocks jab me places I didn't know existed. Dust flies up and hits me in the face, stinging my eyes. The mountain is steeper than it looked, and damn it, I can't stop myself. The world whooshes past at a dizzying speed. A large bush comes at me so fast I'm unable to change my path. I brace myself for the impact.

Wham!

One moment I'm nearly free falling and the next tangled in thorny branches pricking every inch of my flesh. My cheek hurts. I touch it, and the salt from my fingertips burn the wound. I grit my teeth and pull a sharp twig out of the palm of my other hand.

From where I crashed, it appears I've skidded at least a couple hundred feet.

After I untangle myself from the brush, I scoot on my butt, bracing my feet on rocks, clutching vines, anything to keep from spiraling downward.

Cicadas chirp around me. Something rustles in the foliage nearby. I stop for a moment and listen. Whatever it is stops, too. After a second of indecision, I move on. Nothing in the forest is as scary as what's waiting for me back at the cabin, so moving forward is a no brainer.

I don't know how much time passes, but my skin is clammy and the muscles in my arms and legs are burning by the time I reach the foot of the mountain. On the other side, the silhouette of the tree that marks John's mountain hails from above. The ground appears level, at least for a while.

John Spears.

I love him so much it hurts. Even if I never see him again, I can be happy knowing he's been a part of my life, if only for a short while.

I stumble upon a natural path that appears to lead to the other side of the valley.

"Ace! Where are you?" Cameron's voice is faint, yet still demanding.

I freeze and a shiver creeps up my spine.

"You need to come back. It's not safe to be alone in the forest at night."

There's movement in the not so far distance. A swear word here, a thump and a crack of a tree branch there. He must have discovered where I went over the edge, because it seems he's following the same path.

Without bothering to look behind me, I break into a run. I'll have to move quickly if I want to keep my lead. I sprint hard until my lungs burn and I'm forced to slow down. Why did I have to quit the long distance running team after my freshman year?

As I near the other side of the valley, the path becomes less defined. I walk briskly, ignoring slaps from low branches and thorns from the briars.

Then thwack! Ow.

I'm on the ground, spitting dirt from my mouth. I flex my wrist a few times. Luckily, it only hurts for a moment. I untangle my foot from the vine that tackled me, get up, and brush myself off. With no time to spare, I hobble forward as fast as I dare.

When I reach the river, I stop to regroup. The water is swift, but it doesn't appear deep. And, it's all that's separating me from the foot of John's mountain.

John Spears.

I cautiously place one foot on a large flat stone. The water rushes over my sneaker, wetting my foot.

"Stop running. I won't hurt you." Cameron calls.

"I'll take you home."

I whip around. Above the tree line, in the bluish light of the moon, a figure lurks in a clearing of the mountain I left behind. I'm haunted by mental images of me on the hard ground, him on top of me as I claw at his eyes. An involuntary wail escapes from my lips.

Cameron moves behind a thicket of trees, and I jump to the next rock. It's slippery, but I keep my balance as I make my way across one rock at a time. By the time I near the shore on the other side, my jeans are wet to the thighs. I test the surface of the last rock for traction with the tip of my sneaker and slip on slimy mold, losing my balance. My foot plunges into the water and sinks into deep mud. I brace my hands on my other knee and force myself upward until I'm able to pull my foot free. Then I leap onto the shore.

A few quick steps later, I realize I've lost my shoe. It's must have stuck in the mud. I jerk around, wholly intent on retrieving it, but the water is dark and the mud is deep.

So instead, I shift my focus to the tree that juts out at an angle, I take a step.

Then another.

And another.

Moving faster.

And faster.

And faster, yet.

John Spears.

Nothing can stop me. Not now. Not ever.

Time passes. Time slows.

I'm tired. Don't stop. Keep moving.

Something stabs the heel of my bare foot. Pain shoots up my calf all the way to my hip, and I crumple to the ground. A root shaped like the head of a spear is sticking up, and stupid me managed to stomp on it. Blood seeps down the sole of my foot and between my toes. I wiggle my backpack off my shoulders and pull off my T-shirt, then tie it around the puncture wound.

Taking the time to stop and treat my injury comes with a cost. The sheer adrenaline that had been driving me forward seems to have disappeared. Flesh bumps sting my skin, and I shiver so violently my clacking teeth are hurting my jaw. The night air already felt cold, and now that I'm shirtless, the chill is unbearable.

I rifle through my backpack. Rolled very neatly is the sweatshirt John gave me the day we went to Sliding Rock. It could have gotten me in big trouble with my mom, but I kept it anyway. I pull it over my head.

John Spears.

It smells of his cologne and my belly flutters, the way it does when he is near.

Quickly, I gather my scattered belongings and rise to my feet. Heart pounding, I move forward with as much speed as I can muster on the ball of my foot. With Cameron so close behind, choosing a less trodden path would be better, but my foot hurts too much to even consider that. Instead I follow a ribbon of a trail which was made perhaps by animals—what kind I dare not contemplate. Maybe, if I'm lucky, it holds the scent of man from occasional hikers.

Deep in the silence of the night, with only my footsteps to accompany me, I trek upward. The forest thickens, forming a canopy over my head. My legs are weak and my pace is slow. Shadowed in darkness, I can't determine how much farther I have to go. Luckily, I find a large stick that serves well as a cane.

My determination pays off, and soon I'm out of the thick of the forest and bathed in moonlight. The tree that mark's John's mountain is in clear view. I move faster, and finally reach the area where the mountain plateaus.

Minutes, maybe hours later, I round a bend, and John's *asi* is before me. Tears stream down my cheeks, washing dirt and salt into my mouth. My foot is throbbing and when I dare to look, I note my T-shirt bandage is no longer white, but stained red with blood. The pain from my heel pulses through my body and straight to my brain, leaving me to hobble to the little dome house.

Dawn can't be far away. Perhaps I can rest until morning.

But what if I can't walk? How will anyone find me? The tree that juts out like a fallen flagpole gives me an idea.

My leg buckles and I stumble and fall. On hands and knees, I crawl to the tree. I latch onto a vine wrapped around the trunk and pull myself up. My legs tremble as I teeter on tiptoe and wedge my good foot in the Y of the trunk. An overhead branch provides the support I need to swing my leg over the fallen limb. Hugging the trunk like a bear cub, I inch out to the end. All that lies below me is sky and rugged terrain. The wind whips my hair, and my head spins.

Anchoring myself with my knees, I wiggle out of John's sweatshirt, and tie it so it hangs like a flag. If he looks from afar, even if he doesn't know I'm here, surely he's got to wonder how something ended up tied to his tree.

Inch by inch, I back off the limb, and lower myself

to the ground. Then I crawl back to the *asi*. I grab John's bow and quiver, climb into one of the sleeping bags, and scoot back until I'm propped against the wall.

With the bow between my knees and an arrow laced on the string, I lean back and rest. A sharp pain shoots up my leg. I breathe deeply and evenly, willing the pins and needles to settle. My foot is hot, but even the throbbing can't keep my eyes from closing. What's the big deal if I close them for a moment? Nothing bad can happen in a moment…

## Chapter 25
John Spears and Ace McAllister

My phone vibrates. I stiffen and my head bangs the wall. The lack of fresh air reminds me I'm holed up in a closet. Gauging by the ache in the back of my skull, if there's anyone else in the cabin they'll know I'm hiding here, too.

My phone vibrates again. I take it from my pocket. A text from Simon flashes on the screen.

*Call me ASAP!*

Since scoping out the current situation is a little more important than returning texts, I rise to my knees and inch open the door. If Cameron is waiting for me, the element of surprise will probably work best. I take a deep breath and leap into the room.

It's empty.

I'm almost glad since I'd feel like a fool if anyone saw me crouched in this idiotic ninja pose. Still, I remain frozen and listen.

Not a sound.

This isn't good.

I creep from room to room, only to find the place empty.

Why the hell did I sleep so long? Ace is in danger and I'm busy sawing logs in a stupid closet. I'm a fool.

I head out into the backyard and phone Simon, while I take a whizz in the bushes that line the side yard.

Simon answers. "It's about time you called. You've got to get home. Now."

"What's going on?"

"Rae called. She's losing it. Officer Stomper came to your house last night looking for you. He's coming back this morning. Rae says she's going to kill you once she finds you. Where the hell are you anyway?"

"I'm about to leave the cabin. Ace and Cameron never came back."

"Oh, no. This is bad. Real bad. Word is Ace's parents are pushing to have you hauled in."

"Did you tell anyone where I am?"

"Hell, no, but if Stomper comes around here…I don't know, John. He won't believe I'm clueless. He knows how tight we are."

"If he shows, stall him for an hour or two until I figure out what to do, 'kay, Simon?"

"Okay, I'll make myself scarce. But only 'cause you're my brother-by-another-mother."

"Thanks, man," I say as I end the call.

I walk to the edge of the yard where the mountain falls off into the valley. The rising sun sheds new light on the situation. From the look of the freshly-broken twigs and scuffed ground, I'd guess someone or something must have gone that way. Miles of endless horizon span before me. Trying to find Ace in these mountains is like looking for a small piece of gold in a quarry filled with sandstone. It would probably be easier to get my mom to quit drinking.

Maybe I should go home and wait for Officer Stomper. I can show him what I found at the cabin. Then he might believe Ace is in real danger and not off on some sex-fest with Cameron.

But what if he thinks I did something to them? My prints are all over the place. I'm totally screwed either way so I might as well keep looking for her.

What was it Uncle George told me when he taught me to hunt? Rely on my instincts and pay attention to my environment. You can't track game by just looking at the obvious.

I pan the mountains, following the miles long dip into valley and up to the highest peak on the other side. I see nothing. I make the decision to follow the trail on the ground, when motion from the tree that marks my land catches my eye. Someone has tied a piece of cloth or something on the end of it. No one ever bothers our property. At least I don't think they do. But there's no mistaking. Something is flapping in the wind, waving at me, and it had to have been put there on purpose. Ace McAllister. Maybe?

I've got to check it out. How can I not? It's the first time today I feel like I stand a chance of finding my girl.

I race home, pushing Old Blue to the limit. I leave her, keys and all, in the front yard and jog out back to fetch Billy from the barn.

Rae tears out the back door, followed by Aunt June and Lenny.

"What the hell is going on, John?" she shouts, her arms pumping as she runs toward me.

Having a bossy twin like her is really getting to be a pain. I turn and hightail it into the barn.

The three of them stand in the doorway, their mouths hanging open as they watch me slip the harness over Billy's neck.

Aunt June huffs and props her hand on her hips. "Your grandmother is coming home tomorrow and we have police pounding on the door demanding to know where you are. You are going to send her straight back to the hospital in cardiac arrest."

I loop Billy's harness around a post and lay a reassuring hand on Aunt June's arm. "Don't say anything to Elisi. I'll be home in a few hours to straighten everything out. I promise."

Aunt June shakes her head. "Go on. Get yourself in trouble. You've always been too stubborn for your own good."

Lenny looks up at me from beneath the thick lashes that cover his dark brown eyes. "Can I come with you?"

I pick him up and hug him to my chest, then just as quickly, set him down and give him an affectionate spank. "Not this time. You need to stay home and take care of your mother."

Rae glares at me. "I want to talk to you alone."

I laugh. "Talk to me alone? Sounds like you stole that line from a black and white gangsta flick."

Rae frowns.

Aunt June, obviously tuned into the same channel as Rae, hustles Lenny into the house, leaving my sister and me to hash it out.

I grab my backpack and fill it with essentials. "Whatever you have to say, do it fast 'cause I've got to go."

"Rumors are swirling you've done something bad to Ace and her jerky friend. Have you gone stark raving mad?"

I don't know why I'd expect she'd hold back. She never has. "You believe the rumors are true?"

"Of course not, and I've told Stomper the same, but your behavior isn't helping to prove your innocence."

I unhook Billy and lead him out of the barn.

Rae follows and gives me a shove from behind. "Don't ignore me. Tell me what's going on."

"I would if I were sure myself. All I know is that I have to find Ace before something really bad happens." I hop onto Billy's back.

"Let me come with you."

No way I'll let Rae anywhere near Cameron. I'd hate myself if I put her in a situation where she might get hurt. Besides, I need to focus on Ace and only Ace. Like in a football game running the ball to the end zone, tunnel vision is the only way to score. Only this isn't a game. The stakes are much higher. The thought of losing Ace makes me feel like someone punched a hole in my chest and ripped out my heart.

Officer Stomper is wrong. She and Cameron haven't run off for a few days alone together. I'm not going to stop searching until I find her.

"Quit ignoring me." Rae's voice brings me back.

"You can help more by staying here. Someone has to look after Elisi. I'll be back to deal with the police later." I lead Billy toward the trail.

"She was my friend first," Rae calls behind me.

I ignore her and kick Billy into a trot.

"You're a stubborn jackass. You know that, don't you?" she shouts.

"Sticks and stones may break my bones, but look the hell who's talking," I say before disappearing under a clump of trees.

****

"Well, well, well. Thought you'd lose me, didn't

you, Ace?"

I jerk awake. Outside the *asi,* light from the rising sun comes at me like laser beams, hazing my view. Cameron looms in the doorway.

I open my mouth to scream, but nothing comes out.

He squats and peeks inside, prompting me to grip the bow and rise to my knees. With the arrow already in place, I draw back the string. My injured foot throbs and my leg shakes, but I push through the pain and tighten my stance to keep from toppling to the ground.

"Come on, Ace. What are you going to do? Kill me?"

He's not leaving me much of a choice. I draw back the bowstring a little further. I'm shaking so badly, hitting him even that this close range would be a miracle. "I'm warning you. Leave me alone."

"I love you Ace. All I've ever wanted was for you to love me back." His voice sounds like he's pleading, but his face is lifeless.

I grit my teeth while I drum up the courage to fire.

In the next instant, a cry rings out—a cry so guttural I'm not sure if it's human or animal. Cameron turns, and a flash of something flies from out of nowhere and knocks him out of the doorway. I sling the bow and quiver over my shoulder and scoot toward the light, dragging my injured foot behind me.

John Spears.

Outside, he and Cameron are rolling on the ground. Cameron raises his hand and a flicker of silver catches my eye.

"Watch out! He has a knife," I scream.

Cameron jabs the knife at John's side and catches the flesh of his forearm instead, leaving a gaping slice.

John grabs his wound and Cameron pushes him off and jumps to his feet.

John rolls away from him and scrambles to his feet. Blood runs like a slow river down his arm. The red drops coagulate in the dust, forming tiny blood pebbles.

He's really hurt and it's because of me. "Run, John. I'll be fine."

He ignores me. His glare never leaves Cameron. The two men circle each other like wrestlers going in for the kill.

Cameron sneers. "So you feel like dying today?"

John flashes his empty hands at Cameron. "I don't want anyone to die. I want to take Ace to the hospital. Can't you see she's hurt? Come on, man, put down the knife."

"Don't tell me what to do. I'm the one doing the talking. You're the one who's going to listen. Get it?" He steps toward John and swipes the blade at him.

John jumps backward out of range, hands up. "If you give up now, Ace and I won't press charges. You can move on with your life."

Cameron glances at me for a second, then snaps his attention back to John. With his eyes glued on John, he walks backward toward me, holds out his hand, and crooks his finger. "The bow, Ace."

If I do what he asks, I'll be defenseless.

John looks at me, his dark eyes unyielding. "Give it to him."

I use my good leg as a lever to rise to my knee and place the bow in Cameron's hand. He side-arms it toward the edge of the mountain. It falls short of the overhang, but lands far enough away that neither John nor I can get to it easily.

As much as I want to be brave, I can't hold my emotions in any longer. I burst out crying.

Cameron shoots a glance at me and turns back to John. "This is your fault. If it wasn't for you, Ace would be safe at home. She wouldn't be hurt."

"Maybe you're right. Kick my ass, but make it a fair fight. Put down the knife. Unless you're scared."

"Do what he says, Cameron." I say. "Only a coward would attack an unarmed man."

"You two think I'm stupid, don't you?"

John steps back and laughs. "Not stupid, but you sure are a pussy."

Cameron lunges and jabs the knife at John.

John leaps to the side and circles around until his back is toward me.

He purposely put himself between Cameron and me. His bravery makes me cry harder.

"You leave," Cameron says to John. "I'll bring Ace home."

"Sorry, man, but under the circumstances, no can do."

Cameron's face twists into a scowl and he advances, knife out in front of him. John grabs his wrist and the two fall into a struggle.

John lands a punch into Cameron's gut. Cameron staggers backward and buckles over. In a move too quick to register, John throws a kick and the knife flies out of Cameron's hand. Time slows as it flips end over end through the air and stabs the ground.

John lands another fist hard on Cameron's jaw.

Cameron spits a glob of blood from his mouth. His expression freezes and his eyes turn fiery.

If I can engage Cameron, maybe I can distract him.

I wail and grab the ankle of my injured foot.

He pivots toward me. “I don’t feel sorry for you, Ace. You deserve everything you got.”

“I don’t want your pity. I’m worried about you. You haven’t slept and you’ve hardly eaten anything since we left.”

“Don’t patronize me. It’s not going to work. You’re on his side. Not mine.”

“No, Cameron that’s not true.”

“Shut up. I’m sick of your lies,” he says between labored breaths.

He glares at John, then charges and grabs him around the waist.

The two slam onto the ground. Cameron reaches for the knife. Just as his fingertips meet the handle John rolls him onto his back.

I crawl to the knife and pull it from the ground. It’s a large fishing knife and the tip bears John’s blood to prove how dangerous it can be. I throw it as hard as I can and it disappears into a clump of trees.

John notices me, and his eyes go wide. “Stay back.”

Cameron lands a punch to his jaw, then scrambles to his feet and stumbles in the direction of the woods. He’s going for the knife.

John runs after him, and just as Cameron reaches the tree line, John dives for his feet. Cameron falls forward and bangs his head on a tree. He crumples to the ground in a limp mess.

John crouches over him and jostles his shoulder.

“Is he dead?” I ask.

“No. He’s breathing. We have to hurry before he comes to.” John runs and grabs his backpack. He takes out some rope and a hunting knife. He saws the rope, cutting two long pieces. Then he rolls Cameron onto his stomach and ties his hands behind his back.

Cameron stirs and starts writhing. “What the hell are you doing?”

John lifts him to his feet. “Nothing you don’t deserve.”

Blood seeps from a wound on Cameron’s forehead. He glares at me though the streaks of red. “You happy now?”

I don’t answer. If my foot wasn’t in such bad condition, I’d jump up and punch him in the nose and make him even bloodier.

John drags him to the *asi*. He pushes him inside. “I’ll be back in a minute. I need to tie his feet.”

At the rate my heart is pounding, it feels like hours, but it’s probably only a few minutes before John emerges from the hut.

His mouth is turned down and dark circles color the skin below his eyes. For a brief moment, we stare at each other. Then he kneels beside me, swoops me in his arms, and maneuvers me into his lap, cradling me like a baby. I rest my head on his chest, cherishing the thrum of his heart, while he kisses the top of my head over and over again.

“Are you just going to leave me here?” Cameron cries from inside the *asi.* “Wild animals will eat me.”

“Shut up,” John shouts. He lifts my chin. “Will you be okay alone for a minute?”

I nod and he eases me onto the ground, then goes to the *asi* and peers inside. “You’re lucky I don’t tie you to a tree and leave you for bear food.” He lifts the board and slides it in front of the entrance. “You’ll be fine until the police get here."

"It's dark," Cameron wails.

John shakes his head, then retrieves a flashlight from his bag and slips it inside.

Cameron hurls a string of insults at John, but John ignores him and kneels beside me. He removes his shirt. "Let me help you put this on."

Until now, I'd forgotten I was only wearing a bra. Despite all that's happened, my cheeks are on fire.

He helps me slip in one arm then the other. His shirt is warm and has a woodsy scent mingled with John's magical pheromones. "Thank you for taking care of me," I say, meaning it more than I've ever meant anything in my life.

He kisses my cheek, then gently examines my foot.

My leg is swollen below the knee and feels hot. "It really hurts."

"We need to get you to the hospital," he says. "Billy is a little ways down on the trail. I'm not leaving you here with Cameron." He hooks a thumb in the direction of the *asi*. "Can you walk?"

He holds me under the arms, and I try to stand.

A sharp pain takes my breath. "It hurts too bad. I'll be okay here."

"I can carry you. Put your arm around my shoulder."

"Okay, but be careful not to hurt your back."

John gives me a look, somewhere between a smile and concern, and hoists me into his arms with surprising ease. I melt against his bare chest and run my fingertips over the curves of his bicep. With every step he takes, my foot throbs a little harder. The pain is like something I never felt before. It's excruciating. But at this moment, I wouldn't trade places with anyone. No. Not today.

## Chapter 26
## John Spears and Ace McAllister

With each clop of Billy's hooves, Ace leans harder against my chest. I tighten my grasp around her middle. The mid-morning sun burns down on the earth and sweat rolls from my temples. Though a load of problems awaits us, I kiss the sky, the wind, and I'll kiss the ground the first chance I get to thank the universe for returning her to me.

She moans and bites down on her lower lip. I'd rather have my heart ripped from my chest than for her to be in pain, but the only thing I can control is how quickly I get her help.

I nudge Billy with my knees, upping his pace to a fast walk. Any more and I fear he will stumble on the rocky path and hurt Ace worse.

I take my phone from my rear pocket. Her mom wants me in jail, but Ace is the only person I'm worried about right now. "We need to call your parents. What's your mother's number?"

"I don't want to talk to her."

"She's worried. You have to."

Ace mumbles the number and I punch it out with my thumb of one hand, while cinching her tight with the other. When her mother answers, I pass the phone to Ace.

"Mom?" she says.

"Oh Ace!" Her mother screams so loud I can hear every word. "Where are you? Are you okay?"

"I'm fine. I'll be home soon." Ace's voice is weak, even though I can tell she's trying hard to be strong.

"Where are you? I'll come right away."

There's a momentary silence before something between a cry and a scream comes from the phone. "Why won't you answer me? Are you being held against your will?"

Ace tenses before she responds. "I'm with John. Everything is good."

"Is he making you say this? Tell me the truth, baby. Don't be afraid. Tell him the police are going to lock him up for a long time, and if he wants any mercy, he'd better let you go."

"You've got to calm down and listen. John's didn't do anything. Cameron kidnapped me."

"I don't believe you. That boy's brainwashed you. He's making you lie."

"Stop it now. You're screaming so loud he can hear every hateful word you say."

I rub Ace's arm to let her know it's okay.

"Make sure he knows he won't get away with this evil game if I have anything to do with it."

Ace ends the call and gives me my phone. "I hate her."

The veins in her neck are bulging and her eyes are glazed. She wiggles and kicks Billy in his side. He whinnies and side-steps. If I want to get Ace back safely, I have to calm her down. "Try to relax. Your mother loves you. She'll chill out once she sees you're all right."

"You don't know her." She buries her face in her

hands. “I’ve ruined your life. I’m so sorry.”

She’s burning with fever. No wonder she’s talking crazy. I look at her foot—the one wrapped in her blood-soaked T-shirt. The cloth is rust colored and crusted with dirt. Hardly sanitary. “We’ve got to get you back. Nothing will happen to me. I promise you.”

She doesn’t respond. Her chin droops to her chest and she closes her eyes. Her shallow breaths deepen. I don’t know if she’s sleeping or in shock. I’ve got to do something.

My hand shakes as I scroll through my recent calls. I find Officer Stomper’s number and press call.

At the hospital on the Rez, the medical techs unload the stretcher from the ambulance and wheel it toward the emergency room. I jump out of Old Blue. Ace calls my name in a voice so desperate it cuts me to the marrow. Officer Stomper barred me from the ambulance since I’m not family, but he can’t stop me from going to Ace now.

“I’m here,” I shout as I run to her.

The policeman with Officer Stomper holds out his arm and orders me to stay back. I’m reduced to following like a sickly calf straining to keep up while Ace continues crying my name.

As soon as we pass through the automatic doors, the hospital smell hits me. I’ve lived with it since Elisi was admitted but will never get used to it. I’ll be so glad when this place is only a bad memory.

Ace’s mom stands at the nurse’s station in the waiting room. She spins around and barrels across the room with a scowl so fierce it would frighten a cougar. I hold out my hands to stop her from crashing into me. She swings a closed fist and hits me in the chest. The smell of booze on her breath makes me gag. She takes a swipe at my face with her long red nails. I throw an arm up, blocking the attack right before she can gash my cheek.

She stumbles backward. I grab her to stop her fall.

"What have you done to my daughter?" She jerks free and wipes her arm like I've slimed her.

Ace strains against the straps holding her to the stretcher. "Mom, stop."

Her mom comes at me again. I duck to avoid the blow. Simultaneously, Officer Stomper leaps between us and takes the hit himself. He grabs her wrists and pins them together. "Calm down, or I'll arrest you for assault."

She points her chin at me. "Arrest that…that thug, not me. He hurt my daughter. If you don't do your job, I'm going to file a complaint and have you all prosecuted for shirking your duty."

The EMT whisks Ace through two swinging doors in the back.

A tall man with dark hair rushes through the automatic doors. He has the same blue eyes as Ace, and he looks so much like her he's got to be her father. An older woman, maybe Elisi's age, accompanies him. She's dressed in mom-jeans and a short-sleeved western shirt.

"Where's my daughter?" His voice carries throughout the waiting room.

Ace's mom writhes in Officer Stomper's arms. "Your daughter was nearly killed by that boy, and you're too busy running around with a whore to even care."

Officer Stomper frowns. "Please. Calm down. I

spoke with your daughter. John didn't hurt her. He rescued her."

"It's a lie. Can't you see she's brainwashed? Now let go of me, you idiot."

"Ma'am," Officer Stomper says, "I can't allow you in the hospital in your condition. You'll have to leave and come back when you've sobered up."

The older woman next to Ace's father throws up her arms. She glares at him. "Bradley, I've had enough. You need to grow up and face your responsibilities. Start by getting your wife under control. Either she goes to rehab or you don't get another dime from me. Do I make myself clear?"

Ace's dad turns Corvette red. "Not here, Mother."

The older woman points at him. "I mean what I say. Take care of her."

After a second of hesitation, he pries Ace's mom from the officer's grasp and holds her by the waist, pinning both her arms to her sides. A stream of foul language spews from her mouth and echoes off the stark, white hospital walls as he drags her from the building.

"Excuse me, sir," the older woman asks Officer Stomper. "I want to see my granddaughter."

"She's being treated for her injuries. I'll have the nurse take you to her."

"Hurry, please," the woman says.

"John," Officer Stomper says, "I have a few more questions to ask you. Do you mind waiting with Officer Douglas?"

The older lady cocks an eyebrow. "I know who you are. You hear me, young man?"

"Yes, ma'am." I don't know what she has in store

for me, but it can't be worse than anything I've already faced.

They disappear down the hallway, leaving me behind again. The registrar stares at me with a curious expression. I shrug, then I plop down in a hard waiting room chair next to Officer Douglas—and wait.

****

*One day later*

Pain creeps up my leg and pricks the tip of my spine. My eyes pop open, and I'm nearly blinded by an overhead florescent light. Where am I? And where is John? I scream for him.

Someone's hand clamps down on my arm. "Settle down, sweetie. You're all right."

My heart is a sledge and anvil, hammering between my ears, but it's not loud enough to drown out the familiar voice of the person speaking. "Grandma? What are you doing here? Am I dead?"

"No, honey, not unless I am, and I'd like to think I have a few good summers left."

I suck in a gulp of air and blink until my focus returns. The corners of Grandma's mouth tip up into a smile and crinkles form around her gray-blue eyes. She smooths her salt and pepper bob, even though, as usual, not a strand is out of place.

I latch onto the flesh of her arm to assure myself she's real and not an angel. The thin skin on her wrist twists on the bones beneath my fingers, and she winces. I loosen my grip.

It's really her.

Tears flood my cheeks, run past my ears, and soak the back of my neck.

"Go ahead and cry, dear. It's good for the soul."

Grandma brushes the wet tendrils of hair from my face and arranges the rest of my hair into an untied ponytail behind my head. Her light touch on my scalp sends flesh bumps shimmering across my skin, reminding me of times I'd awake from night terrors, and she'd be there to comfort me. Only this time the terror was more real than I care to remember.

"Grandma, I've been so scared."

"You've got nothing to fear. Cameron's in jail. He can't hurt you." She sits gingerly on the bed and pats my arm. "I flew in as soon as I heard you were missing."

"How long have I been here?"

"You were admitted yesterday afternoon. You've been sleeping for quite some time."

"Where's Mom and Dad? Where is Zack?" I struggle to sit.

Grandma eases me back down. "Zack is with a sitter provided by the hotel. I've met her and she's very nice, so don't go worrying about him. Your father and mother stepped out for a moment. They wanted to be here when you woke. I'll go find them."

"I'm not sure if I can handle my mother right now. Is she…"

"Sober? Yes. And she has something very important to tell you. I think you will be pleased."

I bite my lip. My mother has not said or done much to please me in quite some time.

"Don't look so worried. I wouldn't let her anywhere near you if I thought her news would upset you."

As soon as Grandma leaves, I'm hit with a strong urge to run. In my condition that would be next to impossible. Besides, I've been acting like a child, avoiding confronting both parents about their behavior for too long now. It's time we had a talk.

My mother appears into the doorway. Her hair is impeccable, but she's makeup-free, and her eyes are puffy and red. She looks as if she's been up all night crying. Dad's close behind, his usually boyish face creased with worry.

"Can we come in?" he asks.

I nod and they both rush to my bedside with their arms wide. I cross my arms on my chest and lean away. We fall into an awkward silence with them staring, mouths wide as if they've just seen a ghost. I've lived with these people for all of my life, but right here and right now it feels as if we're meeting for the first time.

"Ace, baby…" My mother pauses as if she's waiting for permission to speak.

I nod my approval.

"I'm so sorry. Had I known what a dangerous boy Cameron was, I'd have never brought him near you. If he's done something bad to you I will never forgive myself." She covers her mouth to stifle a sob.

If she's concerned I may have lost my virtue, she'll have to wait. I am not going there, especially with my father in the room.

Her face crumples with pain as if she takes my silence as a yes. I almost give in and tell her that no thanks to her, I'm intact, but there are more important subjects on my agenda. "Maybe if you didn't drink so much you would notice things like that. I love you, Mom, but I'm not going to take care of you anymore. You need help."

Mom sobs harder.

Dad rubs her back. “Ace, your mother and I made arrangements for her to check into the Life Recovery Clinic immediately. We’re going to get family therapy, too, and whatever else it takes to make your life and Zack’s better. I’m sorry it took almost losing you to get us there.”

Now Dad’s crying. Calling him out for his lying and his affair can wait. Mom’s a wreck, and I don’t want to hurt her. I’ll confront him when we’re alone or maybe when we’re in family counseling.

“What about Zack?” I ask Dad. “Will you be able to help me care for him?”

My dad shifts and clears his throat. “Actually, we’ve been speaking with a social worker. We’ve come up with an alternate plan. I’m busy with work, and you’re still in high school. Zack’s a big responsibility.”

Oh, no. Social services threatened to take Zack and me the last time Mom crashed and burned. I’m eighteen, but Zack…

I throw off my covers. “No way. I won’t let you get rid of him.” Both Mom and Dad hold me to the bed. “You can’t let them take Zack. I’ll care for him. I’ll drop out of school…”

Dad turns toward the door. “Mother, will you come in here, please?”

My grandmother hurries to my bedside. She elbows Dad. “I knew if I left you alone you’d make a mess of things.” She strokes my cheek. “No one is taking Zack. Your parents and I have reached an agreement. You kids will come live with Grandpa and me while they work on their problems. Grandpa’s already picked up your belongings. He’s at home getting your rooms ready as we speak.”

So much has changed since I entered the hospital—too much for only a day. My summer memories rush back—some of them are bad—but the ones that include John and Rae are the happiest of my life. I bolt upright and jerk my sore foot. I take a few labored breaths, while I wait for the pain to subside. “No! I can’t leave. Not now.”

Grandma’s brows knit together and the smile melts from her face. “I expected you to be a bit concerned with the arrangement but thought you might want to live with Grandpa and me.”

I’ve hurt her and that was not my intention. “No, I think living with you is a great idea when school starts. It’s just…I’m not ready to leave Cherokee. Not yet.”

Mom’s sorrow rapidly molds into anger. “It’s that boy from the reservation. You have to forget about him. Whether it’s now or later, you’re going to have to leave. There are plenty of boys at home. Ones you’ll have…well…much more in common with.”

“Don’t call him ‘that boy.’” I grind the words out between my teeth. “His name is John, and I’d appreciate you using his name from now on.”

Grandma turns to Mom. “Are you proud of yourself, Dawn? You’ve been in the room less than five minutes and you’ve already caused a stir. Why don’t you and Bradley say goodbye. If Ace is staying with me, it’s important she and I see eye to eye. I’ll keep you both informed of her decision.”

My parents take turns hugging me goodbye. While it feels somewhat superficial, I relent and hug them back. Even after all that’s happened, I still love them.

As soon as they’re gone, Grandma crosses her arms and says, “That young man you think is so special hasn't left the waiting room since you were admitted yesterday."

Young man? My heart does a backflip, then flutters like a butterfly who fell in a cup of espresso. "John's here?"

"Last I looked."

"Get him, please? I have to see him. I just have to." I throw the covers off and ignore the pain as I maneuver my legs over to the edge of my bed.

Grandma stops me. "If you don't hold that foot steady, it will start bleeding again."

I glance at my injured foot. The blue pad at the end of the bed has a rusty stain. My stomach churns and dizziness overcomes me. I fall back and plop my head into the pillow. I lie perfectly still until the world quits spinning.

Grandma gives me a sideways glance. "Honey, you're in love, aren't you?"

My face heats, and I tingle all over. I'm embarrassed, but it's far past time I stop acting like a child. I tell Grandma how I met John and Rae, and how good both of them have been to Zack and me. I tell her about John's plans for the future and how much he cares for his family. I even tell her how a kiss from him shimmers all the way from my lips to my toes.

Grandma nods. "He sounds like the real deal."

"Oh, he is. I love him so much it hurts. We have a few weeks until he goes to college, and I have to go back to school. I want to stay here until then. Please?"

"Well, the suite is rented, so I suppose we can stay for the rest of the summer. You've been through so much with those darn parents of yours. You deserve a real vacation. Your grandfather will survive alone for a few weeks."

"Thank you so much. You're, like, the best grandma ever."

"More like a sucker for my grandkids," she says flatly.

"Please, can you get John?"

Grandma stands. "I suppose it would be okay as long as you don't get all riled up."

"Oh, no. I won't move a muscle. I'll lie here like a stone."

Grandma shakes her head. She knows me too well.

As I watch her disappear into the hallway, it hits me. I'm about to see John, and I have a serious case of bed-head. I pull myself upright and straighten my greasy hair the best I can. Then I prop my pillow behind me, arrange my covers neatly over my lap, and wait, chest aching with anticipation, for the love of my life to walk through the door.

****

*Yikes. Here comes trouble.* I thought I was home free when Ace's parents waltzed past with just a wave and a handshake. But I'm not so sure any more. Her grandmother's awful stern-faced, and she's marching straight for me. Well, I've got news for her. No matter what she has to say, I'm not quitting on Ace.

I stand and wipe my hands on my pants.

Instead of laying into me like I expect, she says, "Hi, I'm Ann McAllister, Ace's grandmother."

I accept her outstretched hand. She's not very big, but her grip is as firm as any man's. "John Spears, ma'am."

She huffs. "I already know who you are and how you kiss, so let me get straight to the point. My granddaughter is fragile right now. She doesn't need any more heartache or boyfriend drama. Not only is she recovering from being kidnapped, she has family problems, of which I presume you are aware."

I nod, but don't speak. I'm too busy thinking of something diplomatic to say when she tells me to take a hike.

Ace's grandmother crosses her arms and taps her fingers on her elbow. "I want to know your intentions where my granddaughter is concerned. Be sure to look me in the eye, so I can tell if you're lying."

Geez, this woman reminds me of Elisi. Are all grandmothers this bossy?

*Concentrate, John, this is too important to screw up.*

I roll my shoulder to relieve a crick in my neck. "I don't see Ace as weak at all, ma'am. She escaped from Cameron all on her own, and trekked all night in the woods. She takes care of her brother as well as any mother would. She's the strongest, most amazing girl I've ever met. I love her, and I plan to hang around as long as she will have me."

There, I said it all and damn well if I do say so myself, but the shellac on Ace's grandma's face fails to crack. I brace myself for the fallout.

She cocks her head. "You know, I can sniff out a liar in a skinny minute."

Here it comes. "Ma'am, I—"

"Wait, let me finish. As I was saying, I have radar for liars and there are no blips going off here. My instinct tells me you're speaking the truth. And I can see why Ace is head over heels for you. You're polite and you respect your elders. You're certainly brave.

You're…" Grandma purses her lips as she sizes me up. "Let me put it this way, if you are half as good a person as you look, you're a keeper."

I choke back a laugh, while flames rise up the back of my neck and burn the tips of my ears. Practically tongue-tied now, I manage a simple, "Thank you."

"You're welcome, but you're still on probation," she says in a business-like manner. "Now, Ace asked that I bring you to see her. I expect that's okay with you?"

"It sure is." I exhale and the warmth of acceptance replaces the hollowness in my chest.

"Well, then, what are you waiting for?" She motions for me to follow. "Let's go."

Not wanting to jinx my good luck, I force myself to walk beside her even though my legs are aching to burst into a sprint.

As we near the room, Elisi's voice blares out the door and into the hallway. Oh, no, she's in there with Ace? Just when I thought everything was going to be okay. I try not to trample Ace's grandma on the way in.

Rae sits on a chair with her feet resting on the bed rails. Elisi is beside her in a wheel chair, dressed in her hospital gown, clutching magazines to her chest.

Ace's eyes capture mine, and they shine as she whispers, "John Spears."

Her soft, husky girl-voice causes the skin on my neck to buzz. I plant my feet firmly on the ground to keep from gathering her up in my arms and carrying her away.

Rae turns to face me, and Elisi spins her chair around at the same time. "Hi, John," they say in unison.

"What are you two doing here?" I demand. "Hasn't

Ace been through enough?"

"Chill, brother, we come in peace." Rae flashes a peace sign. Her eyes dart to Elisi and then back at me.

She's trying to signal everything is cool, but believing it is another thing. I gently jostle the handle of Elisi's wheelchair. "And you? Why are you out of bed?"

"The doctor said I was almost good as new. I'm going home tomorrow, and I'll be walking all over the place so you'd better get used to it."

Ace's grandma lets out a hearty laugh.

*Outnumbered by matriarchal mastery once again.*

They're not going to win. Not this time. "The doc may have told you to get up and move around, but I'm sure he didn't tell you to come bother Ace."

"John," Ace says, "it's all right. Really. We're having a nice visit. Grandma, this is John's grandmother, Mrs. Youngdeer, and his sister, Rae."

Elisi raises her chin. "Call me Pearl."

The three of them exchange greetings.

Am I on the same planet? I wrinkle my nose and stare hard at Elisi, questioning her with my eyes.

Elisi gestures a sarcastic "what" like I'm the one who's acting out of sorts. Then she peels the magazines away from her chest and lays them out on Ace's bed. The first one is a Native American journal with stories covering Cherokee culture, the second a gardening magazine, and third is a fashion magazine. "I thought you might like these," she says to Ace. "I'm done reading them, and I hate to waste paper."

Rae snatches the fashion mag and flips through the pages. "This looks brand new. You bought this especially for Ace, didn't you?"

Elisi frowns. “No, I didn’t. You think because I’m old I don’t care about the latest trends?”

Rae rolls her eyes. She knows as well as I the magazine is a peace offering, and Elisi is too hard set in her ways to admit it.

Ace must think the same because she offers a stupefied thank you, places her hand over her heart, and looks at me misty-eyed. She is overwhelmed, and I’m with her one-hundred percent. This sudden acceptance feels like a full belly after visiting an all-you-can-eat buffet. The kind where you stuff yourself to the point food comes out your eyeballs.

Ace’s grandmother doesn’t waste any time trading stories of ailments with Elisi. I ignore all the chatter going on around me and weave to the other side of the bed to be near Ace.

When I’m close enough, she takes my hand, and peeks up at me from under her golden lashes. Pleasure zig-zags through my body, and I swear the room glows brighter. Then it hits me hard. Ace is my sunshine. She erases the darkness from my life. How lucky am I to have a sun goddess for a girl friend?

Not caring who is looking, I sit on the edge of the bed and kiss her. Her sweet candy-cane tongue slips between my lips and meets mine. If I could hold onto this moment forever, it wouldn’t be long enough.

Someone clears their throat. As much as I hate to do it, I pull away. Rae, Elisi, and Ace’s grandma are staring at us. The silence is thick and hangs in the air like humidity after a hurricane. The room becomes incredibly small.

Ace’s cheeks are the color of pink lemonade. “Excuse me,” she says, “I’d like to talk to John for a moment."

"Oh, go right ahead, dear," Ace's grandma says. "Don't mind us."

"*Alone*, Grandma, I want to speak with him alone."

It's about time one of us was brave enough to tell the intruders to leave.

Her grandma's eyebrows scrunch together but then separate once as she processes Ace's request. "How silly of me, of course you do. Come on, girls. Coffee's on me." She grabs the handles of Elisi's wheel chair. Elisi plants her feet on the floor long enough to give me a "you'd-better-behave-yourself glare" before allowing herself to be pushed from the room.

Rae kisses Ace on the cheek. "I'm going home. It's John's turn for hospital duty. I'll see you when you get out of here." She pulls an envelope from her shoulder bag and hands it to me. "Here, this came today. It's from Mom. I thought twice about giving it to you today, but I heard messing with someone's mail is a federal offense."

My insides burn. What part of "I no longer want you in my life" does Mom not understand? "Toss it in the trash on your way out."

I try to pass the envelope back, but Rae shakes her head, not having any of it.

"Nope," she says, "that's something you'll have to do yourself."

I crumple the letter into a ball, but when I go to hurl it into a nearby trash can, but something stops me.

"You coming, Rae?" Elisi calls from the hallway.

"On my way." Rae winks at us. "Behave yourselves."

*Like Grandmother, like Granddaughter.*

As soon as she's gone, I fall into Ace's waiting arms and plant tiny kisses on her neck. Her skin smells mossy like the outdoors and her hair like the wind. Too bad life can't always be like this moment. Whenever I get too happy, life throws fireballs my way. The letter in my fist is a reminder of that.

"What's wrong?" Ace asks.

It's almost scary how well this girl can read my emotions. "Nothing important."

"You're worried about your mom, aren't you?"

I dip my head.

"It couldn't hurt to read the letter?"

"She's dumped on me so many times. I told everyone I was done with her. What will my family think if I let her make a fool out of me again?"

"John, you have a great family. They'll love you regardless, and I will too."

I slowly uncrumple the letter and break the seal. When I remove the single sheet of paper, a wrinkled twenty-dollar bill falls into my lap. Inside is a brief note. I read it aloud.

*Dear John,*

*Hope all's well at home. I'm in rehab trying to get my life together. I know I don't deserve your forgiveness, but if you can find it in your heart to try again, I want to make it up to you. The twenty dollars is a first payment for all the money you have loaned me. Please don't give up on me. I will be a mother to you again. I promise I won't disappoint you this time.*

*Love you always, Mommy.*

Ace smiles. "That's positive."

"Yeah, but we've gone down this highway so many times."

"What does your gut tell you?"

My gut tells me not to write her off just yet. "Would you think I was a fool to call her?"

"She's your mother, John, and she's reaching out to you. If you want to call her, it's allowed."

"I'll think about it." I stuff the letter into my back pocket.

She places her hand over mine. "Now, why do you still look so bothered?"

"I'm worried about us."

"Us? Why?"

"My heart is set on becoming a lawyer, but I may never be rich. I intend to return to Cherokee and offer my help—even if it means pro bono. I'll probably live on the Rez or at least nearby. It's nothing like the life you are used to."

Ace frowns. "Don't say another word. I was really enjoying being with you until now. Do you think I'm shallow?"

"No, I'm sorry. I just want you to have the best, and I'm afraid I'll never make enough money to give you what you deserve."

She sits up and adjusts her pillow. "Material things sure haven't done anything to make my life better. Your love is the only thing that can do that. Since I've been in Cherokee, I feel alive for the first time in my life. It's as if I belong here."

"Really?"

She nods, and we exchange ginormous smiles. I take her hands into mine and hold them to my heart, which is about to burst out of my chest in celebration.

"Oh," she says, her eyes wide. "There is one condition."

Oh, no, here it comes. That one thing. The one thing that breaks the deal. The one thing I won't be able to give her. The bow that puts an arrow through the center of my chest. "What is it?"

"I'd want to bring Zack with me."

I shake my head to make sure I heard her right. "What?"

"Zack. I'd want him to live with us."

I grin. "Why would you think that would be a problem? I wouldn't take you without him."

"You wouldn't, huh?" She bumps me with the side of her knee. "Then I suppose it's a deal." She pulls me close and kisses me once more, filling me with her everlasting sunshine.

## Chapter 27
## Ace McAllister

When I was released from the hospital, Grandma got me into therapy because I couldn't find the nerve to leave the hotel suite. I saw danger lurking in every corner. Needless to say, John's and my activities were reduced to watching TV and playing cards with Rae and Simon in the casino suite. Through it all, John Spears never complained.

After a few weeks of at-home therapy visits, I felt safe enough to venture out. At the therapist's suggestion, John and I attended a teen Al-Anon meeting in a nearby town. It was nice to talk with others like us who understand what it's like to live with an alcoholic parent. I think I'll keep going to meetings when I get home.

Today my therapist was thrilled when I told her John and I planned to go on a camping trip with Rae and Simon. She thinks it's a milestone in my recovery. She's still concerned about my nightmares and asked if I was getting enough sleep. I let her know I'm making it through most nights undisturbed, but that's not the truth. The nightmares haven't disappeared. Only now they're about having to leave Cherokee—and John.

I'm almost done packing my bags when Grandma enters my room and closes the door.

"Ace, I want you to enjoy your last night here, but

we need to talk."

The fact that I have only hours left with John is bearable only because I look forward to our trip. Grandma can't back out on her promise to let me go. Not now.

"I've got all my packing done. My friends will be here any minute. Please don't change your mind."

"Calm down, I'm not changing anything." She glances at a box she has in her hands.

Oh, no. Condoms. A really large box of condoms. I could die.

She waves them in front of my face. "I wouldn't feel right if I sent you off to spend the night with John without protection."

My cheeks are so hot they're tingling. I take the box from her hand and place it in the front pocket of my backpack where I've already stashed a condom, just in case. Grandma's right, I need to be prepared, but losing my virginity is not something I'm comfortable discussing with her. "I'll be sharing a tent with Rae, but thank you anyway."

"Oh good, so you haven't done anything—yet."

Again, I pray for the floor to open up and swallow me whole, but as usual it doesn't happen. "No, Grandma, we haven't."

"Okay, but I'm not so old I don't remember what it's like to have hormones clouding good judgment. You're old enough to make decisions for yourself, but as your grandmother, it's my job to make sure you do so wisely. Sexually transmitted diseases aside, it's a rough world out there for single mothers."

As embarrassing as this whole conversation is, it's cool she understands. I hug her, partly because I desperately want to change the subject and partly because I love her for not treating me like a child. "Thank you for letting me go. I promise I'll be careful."

Never one for outward affection, Grandma pats my back, albeit awkwardly, then steps out of my path. "Make sure you are home by noon tomorrow. I don't want to miss our flight."

Ugh…tomorrow. A small ache carves a divot in my chest and tears prick at the corners of my eyes. I breathe deeply until I'm able to erase thoughts of saying goodbye to Cherokee and everyone I love here.

Someone knocks on the front door. Zack's footsteps pitter-pat down the hallway.

Grandma slings open the bedroom door and rushes to catch him. "Wait a moment, son. Remember you have to look through the peephole first."

Zack stands on his toes and cups his hands around the tiny hole. "It's John and Rae and Simon."

Knowing John is seconds away makes my insides warm. I straighten my shirt and smooth my hair.

Zack throws the door open so hard it bounces off the bumper on the wall. He drags John inside.

Rae and Simon follow. Grandma moves behind me and rests her hands on my shoulders. "Take care of my girl. She's special."

I sigh. "Please stop. You're embarrassing me."

John takes my hand and pulls me into his arms. "What's wrong with everyone thinking you're awesome?"

Being the center of attention is not my thing, and *everyone* is smiling at me with twinkly eyes. I wiggle free. "I'll be right back." With my head down, I hurry to the bedroom to retrieve my backpack.

"She can never take any praise," Grandma says, loud.

"I heard that," I say as I return.

Zack's shoulders slump. "You're leaving without me again."

"Zack," I say. "We are going to be sleeping outside on the ground and eating fish cooked over the fire. There's no place to take a shower."

"Ew." He wrinkles his nose.

"I didn't think you'd like it."

John covers his mouth to hide a smile, then collects himself and turns to Zack. "I promise, next time you come to Cherokee, I'll take you white water rafting again. You liked that, didn't you?"

"Yes. But just you and me. Ace has to stay home."

"If it's okay with Ace," John says a bit too eagerly, even if it is to appease Zack.

I cut my eyes at the two of them. "I suppose."

"Well," Grandma says, "*I* suppose you all should be on your way."

"Come on, guys," I say, "she's trying to get rid of us."

"You bet I am," Grandma says as she herds us to the door. "I've got a ton of packing to get done before tomorrow."

When we reach John and Rae's house, Billy is bridled and waiting. We load our supplies onto his back and hike the trail. The sunlight peeks through the treetops, baking the already oppressive air. John removes his shirt and stuffs it in his back pocket. His muscles flex and release in rhythmic patterns beneath his summer-brown skin as he leads Billy into the mountains. Who knew I'd become a muscle junky? I can't help myself. I'm transfixed. My boyfriend is so gorgeous; one thousand summers wouldn't be enough to make me take my eyes off him.

We hike for over an hour before the trail opens up into John and Rae's family land and a full blue-sky day.

The late summer sun's amber rays bear down strong, and the land blossoms green with life. Happiness bubbles inside me until I swear I'll take flight. Though it's not in my birthright, I long to be a small part of Cherokee and its people. Will I ever be so lucky?

John and Simon unload the supplies while Rae and I gather firewood. Though the weather is close to blistering now, come nightfall the temperature will drop. By the time we return with our arms full of broken limbs, John is driving the last stake for the tent into the ground. He raises his sunglasses and smiles so sexy, I drop the firewood where I'm standing and run to him.

He catches me and presses his lips to mine. They are soft and taste salty and a bit gritty, but none of that matters. He could woof down an entire bottle of castor oil and I'd still drink him in.

Rae thumps her knee against John's back. "Get a room."

With his lips still locked to mine, he pushes her to the side. An eternity later he gently takes my lower lip hostage between his teeth for a nanosecond before breaking away. He gazes into my eyes through hooded lids and brushes the skin above my mouth with his thumb. "You have dirt on your face."

I wipe my mouth with the back of my hand and note mud streaks. All around John's mouth is the same.

"Omigod, my face was dirty. I'm so sorry."

John's mouth curves into a lopsided grin. "That's okay. I still love you."

Simon and Rae lean against each other and giggle. I try to use my finger to wipe the dirt from his mouth, but it smears. The two of them roar.

He stands and removes his shirt from his pocket to clean his face.

"Better?" he asks me.

"Yes." I press my lips together to stifle a laugh.

He wipes my mouth with his shirt before tossing it into the tent. Then he rises and playfully slaps Simon's stomach with the back of his hand.

"Oof," Simon croaks.

John squeezes Rae's cheeks between his pincher fingers. "Now that you've had your fun, we better get to the river if we're going to catch any trout for dinner."

Rae struts over to a log near the fire pit and sits. John marches up behind her and lifts her to her feet. "What do you think you're doing? This is an equal rights camping trip. If you want to eat, you fish."

"Okay, brother, I'll bite." She twists her lips and rubs her chin. "We'll have a fishing contest. Girls against guys. Loser gets canteen duty."

"Cooking and cleaning up everything? Even the fish?" I ask.

"Yep." She nods.

Is she crazy? We'll be working all night. I start to say something, but she shushes me.

"Sucker's bet." John high-fives Simon. "You got a deal."

Rae and John shake on it.

"Well, what are we waiting for, John?" Simon

says, “Let’s go kick some butt.”

I shake my head. Looks like Rae and I will be busy tonight.

When we return, no thanks to me, the guys get busy cleaning the fish. Rae must be some sort of fish charmer because she managed to catch double the rest of us. I’ve never been so relieved. While I’m embracing the great outdoors, cleaning fish is a task I’m more than happy to put off learning until later.

I use our moment of leisure to pull Rae to the side. “I’ve been thinking, if it’s okay with you, I’d like to spend the night with John tonight. But if you don’t want to sleep with Simon, I…”

“Don’t say another word. I’m with you, girl. I was thinking of asking you the same thing. It’s about time John finds out about me and Simon anyway.”

Rae and I pinky-shake. I’ve never had a close friend like her. Until I came to Cherokee, my life was filled with people my mother decided were appropriate, and like a dummy I went along with it. Whole lot of good that did me.

I’m near giddy, but once it sinks in what we’ve agreed to, my mouth goes dry. “Rae, have you ever done it before?”

“I usually don’t kiss and tell, but since I can practically see your knees knocking, I’ll talk. The answer is yes.”

“What do I do? Is it hard?”

“Let me put it this way. Once you get there, you’ll figure it out. It sort of comes naturally. I can’t imagine why you want to do it with my brother,” she winks, “but I know he loves you so you’ll be fine.”

I let out a long breath I didn’t realize I’d been

holding. "I'm going to miss you so much when I leave."

"I know, I feel the same, but I'm not going anywhere. I'll be here in Cherokee. You can visit anytime you like. Until then, we'll burn up the internet on FaceTime."

It's near twilight by the time we finish our meal. Pink mist frames the mountaintops and the stars twinkle in the violet sky. As promised by the spirit of nature, a chill takes over the air.

John sits on a log by the fire, prodding the embers with a stick. I snuggle between his legs, and he wraps his arms around me, encircling me with his love. Poor Rae and Simon are nearly a foot apart. I couldn't imagine being so close to John and not touching him.

Simon side-eyes Rae, tosses a stick into the fire, and yawns. "I'm getting tired."

Rae stretches. "Yeah, me too."

John frowns. "It's early."

Simon stands. "We've been busting our butts all day, man. I'm beat."

If looks could kill, the one John gives Simon would send him six feet under in a skinny minute. "I guess the girls can have the *asi*." John kisses the top of my head. "You're not ready for bed yet, are you?"

"Actually, I am."

John's arms drop to his side. "I was hoping we could spend a little more time together."

If I let this go on much longer, he'll totally bum out. I take his hand and kiss his knuckles. "I want us to go together."

He looks puzzled, so I spell it out. "I want to sleep in the tent with you tonight. Just you and me."

John's eyes widen, and he manages a loopy smile.

"If we take the tent, where will Simon sleep?"

Simon offers Rae a hand and pulls her to her feet. He drapes his arm over her shoulder, and she circles her arm around his lower back.

John jumps to his feet. "You've got to be kidding. That's my sister."

Simon's expression flattens. "What's that supposed to mean? Do you think I'm not good enough for her?"

John smooths his hair. "You're like our brother. How can you even look at her that way?"

Rae's eyes narrow. "What way, John?"

The last thing I wanted to do was start trouble. "Please don't fight. Rae and I can sleep in the *asi*."

"No, Ace," Rae says. "Just because he's the male twin doesn't mean he's my keeper."

John lifts his hands, palms up. "So my best friend snags my sister behind my back, and I'm supposed to be okay with it?"

"Yes." Rae says. "If you'd been paying attention, you'd have noticed earlier. Besides, you love Simon. Why can't you be happy for us?"

He glares at Simon.

Simon squeezes Rae tighter. "Listen, I know I've been a bit of a player in the past, but I'm not playing around this time. Rae's the real deal. We have high voltage love. I'd never do nothing to hurt her."

"So you two thought it was okay to lie to me. The two people I thought I could trust."

"Man." Simon shakes his head. "We haven't done nothing to you. I knew you'd act this way, that's why I didn't tell you earlier."

John scowls. "How did you expect me to act?"

"You know what, man? I think you're jealous."

"You're crazy. She's my sister."

"You're jealous because I like her more than you."

John rubs his forehead with the heel of his hand and he kicks the ground. A dust cloud covers the toe of his boot. "Damn it, as much as I don't want to admit it, you're right. I am jealous, and I'm acting just like Elisi. It's just…when we were kids and I wanted you two to like each other, all you did was fight."

Simon takes Rae by the shoulders and holds her in front of him as if she's on display. "That was then. Look at her now, bro. She's hot."

Rae looks over her shoulder and gazes dreamy-eyed at Simon.

John lets out a one-syllable laugh without humor. "I never figured you'd look at my sister that way."

"Remember I'm your brother, but a brother-from-another-mother, and come to think of it, father too."

"Okay, okay." John slaps Simon on the back. "I suppose you won't make such a bad brother-in-law."

Simon chokes. "Slow down, we're not planning any wedding yet."

Rae laughs. "Tell you what, John. Let us make it up to you. Since you and Ace are on borrowed time, I'll forget our bet. Simon and I will finish cleaning up and we'll take care of Billy."

"Now that's an offer I can't refuse." John helps me to my feet. "Thanks, Rae."

I snag my backpack off the ground.

"'Night, kids," Rae calls to our back. "Don't do anything I wouldn't."

John tenses for a moment, then shakes his head before taking my hand.

As we head to the tent, my heart thunders in my

chest and my scalp pings with electric energy. I hesitate. Then for a reason that can only be attributed to nerves, I open the front pocket of my backpack and hold open the flap so he can peek inside.

His eyes go wide. "Wow, that's a huge box of condoms. I don't think I could use all of them in one night if I wanted to."

My jaw drops. Fire burns beneath my sunburned cheeks. I glance over at Rae and Simon who are tending to Billy across the way. "Shh! They'll hear you."

He presses his lips together, but in the next instant he bursts out laughing.

Simon looks up, "What so funny?"

John opens his mouth to speak.

I point at him. "Don't you dare."

He shrugs at Simon and Rae who are both smiling at us now.

"Ha, ha, very funny. Maybe I should find some other guy who's not intimidated by a few condoms."

"Oh, Ace, don't do that. I'd have to kill him and then you'd have to wait until I served my sentence."

"Hmm…Well, I'm not into sharing you either. So unless you willing to live a life of crime…"

He ticks my chin with his knuckle and thumb. "You are the only girl I want."

His gaze is so steamy, I dip my head, unable to look at him. "Really?"

"Really," he says. "But I'll love you no matter what, so you don't have to do anything if you're not ready."

"I want to. Don't you?"

He brushes a strand of hair behind my ear. "Of course I do. I've spent days fantasizing about us making love. But I must admit I'm a little scared."

"Scared? Haven't you done this before?"

"Not with you. What if you change your mind about me and we don't end up together? What if you don't like it? You'll be giving up your first time, and you can never get it back."

"Sucks to be you, huh." I giggle.

"Go ahead and laugh, I deserve it. But seriously, I love you so much I could never stand to be your regret."

I lace my hands around his neck and pull him to me until we are cheek to cheek. "I've been dreaming about this moment since I met you, and it's almost exactly as I'd envisioned—in a place where sun-showers rain pure magic. Whatever happens in the future doesn't matter. I want to be with you now, and I've never been so sure of anything in my life."

He cups his hand behind my head and kisses me. His wet warm tongue circles my lips and I open my mouth, inviting him in. He groans into my mouth, blasting me into orbit. As our kiss deepens, we float weightless among the stars. Family problems cease to exist as does war, because there is no room for war in our world. Our love consumes every molecule of this vast universe and it's a fantastic, humbling, incredible, eternal, and sacred place to be.

Our kiss continues until there's no place here left for our love to go and I'm forced to pull away. His smoldering eyes capture mine. He doesn't speak, but he doesn't have to because I read forever in his eyes. I flashback to our first kiss. The one that wasn't supposed to mean anything. Even then, I knew we had it all wrong. It meant everything.

Without a single regret, I lift the flap to the tent, then take his hand and lead him into our future.

## Chapter 28
## John Spears

Ace, her grandmother, and Zack exit the hotel with me behind them, luggage cart in tow. The limo driver pulls up in front and gets out to load their stuff. I help him—anything to distract myself from the thought of saying goodbye. I was raised to be strong, but it's hard when I'm dying inside.

When the bags are loaded, I wander back to the curb to stand by Ace. The rims of her eyes are red and she smiles at me with quivery lips. I wrap my arm around her and pull her close into my side. The need to protect her from this pain is strong, but minutes from now, I'll no longer have that option.

Ace's grandma checks her watch. "Okay, kids, it's time to get going. Zack, say goodbye, please?"

Zack tiptoes to me. His eyes are watery and he's biting his lip.

"Move, Ace," he demands.

Ace shoots him a look, but steps aside anyway.

Zack throws his arms around me but lets go before I have a chance to hug him back.

"Bye," he blurts, then jumps in the car and slides to the far end of the seat.

I rest my forearm on the roof and lean down into the cab. "We'll see each other soon. Okay?"

He turns his head away and rests his forehead on

the window glass. I think he's crying, but I don't push because I completely get how he's feeling right now.

When I turn around, Ace's grandma swallows me in a boney hug. "It's been a pleasure getting to know you, son. You'll have to come visit."

"Thank you. I'd like that."

She glances at her watch again. "Okay. You two hurry up."

When I reach for Ace, her face is blotchy and she's crying. I hug her to my chest, and suck in a deep breath to keep from crying, too.

I stroke the back of her head. "*Ugeyudi.*"

"Ooh-gay-di?" she repeats in her husky girl voice.

"It means you're lovely."

"*Wado,* you too," she returns.

My brain glitches, and I pause a moment. "You just thanked me in Tsalagi."

"Does it bother you? I mean…since I'm not Cherokee."

"Bother me? It makes me love you more, if that's possible. How am I going to survive the next year without you?"

"Next summer is almost ten months away. I'm really going to miss you. I'll miss us."

"I will too. Always remember I love you."

She looks up at me with watery eyes. "We're going to make it, aren't we, John?"

"Of course we are." I reach in my pocket and pull a small box with a beaded turquoise necklace I got from the best jeweler on the Rez. "It's for you."

Ace takes the box from my hand and opens the lid. A smile spreads across her face. "I love it, especially the bear pendant."

"It's the Star Bear. I've finally embraced him thanks to you."

She looks at me questioningly.

"How can I be scared of him when you made the night by the river one of my favorite memories?"

She covers her eyes and sobs.

"The necklace was supposed to make you happy."

"It does." She sniffles. "Help me put it on."

I hook the clasp behind her neck and kiss her lips.

Ace's grandmother knocks on the glass and the tinted window glides down. "I'm sorry, Ace, but we've got to go. The driver says we're cutting it too close."

Ace throws her arms around me and squeezes.

Pain as hot as lava boils in the pit of my stomach. Now I know why we have no word for goodbye in the Tsalagi language. It hurts too much.

"*Stiyu,*" I say. "Stay strong."

"*Stiyu,* John. I promise I will."

Without another word she lets go of me and hops in the limo.

Why does this have to happen when I've finally found love? There has to be another ending to our fairy tale. I imagine it's the old days when eighteen wasn't too young to take a wife. Ace is standing in an open field, and I'm in the distance riding Billy. I gallop toward her and swoop her up behind me. She wraps her arms around my middle, squeezing until our bodies are spooned together. We ride bareback into the hills to the house of wood, vines, and plaster I built myself. We live off the land, just the two of us, and we're happy.

But it's not the old days, and the world has changed. I have no way to provide for her, not yet, and this girl deserves the best. My best.

I have to let her go.

The large black car pulls off, and I watch it drive from view. She's gone. Ace is gone.

My heart rips in two.

By the time I reach the house, my brain is mush and all the muscles in my body have turned to ice. Everything is friggin' numb.

The need to feel alive, to feel something, is the only thing that makes me get out of the truck. When my feet hit the earth, I head straight for Elisi's garden. In the center is a plant I will stop at nothing to get to.

I step over beans, tomatoes, and everything else in my way until I reach the rosemary. I break off a sprig and run it under my nose and inhale. My heart stutters. Images of Ace appear in my mind, images so vivid I feel her in my arms and envision her soft pink lips tipping up into a smile. Despite the huge hurdles we face ahead, no matter how terrible I feel, I'd never take back a minute of the time I spent with her. She has half of my heart and always will.

"John," Elisi calls, "are you eating vegetables without washing them?"

"No, ma'am," I say.

She steps out of the house and into the yard. "Then what are you doing out there?"

"Nothing." Nothing she'd be interested in at least. I twirl the sprig of rosemary between my fingers.

"Ace is gone, isn't she?"

Can't fool her for a minute. I nod and walk toward her.

"Everything will be fine. The world will continue to spin. I promise."

"How can you say that? She's is the most

important person in the world to me. Why does everything in my life have to be so hard?"

"It doesn't. Give up your fight. Forget about college and stay here and work construction or at the forest station with your Uncle George. Meet a Cherokee girl, get married, and raise a family."

"Elisi, you know that's not the plan."

"Ah…so your fighting spirit still exists even though Ace isn't standing by your side? The world *is* still spinning."

"I thought you didn't want me to go away to college."

"I had a lot of time to think when I was laying in that damn hospital bed. I didn't raise you to be a quitter, and I don't want you to give up your dreams. Go to Duke with my blessing, then law school. Pursue Ace if that's what you want. It's not easy to walk in two worlds, mind you, but those who are strong enough can enjoy the best from both. If anyone has the power to do it, it's you, and no one, especially me, should stand in your way."

My eyes prick and I swallow hard.

She crooks a finger, summoning me closer. "Don't look so sad. Ace isn't gone forever. As much as I hate to admit it, I sense that girl is strong enough to walk beside you."

Her words mean more to me than any she's ever spoken. I can't stop a tear from leaking from the corner of my eye. "Elisi, I want to thank you for everything you've given me. You've always been my rock. I love you, old lady, and no matter where I am, if you ever need anything, all you have to do is call."

She purses her lips. I expect she will become

weepy-eyed, too. But then the familiar scowl returns to her face. “And you’d better answer your phone by the third ring because the first time I can’t get through, I’m going to march right up to that fancy-pants school and drag you home.”

I laugh. “Okay, by the third ring. You have my promise.”

She nods and wipes the tear from my cheek with her apron. “Are you hungry?”

My stomach feels a bit knotty, but I need nourishment. I’m still a growing boy. “I think I could eat a little bit.”

“Let’s go. I’ve got *kanuchi* warming on the stove.”

I slip the rosemary in my shirt pocket next to my heart and offer Elisi my arm. She locks on and the two of us walk into the house together.

## Epilogue
## Ace McAllister

I stand in front of the mirror, applying totally too much makeup to attend an event I outgrew a year ago, but I'm going anyway. Grandma says the senior prom is a rite of passage, and I'll regret it years later if I skip out on it. So here I am, relying on her wisdom once again, and praying I won't fall flat on my face in my two-inch, silver, high-heeled sandals that aren't good for anything except making my butt look perky.

Draped over the corner of the mirror is the headpiece I made earlier in the day. I use bobby pins to anchor the band of orange, yellow, white, and turquoise flowers into my hair. The girl in the mirror isn't half bad. She's even pretty in sort of a bohemian way. More importantly, she appears happy. She is happy because she has come to the conclusion she no longer has to fix everything; she has choices and deserves to have fun. The girl in the mirror…damn it…has a massive pimple popping out on her chin.

*I suppose that's what I get for referring to myself in the third person.*

I lean forward to assess the damage to my face. It could be worse. Nothing a tube of cover-up won't fix. I apply the heavy base and blend away until most of the redness is gone, then I get my white lace prom dress from the closet.

I found the dress when I went shopping with my new friend Sarah. Spaghetti straps, a v-neck open to the breast bone, and daringly short-in-the-front skirt that flows to floor-length in the back is not something I'd have typically chosen, but Sarah thought it looked awesome on me. From the reflection looking back at me, I'd have to agree. As a personal touch, I stitched a turquoise and silver beaded pattern around the waist—similar to one I saw in Rae's store.

It seems like a lifetime has passed since my Cherokee summer. Cameron is in a psychiatric hospital, hopefully getting the help he needs. Thankfully, I'll be long gone before he gets out. Mom's out of rehab. She's cranky, but sober. She and Dad seem to be headed for divorce, but I keep out of it. I can't help them; that's something they have to figure out for themselves.

Thanks to Grandma and Grandpa, Zack and I have a stable home for as long as we need. Since Zack is finally being cared for properly, I'm going to college. Best of all, I have gobs of fantastic memories from last summer to keep the warm, fuzzy feeling going.

However, tonight is not a night to reflect on the past, or the future or even what will happen tomorrow morning. Tonight I'll experience another first, and first experiences have been my forte this year. Tonight I'll charge forward into the unknown once again without fear or regrets—well, maybe the high heels.

The doorbell chimes a pretentious Big-Ben-like bong, bong, bong, bong—bong, bong, bong, bong when a simple ding-dong would be much nicer. I really have to talk to Grandma about that.

I clasp my stomach, take a deep breath, and head

for the bedroom door. Then I remember something I've forgotten. The turquoise necklace John gave me is still on the dresser. I retrieve it and clasp it behind my neck. I run my fingers along the blue beads and the image of his face appears in my mind—though slightly clouded. I squeeze my eyes to conjure up the missing details.

"Ace," Grandpa calls, "your date is here."

My date? Geez, does he have to be so old fashioned?

The wall serves as a crutch as I wobble my way to the staircase. I should have listened to Grandma and practiced in these new shoes before tonight.

When I reach the end of the hall, I stop, take a deep breath, and round the corner. At the foot of the grand staircase, on the black and white marble tile, stand Grandma and Grandpa staring at me with silly smiles on their faces.

Oh, no. I think my hard-as-nails Grandma just wiped a tear from her eye. This situation couldn't be more awkward if I had a bowl of fruit on my head.

Conspicuously missing, is "my date." "Didn't I hear the doorbell?"

"Oh yes. I almost forgot. He's on the porch with Zack." Grandpa sticks his head out the door. "Hurry up, son. She's waiting."

Grandpa opens the door wider, and "my date," enters the foyer, looking really hot in a fitted, gray suit.

He looks up at me and flashes a beautiful white smile. His dark eyes are sparkling and his shiny black hair is tied back slick in a braid. In one hand he holds a corsage, in his other a black bowler with a beaded band and a feather sticking up from the side. My heart does a triple axel.

I forget about my shoes and tramp down the stairs and tumble into John's waiting arms. He stumbles backward but doesn't let go. Oh, what I wouldn't give to be alone with him now.

"Ace, be careful," Grandma says. "You'll break him before you get to the prom."

John and I laugh and let go of each other, but not entirely. He leaves his arm around my shoulder and cinches me close.

"Grandpa," I say. "This is John."

"Son, she's been talking about you coming for days. Welcome to New Jersey. Welcome to our home."

"Thank you, sir," John says. "You don't know how happy I am to be here."

Grandma looks at her watch. "Hurry up and pin that flower on her or you two will be late."

John removes the corsage, hands the empty box to Grandma, and with his hand shaking slightly, pins it to my dress. His fingers brush my skin, sending tingles across my chest and down my arms.

"You're beautiful," he says.

Grandpa raises an eyebrow. "She certainly is."

Zack bursts in the front door half-carrying, half dragging a duffle bag. "Where do you want it?"

Grandpa points to the staircase. "In the guest room."

"Which one?" Zack asks.

"The one furthest from Ace's room." Grandpa eyes John, then me.

My cheeks sizzle. I wonder if he knows about our camping trip?

"Oh, good," Zack shouts. "John will be in the room next to me."

“I’d like that buddy.” He answers Zack with such conviction even I believe he means it.

Zack lugs the bag up the stairs one step at a time.

“So, John,” Grandpa jingles a set of keys in front of us. “Can you drive a clutch?”

“Yes, sir.”

“Good. Take my ’67 Mustang.” He tosses the keys, and John catches them in one hand. “I want you two to go in style.”

“Wow, thanks. Are you sure?” John says.

“I certainly am. Nothing is too good for my beautiful girl.”

I throw my arms around him. “Thank you, Grandpa.”

He pats my back. “The only thing I ask is for you two to behave yourselves tonight.”

My cheeks flame. “Of course.”

“Now, shoo!” Grandma says. “That prom will be over before you get there.”

Thanks to Grandma, I have an escape from Grandpa’s watchful eye. She’s always been my champion.

I grab my clutch from the foyer table and we’re off.

Once we’re out of the view of the front door, I pull John off the walkway. My high heels dig into the earth as I drag him around the side of the house behind a large elm tree. There, I stand on my tiptoes and kiss him. He wraps his arms around my waist and crushes his lips into mine. He tastes sweet, like he just popped a mint candy. Our tongues do an intimate dance and every nerve in my body awakens, causing shooting stars to fire from my head to my toes. I would gladly stay right here like this for the rest of my life.

He breaks away from our kiss, lifts my chin, and holds my cheeks with his long, lean fingers. "We better save some of this for later or we'll be late for your prom."

"Let's play hooky."

"Nope, I'm here to make memories and that's what I'm going to do."

I sigh. "All right, but at least let me show you something first?"

He looks at me from under hooded eyes. "You're making me nervous."

"It's just a little something." I open my clutch and take out the letter I folded into a square so it would fit. I hand it to him and he raises an eyebrow.

"Go ahead, open it."

He unfolds the paper one side at a time. His lips move as he reads the page. When he looks up, his eyes are wide. "You've been accepted to Duke."

I nod and my heart booms a crazy beat while I wait for him to scream, "Hell yeah."

He opens his mouth, but no words come out.

Maybe he doesn't want me to go to the same school? Maybe he thinks two's a crowd. I paste a smile on my face as to not show disappointment. "I've been accepted to other schools too so if you'd rather I not go there…"

"Not go?" He tosses his hat, grabs me under the arms, and swings me in a circle. "It's the absolute best news you could give me. I friggin' love you."

Once I'm on my feet again, I bat my lashes. "How much do you love me?"

"More than the moon and the stars. More than the sunrise on a cool summer morning. More than the river that contains the water of life."

"More than the universe? 'Cause that's how much I love you."

His face lights up. "I just thought of something. We can be roommates. We can get off-campus housing. We can—"

I hold a finger to my lips. "Shh…Not so loud. I'll have to clear that with my grandparents first. I think Grandma will be okay with us living together, but Grandpa's going to need some convincing."

"It doesn't matter. The dorms are okay. Where ever you live works for me—as long as you are nearby." He shakes his head and smiles. "I sure hope you like dancing, 'cause I'm going to keep you on the floor celebrating all night." He takes my hand and practically drags me toward the garage.

"Wait." I wiggle loose. "You forgot your hat." I scoop it up and brush it off, then I place it on his head.

"You don't think it's too much?" he asks, running the feather between his fingers.

"It's perfect," I say. "You're perfect. I wouldn't have you any other way."

With that, he takes me in his arms and kisses me again, and I cling to him while the earth falls away.

**A word about the author…**

Susan Antony is an IT by day, hip-shaker and writer by night, artist whenever possible, and an internet addict. She lives in the sunny south with her teenage son and two Cairn Terriers.

Thank you for purchasing
this publication of The Wild Rose Press, Inc.

For questions or more information
contact us at
info@thewildrosepress.com.

The Wild Rose Press, Inc.
www.thewildrosepress.com

To visit with authors of
The Wild Rose Press, Inc.
join our yahoo loop at
http://groups.yahoo.com/group/thewildrosepress/